By Allegra Goodman

SAM

SAM

A Novel

Allegra Goodman

THE DIAL PRESS

NEW YORK

Published in the United States by The Dial Press, an imprint of Random House, a division of Penguin Random House LLC, New York.

THE DIAL PRESS is a registered trademark and the colophon is a trademark of Penguin Random House LLC.

LIBRARY OF CONGRESS CATALOGING-IN-PUBLICATION DATA
Names: Goodman, Allegra, author.
Title: Sam: a novel / Allegra Goodman.
Description: First edition. | New York: The Dial Press, [2022]
Identifiers: LCCN 2021048346 (print) | LCCN 2021048347 (ebook) |
ISBN 9780593447819 (hardback; acid-free paper) |
ISBN 9780593447826 (ebook)
Subjects: LCGFT: Novels.
Classification: LCC PS3557.O5829 S26 2022 (print) |
LCC PS3557.O5829 (ebook) | DDC 813/.54—dc23/eng/20211018
LC record available at https://lccn.loc.gov/2021048346
LC ebook record available at https://lccn.loc.gov/2021048347
International ISBN: 978-0-593-59682-1

Printed in the United States of America on acid-free paper

randomhousebooks.com

2 4 6 8 9 7 5 3 1

FIRST EDITION

Book design by Dana Leigh Blanchette

To Miranda

I

Umbrella

1

There is a girl, and her name is Sam.

She has a mother named Courtney and a dad who is sort of around, sort of not. He lives ten minutes away, but he is not always home. Courtney says that's the whole point.

"What is?" Sam asks.

"He's never anywhere."

"Yes, he is. He's *some*where."

"Very funny," Courtney says.

Sam is seven and she never stops. She never helps either. Courtney is exhausted all the time—but it's not just Sam. It's Noah!

Noah is two and he has a teddy named Bill. He got a plastic ark for his birthday, but he only has one lion and one zebra left. You can't teach Noah. You can't even scare him. He thinks no is his name. Sam climbs up inside the doorjambs to get away from him.

If you want to know how, just take off your shoes. And socks! You have to be barefoot.

Stand in the doorway to the kitchen and spread your feet as far apart as they can go.

Wedge your feet into the frame.

Inch one foot up. Then the other.

Inch up some more.

Stop, or you'll bang your head! Just stay there. Brace your feet against the wood.

Courtney says, You know what, Sam? This is getting old, because Sam likes to stay up there so long. It is not cute.

The day her dad comes over, Sam tackles him. "Where were you? Are you back? When did you get back?" Before he can answer, she wedges herself into the doorframe.

"Hey, monkey," her dad says. "When did you learn to do that?"

Courtney frowns. "A long time ago."

He just looks up at Sam. "Ready?"

"Yes!"

"Okay, let's go!"

Sam jumps down on him. "Where?"

"I don't know!" He's teasing, but she doesn't care. He's a jet. He's a plane. He's a parachute. He holds Sam by the heels, and pennies start falling from her clothes. She is raining pennies that were never there before—but that's what happens with her dad.

"Stop that!" says Courtney. "Come on. Mitchell."

Noah lifts his arms, even though Mitchell is not his dad, and calls out, "Me!"

"Mitchell. Stop!"

Sam is wobbly when Mitchell sets her down, but she recovers fast. "Where? Where?"

"Topsfield."

"*Yes!*" She picks up the pennies. Then she runs to get her purse, and Noah runs after her. Sam sits on her bed and counts out her dollars. When Noah tries to climb up, she explains, "Noah, when you get older, you can go to the fair."

"Where's your hoodie?" Courtney asks Sam. It's going to be cold, and Sam will be sick if her dad stuffs her full of junk. Cotton candy is not dinner.

Sam races out to Mitchell's car, which coughs a lot.

"What's wrong?" Courtney asks from the doorway when Mitchell tries to start it.

"It's fine," says Mitchell. The car coughs again and then again. In the back seat, Sam shuts her eyes and prays silently, Please please come on I'll be your best friend.

The car keeps wheezing and coughing. Courtney picks up Noah to prevent him from running off. There are leaves everywhere. Two oaks fill the front yard, and a beech tree spreads out on the side. One rake isn't enough. It's an ocean. It's a tidal wave of leaves.

"You've got a dead battery," Courtney says.

"No, it always does this."

Before Courtney can say anything else, the engine catches.

"We're outta here!" shouts Mitchell, and they are hurtling down the road. The day is faster. The trees are brighter, the road is twistier. Sam's house is gone, along with Courtney holding Noah up above the leaves.

The fair is bigger than a hundred football fields. You have to park miles away and take shuttle buses. On the bus, Sam gets the window and Mitchell sits next to her. They are both wearing hoodies. Mitchell's is Red Sox. Sam's is gray but warm. The pockets in front are connected so you can tunnel your hands inside. She is holding her money in her pocket between her hands. Her money is $9.26 folded into a calico change purse with the face of a cat. The clasp snaps shut between pointy ears.

Mitchell pays admission and then he buys tickets. He and Sam stay away from the games because that's how they get you. They head straight for the rides. Not the Zipper because it makes you sick. Not the Ferris wheel, because it's a waste. They ride the Pirate Ship, the Vertigo, and the Raptor twice. You fly over all the people and the arcades and the food trucks and the kiddie roller coaster. When Sam is a velociraptor, she doesn't care about the cold.

It starts drizzling, but Sam and her dad ignore it. They lick cotton candy and their tongues turn blue. They share a fried onion exploded like a flower. They gorge themselves on kettle corn. Mitchell holds the bag as they walk through barns of fancy chickens and weird rabbits. There's a milking demonstration, but it's postponed, because the cow sits down and won't get up again.

Rain pings the metal roof of the exhibit hall, and Sam buys red whips and a miniature china sheep. She can eat the red whips now and have the sheep forever.

Mitchell and Sam sit in the competition barn and Sam knots the long thin strands of red whips together. Then she eats the knot. Her delicate sheep is wrapped in tissue in a brown paper bag. She's carrying him kangaroo style in her front pocket.

Outside, the grounds turn to mud. The competition barn smells like wet sawdust, but the horses in the ring are decked in braids and silver.

When the rain stops, it's cold and soggy, and mud sucks your shoes, but so what?

Sam and Mitchell watch men climb a sky-high ladder to dive into a tiny wading pool.

They go to a pig race with little white pigs, the cartoon kind with corkscrew tails. "It's Porkchop by a nose!"

"Can I get a pig?" Sam asks.

"What do you think?" Mitchell answers. He always does that, asking questions back at you. He never says no.

Courtney says no to everything. She is allergic to all animals, including fish.

"Can I go up there?" Sam asks. It's a giant trampoline, but the lines are long.

Mitchell says, "Do we have time?"

Then all at once, he sees the tower. They both see it. You have to tilt back your head to see the top. Handholds on the tower look like confetti. The idea is you strap on a rope and climb up any way you can, and if you get to the top, you ring a bell. "I want to do that," Sam says. "Can I do that?"

It's annoying because it costs extra. That's how they get you, even after you pay admission and buy tickets. Also, it looks wet.

"You really want to go up there?" asks Mitchell.

"Yeah!"

"You think you can get to the top?"

Sam catches the excitement in his voice. He wants her to try. He thinks she can get up there, even though he says it's harder than it looks.

They wait a long time—almost as long as it would have been for the trampoline. Sam shivers in her rain-soaked clothes. Mitchell would give her his own hoodie, but it's wet too.

He says, "Maybe we should try something else."

Sam hands Mitchell her china sheep in its soggy paper bag. She isn't trying something else. She's got her eyes on the wall and the people trying to reach the bell. One guy makes it. Then there's a kid who gets stuck. When you can't climb anymore, the man with the other end of your rope starts bringing you down.

Huddled together in line, Sam and her dad inch forward until finally, finally one of the ropes people calls out, "Young lady!"

Sam runs up the stairs to the platform where they hand you a helmet and strap ropes onto you. She's wearing a harness around her waist and between her legs. The rope is thick and long, and it will keep her safe if she slips and starts to fall, but that won't happen. She is already climbing with her right foot on the lowest foothold. The holds are big and close together, so she can climb foot over foot and hand over hand. The hard part is her shoes. They're wet and mushy. She wishes she could take them off, but its too late. She can't get rid of them, even though they drag her down.

She doesn't look. She's concentrating, inching up, one hold at a time. Her shoes are heavy, and her hands are small, but she makes it up halfway, and then the holds start spreading out.

She keeps climbing, foot after hand and hand after foot. Her hands are freezing. Her fingers are so cold she has to stop. She's balancing with foot and knee braced against a big hold, and she takes her right hand and rubs it on her shirt. Then she switches and rubs her left hand. Resting there, she hears the music of the fair, the carousel, the games. A prize for everybody. Everybody wins! From far below, she hears her name. "Sam? Are you done, Sam?"

She's not done; she's just catching her breath. After a minute she feels better, but she's stiff when she reaches for the next hold and slips, heart pounding. Without the rope, she would come crashing down—but that's not what scares her. She's afraid she'll lose her turn. Then she would have to wait in line again.

She grabs a knobby yellow handhold, then a red.

She's up so high she cannot stop. She's beyond everybody but the lights. Gold Zipper lights, red striped lights from the Raptor. She is a cold monkey. Her teeth are chattering. Her arms are aching as she reaches higher and higher. She drags her feet up and each one weighs a hundred pounds.

She lives for every tiny resting place. She stops wherever she can balance. Her fingers are numb. But there it is, the metal bell. She lurches up and slams her palm across its face.

Ding!

In glory, she glides down to the platform where the ropes person unties her. Mitchell and a few people in line are clapping. "Look at you," the ropes guy says.

Her face is streaked with dirt and rain and sweat. Her dad buys her hot mulled cider and a purple glow stick.

Suddenly, it's pouring. Everyone is leaving all at once, but you can't just jump in your car. You have to wait for the shuttle.

The buses are so crowded there aren't any seats at all. Mitchell stands with his arms around Sam to protect her.

"Crazy kid," he tells Sam, as he rubs her frozen hands, and she feels grateful, and powerful, and famous.

When the bus stops, he carries her through the parking lot, because she is too cold to walk. He has a plaid blanket in the car. He pulls off her soggy shirt and wraps her in the scratchy wool.

"Can I sit in front?"

He hesitates and she's afraid he'll ask, Does Mom let you? Then he says, "Sure."

Blanket and all, she scrambles into the front seat. "Can we go back tomorrow?"

"Hold on." He's trying to start the car.

"Please?"

"What do you think?"

"Please?"

"Sh." It's dark, except for Sam's glow stick, shining like a magic wand. It's cold and the rain is pouring down and the car won't start. Maybe they'll just stay. They'll sleep at the fair!

The car coughs and coughs. Mitchell waits a minute and Sam holds still. He is giving the battery a chance to rest.

"Oh, come on," Mitchell says, because the car still won't start. "Fuck." He looks over at Sam and covers her ears. "Wait here." He goes out into the night and finds a guy with jumper cables in his station wagon. Together Mitchell and the other guy hook up cables between the two cars.

When Mitchell gets the car started, he says, "See?"

Sam nods.

"People help you."

"Do you know him?" she asks about the guy with the station wagon.

Her dad says nope—but a lot of strangers know her dad. They go to his magic shows or hear his one-man band. He says you have to know your audience. He also says if you don't talk to strangers you won't meet anyone.

"Dad?" she says, as they drive into the night.

"What?"

"Are you famous?"

"Not yet."

"But you're going to be."

"Oh sure. Probably."

"Me too." She is remembering how people clapped when she came gliding down.

2

Climbing is hard. It's not just a sport; it's an art. It requires your whole body and your whole mind. Humility. Perseverance. Respect! You respect the wall; you learn from the wall, and you know that nine times out of ten you fail. That's the main thing. You will fail. You will fall. Climbing is mostly falling. Mitchell explains all this, and Sam has no idea what he's talking about.

He says, "I'm telling you, so you'll have the mindset."

"Tell me about when you were little," Sam says. They are eating Sunday lunch at Freeda's Pizza where her dad likes the music because it's oldies, like "Singin' in the Rain" and "Fly Me to the Moon."

He tries to remember when he was little. "I got nothing."

"Okay, tell me about when you were seven."

"Seven?"

"Yeah. When you were as old as me."

"Hmm." While he's thinking, the lady at the counter calls fifty-six, and Sam slides out of her chair to retrieve their slices on white paper plates. Her dad starts eating, but she looks at him expectantly.

"I remember my mom wouldn't let me get a dog."

She waits, but he just eats his pizza. "That's all?"

"Red Rocks."

"What's that?"

"Where we went climbing."

"Can I go?"

"Maybe when you're older."

"How old? How old were you?"

"Fifteen, sixteen."

"Fifteen!" She can't wait that long.

He says, "The boulders are like houses; they're so big. And there's no admission."

"What is there?"

"Lichen. All kinds of moss—like velvet—and it's dark. The rocks are granite from the ice age, dropped by glaciers—and there are ferns. Did you know ferns are as old as dinosaurs?"

"How far is it?" Sam asks.

"Gloucester."

"Right in Gloucester?" He made it sound like another planet. "Do you still go now?"

"No, I stopped a while ago."

"Why?"

"Oh, I don't know. I don't remember."

"Dad!"

"What?"

"When I grow up, I'm going to remember everything."

"Okay, remember this."

Gray counters, chrome napkin holders, jars of chili pepper flakes, stacks of pizza boxes piled to the ceiling. She looks all around, and then she looks at her dad, even though she knows him by heart.

His eyes are dark brown. His hair is long. His face is scratchy. His arms are hard. He can run faster than anybody, except he smokes. He shouldn't do that.

He plays every instrument and the harmonica. He can read your palm and, also, he knows magic. He can pull a rabbit from a hat and cards out of your clothes. He can juggle anything you like—for example, a cantaloupe, a whiffle ball, a knife. He is an artist. That's why he travels.

He can write Poems While U Wait. He sits at a little table with a typewriter and Sam draws chalk pictures on the sidewalk.

Each poem is one of a kind and they will have a metaphor like you are my piece of toast. Sam already knows how to make her own metaphors. You just take two things that don't match and put them together. Her best one is my dad is my umbrella.

Her dad taught her like this. He said you are my sun moon stars. She said you are my planet.

He taught her how to ride a two-wheel bike, and he's going to teach her how to ride a unicycle.

Now her dad says, "I'm going to teach you climbing."

"When?"

"Soon."

"Today?"

"Sure!"

She jumps up and throws away her paper plate, but her dad is still eating. "It's hard," he says. "It takes dedication. You have to be very, very patient."

"I *am* patient." She is sitting there with her chin in her hand, waiting and waiting for him to finish his pizza.

Since the fair is over, her dad drives her to the YMCA to see Kevin instead. Kevin has a beard. He is older and taller than Sam's dad, and he smells like cigarettes. Kevin shows them into the gym so they can check out the climbing wall.

"That's *it*?" Sam says.

Compared to Topsfield, this wall is short, but it's got the same kind of handholds—pink, orange, green, red, yellow—all the same colors. Kevin straps Sam into the harness and she sees a letter tattooed on each knuckle. *L.O.V.E.* She can read his hand!

Kevin stands on the ground holding his end of the rope.

"All set," Mitchell says.

She doesn't even glance over her shoulder.

"Careful now," Kevin warns, but Sam is climbing lightly, foot by hand by foot. It's easy without wet shoes and rain and frozen fingers. It's like a toy climbing wall. It feels plastic.

The problem is the middle. You can't climb straight through the middle. Sam stretches above her head to the next handhold, but her arms aren't long enough, and she can't reach.

"You can do it," Mitchell calls out. She's hanging on with one foot resting on a green ledge. "If you can't go straight, just try moving to the side. Go lateral!"

"What's lateral?" she calls down.

He shifts his weight to the right and to the left. "Just be gradual. Come on, monkey. Be a monkey, Sam!"

She gets it now—swing like a monkey—side to side. You have to zigzag to climb higher.

"Smart kid," says Kevin.

Where's the bell? Sam wonders. There is no bell, but she's a sport. She's a queen as she glides down.

Kevin says she's got it. She's a natural.

Her dad is going to be her coach, but she will have to practice for real. She'll need strong fingers. You have to clench and flex your hands to strengthen them, so they walk to Family Dollar to look for putty and a squeezy rubber ball.

Together they walk through all the aisles, but they can't find what they are looking for—only plastic pumpkin candy buckets, and purple glitter bouncy balls, and costumes.

"Hey, do you want one of these?" Mitchell holds up Belle's yellow gown and Ariel's mermaid dress—but Sam's hair is short and brown, so she can't be one of those princesses. "Cinderella?" her dad suggests, but Sam shakes her head, and he keeps searching. "Aren't there any ghosts?"

The Statue of Liberty is a good deal—robe, crown, and torch—but the torch doesn't light up, so Sam says no.

"Never settle," Mitchell says. "I respect that."

They leave the store with just one purple bouncy ball, and Mitchell says he will find putty somewhere else. In the meantime, Sam will swing like a monkey on the playground. She'll practice pull-ups on the climbing structure.

3

The next morning, everybody's gotta wake up and get moving. Courtney has work. Sam has school. School is her job. Everybody has a job. Even Noah goes to Brown Bear Family Daycare. He cries, but Courtney says, Come on, buddy, you can do it. Courtney takes him in the car, and Sam rides the school bus, which is called Bluebird but painted yellow. That's because her mom can't be everywhere at once.

A day in school is like a year.

Morning meeting.

Calendar.

Sit at your table.

Scoot in your chair.

Crisscross applesauce.

Sit down nicely on your carpet square.

You have to learn about blue whales. They are the size of three school buses, but they have no teeth, just baleen, and they suck up tiny krill. Did you know people hunted them until they were almost extinct? They are still endangered.

Think about that.

Do your work. Put everything away. You're in second grade, not pre-K. Line up. Walk quietly to Art. No running no shouting no fighting. If you're making sponge paintings, dipping sponges green and blue, you can't throw your sponge at other people. You can't, but Sam does, so she has to go to the sink quietly. Quietly! And wash brushes. Sponges are for paper, not for people. Why would you throw a sponge?

Because a sponge is juicy-wet. You throw yours and then boys throw theirs right in your face! You duck behind the easels and you've got green paint dripping down your shirt until the teacher catches you.

Sam doesn't have a change of clothes. While she washes brushes, her shirt hardens stiff as cardboard. "Now wash your face and hands—and arms!" her teacher tells her.

She runs (don't run!) to the girls' bathroom and digs in her jeans pocket for her bouncy ball, which she bounces as high as the ceiling. She throws it against every mirror and every wall until the door opens and she thinks one of the teachers is coming to check up on her. It's only a kid, but Sam scrubs herself all over and walks to her classroom—just in time to read a book about a deer.

It's harder than it looks. The pictures are all brown with just a little bit of green. A lot of words look the same and you can't guess. For this reason, she goes to Miss McCabe.

Miss McCabe works in a closet, but she is organized. She's got folders and binders and frog stickers and a big round clock.

You have to sit up and concentrate. Then while you're concentrating, you can read the whole story, one step at a time. When Sam gets to the end, Miss McCabe says, "High five! Now tell me what happened to the deer."

Sam shrugs.

"Tell me. What happened to him in the end?"

Sam feels bad.

"Did you forget?"

Sam shakes her head.

"You read it beautifully," Miss McCabe says. "Were you thinking about the words?"

"Yes."

"Were you thinking about the story?"

"No."

"What were you thinking about?"

Sam looks at the clock. The big hand is on the five and the little hand is on the ten. It's still Monday morning.

By the time Sam gets home, her mother knows about the sponge fight. Actually, it's not a fight; it is an incident. Unfortunately, it's not an isolated incident. The art teacher has concerns. Also, she is trying to teach the whole class.

Courtney says, "Oh come on, Sam."

There are twelve months in the year and seven days in the week, and sixteen words hidden in Sam's worksheet. You have to do it step by step.

The next day and the next day, Sam rides the bus. She loses her bouncy ball, and crawls under the seats to find it. She writes IGHT words. Night, fight, bright, light. She adds numbers and cuts out construction paper deer and trees.

In Art, she squeezes wet clay between her fingers.

At recess, she swings on metal monkey bars. She swings her whole body, bar to bar, until she gets pink blisters on her palms.

At home, she hangs by her fingers from the doorframe to her room. She inches up inside the frame until Courtney screams, "Sam! STOP! Don't break the HOUSE!"

Sam does all this, but by the weekend, her dad has gone away to Boston. That's just how it goes.

"What's he doing there?" Sam asks when she's supposed to go to sleep.

"Who knows?"

"Juggling?"

"Probably." Courtney is sitting on Sam's bed, and they are whispering, because Noah's bed is wedged in next to hers and if they wake him it's bad news.

"Dad's taking me to Red Rocks."

"Is that what he told you?"

"Yeah! When I'm bigger. He's coaching me."

"For what?"

"Rock climbing."

"Oh great."

"I'm going to be a climber."

"You can be a lot of things, but you have to learn to read."

"I *can* read."

Courtney sighs because she is so tired all the time. She stretches out on Sam's bed and rests her head next to Sam's head on the pillow. "You can read, but you don't."

"That's just because I don't like it."

"Which part don't you like?"

"The books."

"Well, let's get different ones."

Now Sam sighs, because they've already been to the library a million times. "I don't like *any* books."

"Yes, you do." Courtney's hair is silk. Her eyes are green. She could be a princess if she wanted, or a mermaid. She reminds Sam, "You like taking Noah to story time."

"No, I don't."

"You write poems!"

"That's different," Sam says, because writing is not like reading at all.

"Fine." Her mom sits up. "Now, close your eyes."

"Don't go!"

"Come on, Sam. It's late."

"But I can't sleep."

"You can if you want to," Courtney says, because if Sam wants, she can read and sleep and do everything the way she is supposed to.

"I'm not even tired."

"Yes, you are."

"No, I'm not."

"What's bothering you?"

"Nothing."

"Are you sad?"

"No."

"Are you worried?"

"No."

"Then go to sleep!"

"I can't!"

"Just pretend. Just close your eyes."

Sam closes her eyes. She almost starts to feel the darkness pull her in. Then she jolts awake. "Mom?"

"What?"

"When do you think Dad's coming back?"

"I don't know."

"Could you ask him?"

"Sure. I could ask him lots of things."

"Like what?"

"Never mind."

Once again, the darkness tugs at Sam, but she fights it. "Do I have to go to school tomorrow?"

"Yeah, if you want to grow up and earn a living."

"Do you have to go to school to be a climber?"

"*Yes.*"

"Why?"

"So you can learn . . . geology."

Sam is slowing down; she keeps getting sleepier, so it takes her a moment to ask, "What's geology?"

Courtney explains that glaciers and ice and fossils pile up. There are rocks, and there are scientists. Some are igneous and some are sedimentary. You have to understand these things. You have to study, because if you don't do your work in school, you'll live in other people's houses. You'll have to borrow a leaf blower. You'll borrow all the time. You will be twenty-six and you'll work all day but then you can't go anywhere. You can't go out at night; you can't even get a good night's sleep. You will never catch a break.

Now Sam is snoring. She is fast asleep and climbing, hand over foot and foot over hand.

4

Sam's house is small and rusty red. Inside, the kitchen is pinewood and all the other walls are gray. The living room has wires in the corners. If you pull them you might electrocute yourself, so watch it. The house is not finished, because Noah's grandpa and grandma bought it as an investment. Grandma B. is rich. She owns a lot of property, even though she wears old golf shorts. Grandma B. lets them live here because of Noah. That's why Courtney and the kids can stay for free. Someday they will have to move, but Sam isn't worried.

For the time being, she climbs the beech tree on the side of the house. It's too tall; it's way too dangerous. If she does it again, her mom is going to kill her, but she climbs anyway. The trunk is smooth but wrinkled at the knees.

Stand on the roots and reach the bumpy knob and then pull yourself up with your arms. With one foot on the knob, you can reach the lowest branch. It sinks under you. All the leaves rustle as it dips, but the branch won't break. It's way too strong.

Climb from one branch to another. They're piled thick, and the tree is full of golden leaves so nobody can see you.

Sam watches Noah's dad arriving in his pickup truck. Jack is moving back because he loves Courtney, and she loves him, even though they always fight. Since he's between jobs, he is going to live with them and be a family, and work on finishing the house.

Sam can see him unloading. He has a duffel bag and he's got tools. For one thing, he has an electric drill. He also has a table saw he can set up outside while the weather is still good. Jack's hair is black and shiny like his truck and he carries a canteen that he calls his flask. He has tattoos all over his arms and shoulders including a bald eagle and GARY, which was the name of his friend in the Gulf War. He's got Noah on there, but not Sam, because she is not his kid. Also, he doesn't like Sam.

This is why Jack does not like Sam. She does not listen she talks back she whines she ruins everything. Noah is just little, but Sam should know better.

When Courtney and Noah come out to help Jack carry his stuff, he looks around, like he's expecting Sam. Courtney even calls, "Sam? Where are you?"

She holds still, hiding in the branches so Jack can't see her. "Sam?"

Her mother glances toward the tree.

Sam hardly breathes. A piece of hair slips out from behind her ear and tickles her. She doesn't even brush it from her face.

She waits and waits until Courtney and Jack and Noah take one last trip into the house and close the door. Then she climbs down backward, hand after foot, branch beneath branch.

When she opens the front door, Jack says, "Where did you come from?"

Sam just looks at him and doesn't answer.

But this is a family. They are all together! Jack calls Courtney babe. He is going to paint the walls.

After school, Jack lets Sam help him with the drill, and he shows her how to use a paint roller. They are painting the bedroom he and Courtney share. The color is white chocolate, but first you mask all the windows and throw down old sheets and paint with primer.

Sam gets primer in her hair, and this stuff does not dissolve in water. "Oh my God, Sam," Courtney says. It's not like poster paint at school. It's permanent. The only way to wash it out is toothpaste.

Sam sits in the tub, while her mom washes and washes her hair. Eventually, Sam asks, "Are you and Jack getting married?"

"No."

"Could you marry Dad, then?"

"No! I'm not marrying anyone."

"Dad's not anyone."

"Close your eyes." Her mom is pouring water over her.

"Why don't you like him?" Sam asks with her eyes closed.

"I like him."

"No, you don't. You never let Dad live here."

"He doesn't want to."

Sam opens her eyes at the wrong time, and she gets a face full of water. "How do you know?" she splutters, because she can't believe that. He doesn't live with them because her mom won't let him.

"Sam." That means don't even start.

But why does Courtney let Jack stay? Just because he kisses her and paints the walls and takes Noah outside in the morning so she can sleep?

Jack never takes Sam anywhere. He yells at her because she steps in the paint tray. He swears at Sam, and Courtney snaps at him—but families help one another, so when Sam comes down with strep and stays home from school, Jack watches her. She has strawberry tongue. This is what Pat, the nurse practitioner, says. Sam takes pink bubblegum medicine and sleeps all morning while Jack paints her mom's bedroom.

When she wakes up, she smells smoke. She knows that smell. It's like dead flowers and wet socks.

"No smoking in the house," she tells Jack, because it's true.

She is standing in footed pajamas in the doorway to the living room. He is drinking from his flask and blowing smoke and watching TV on the couch.

He ignores her, so she stands in front of him. "You can't do that."

"Move," he says, because she is blocking the screen.

"Put it out."

Now he stares at her.

"You can't smoke in our house."

"It's not your house."

"We lived here before you did!"

"I said move." He stands up and he is like a bear on his hind legs.

"You're gonna get it," she tells Jack, but he is big. He is way bigger than she is and he picks her up. She tries to squirm away. She can't. She tries to break his grip. She can't. She bites his arm, instead.

He gasps. "Get off me!"

She holds on fighting, but he throws her off. The room springs sideways and she lands in a heap on the front steps. When she tries the knob, it's locked.

The cement is cold. She's out of breath. If her dad were here, he would break down the door. No, he would pull the key out of his hat. Then he would break Jack.

Her dad hates Jack. Once when he came to pick up Sam, he called Jack a lying piece of shit.

Her mom said, "Watch your language," because Sam was standing there.

He said, "Sorry, monkey," but later, Sam heard him ask her mom, "What are you doing?"

Courtney said, "You're asking *me* that?"

Sam's dad would chase Jack all the way to the highway if he were here, but he is not.

She looks up and down the road, but there is not a single car. She is too cold to sit here on the step. It's too cold to climb the tree.

Sam could go to the neighbors, but they are far, and what if they call the police? They will take her away. Jack will say, Good.

She hugs her knees to her chest and looks up at the sky. She closes her eyes and bows her head and prays, Please help me. Tell me what to do.

Nothing happens. Nobody tells her anything, but she has to get up. Her teeth are chattering. She will walk to the farm stand, all the way at the end of the road. She will ask them to call her mom to come and get her.

As soon as she decides this, the door opens. Jack is letting her back in.

She knows that he is thinking, What will Courtney say?

He starts talking about how he isn't angry anymore. His voice is quiet, but he is a bear, underneath his skin.

He says, "What if we go out for ice cream later?" but she won't even look at him, so he gives up. He turns around and leaves the door open, just a crack.

She stays out on the steps until she can't feel her feet. Finally, she runs to her room and shuts herself in. She drags Noah's mattress over to the door and piles all his toys on top. Then she finds markers and draws on the back of her math worksheet.

In her picture, Jack throws her out the open door. Sam's mouth is open in an O. Her arms are wide with surprise. Jack's hair is thick and angry like fur. Gray clouds are puffing from his mouth.

When Courtney comes home with Noah, she sees the picture. "Okay, what's going on?"

Sam is afraid to tell her.

Jack does instead.

Courtney turns to Sam. "You *bit* him?"

Sam says, "He smoked in the house and I wouldn't move so he picked me up and I bit him, and then he threw me out!"

Now Courtney turns on Jack. "You what?"

Fight, fight, fight all night.

He says, Look at my arm. She bit me like a fucking dog.

Courtney says, You locked her out?

Sam and Noah hide in their room. They pretend that they're in outer space. Mostly Sam pretends, while Noah falls asleep. Sam stays awake, because she is afraid Jack will barge in the door. She sits up until she hears Jack's truck and then she holds still listening to him drive away.

5

In the morning, Sam is still sick, and Courtney has a headache, but Noah is running all around. Sam starts asking what will happen, but her mom is hunting for the pink medicine in the fridge and telling Noah, "Stop it." That's because her head is splitting but she has to work anyway, and who will watch Sam now?

"I'll help you, Mom," says Sam. She has more energy, now that Jack is gone. She finds Noah's socks. They even match. "Sit here," she orders, as she stuffs his feet into them.

Usually, her mom would thank her.

They drop off Noah and then Courtney takes Sam to work at Jennifer Salon. It's because Sam is still contagious. Also, her mom has no choice. "Oh my God, Jen," says Courtney, the minute she walks in the door.

Jen is Cousin Jen, who calls Sam sweetheart. Jen owns the shop and bleaches her hair blond.

The salon is right on Cabot Street. It's purple and green like Easter. There is a big clock that runs backward in the mirror and there are lollipops, but they are very small. You can refill the candy or be an astronaut under the dryer.

The salon is right near Family Dollar, and two doors down, you can buy coffee from the Donut Stop. Sam is the delivery girl. Jen gives her money and Sam buys one black coffee and one latte. She carries them back, walking slowly.

"Thank you, sweetheart! Just put it there," says Jen, because she has a client. Her client is old, and she is there with her daughter who sits under the dryer. Even the daughter is old. She has a tricky knee.

"I'll take mine now," says Courtney, and she drinks long sips. She has a client too, a lady with aluminum foil packets all over her head. She is going lighter. She will have streaks of gold.

Sam watches in the mirror and her mom is like an actor smiling. As soon as her client leaves, Courtney sinks down on the stool behind the counter.

Sam is tired too. She curls up in a big swivel chair.

"Aw, she's sleeping," Jen says.

Courtney whispers something. She talks for a long time, but Sam can't hear.

At last, Jen whispers back, "Do you even want him there?"

Sam holds still, listening. Her mom says, "That's the problem. It's his parents' house."

Jen says, "Fuck 'em. Move to town."

"With what?"

With me? Sam thinks. With Noah?

The door is opening; the bell is ringing. Cold air rushes in.

"Hey."

It's Jack. Sam's eyes open. Then she squeezes them shut. She curls up tighter.

"I just thought . . ." He's being nice again.

Courtney says, "I'm working."

"Can I just?"

"No."

"Just give me five minutes."

Watching through her eyelashes, Sam sees Courtney lead Jack to the back door, EMPLOYEES ONLY.

She sits up and Jen says, "You weren't sleeping, were you?"

Cousin Jen and Sam look at each other in the mirror. Jen is tanned. Sam is pale and freckled. Her eyes are copper brown.

"You're fine," says Jen. "You're gonna be okay."

Sam says, "I have strawberry tongue."

"Let's see."

Sam sticks out her tongue.

"Looks fine to me!"

"It's pink."

"Your tongue is supposed to be pink."

"It's pink with bumps."

"If you say so."

Sam frowns. "That's strawberry tongue."

"Okay, you don't have to get upset about it."

"I still have a fever." Sam glances at the EMPLOYEES ONLY door.

"Listen," says Jen. "Your mom won't let anything happen to you."

"But she can't be everywhere at once."

Jen laughs. "You are a piece of work." She always says this, and Sam can't tell if it is good or bad.

Doorbell. Freezing cold. It's Courtney's next client, a mean lady who carries a rolled-up newspaper, like she's about to kill a bug.

Jen says, "Hi, Theresa! Courtney just stepped out! She'll be with you in a minute! Can I get you some water?" She takes a bottle from the mini-fridge and hands Theresa a short black kimono.

Theresa sits at Courtney's station and starts rattling her paper as Jen says, "You remember Sam."

Sam watches the clock running backward in the mirror. It's supposed to be eleven. Then it's supposed to be two minutes past, but it gets earlier and earlier.

Courtney comes running, and she talks fast. "Hello, Theresa! How are you? Are we doing the same color?" Theresa's hair is light brown and gray, the color of a mouse. "Let me mix that up for you!" She is squeezing out the color into her bowl and mixing it together. You can't tell she has a splitting head-ache. Her hands keep working, even though she never slept.

Jack does not come in again, but when Sam looks out at Cabot Street, she sees his black truck parked there.

6

"Can I sleep over?" Sam asks her dad, the next Saturday she sees him.

"I don't think your mom would like that."

"Yes, she would!" The October sun is shining, and they are driving to a real climbing gym called Boulders. "Please? With Noah? She really needs a break."

He smiles, but then he says, "I have a gig in Salem."

"I can play with you!"

"Then you have to practice."

Sam flops back in her seat and her dad laughs. She has already started drums, accordion, and ukulele—but she only likes playing with her dad. It's the same with magic. "Please, Dad."

"Okay, this is gonna be cool," Mitchell says as they pull up. "This is a whole open house for kids."

The gym is huge. It's a million stories high, all decorated for Halloween.

There is face painting. There is a popcorn machine like at the movies. There is soda in designated areas. There is music, and there are kids running everywhere.

First your parent or guardian signs the waivers. Then you write a name tag for yourself and stick it to your shirt. After all that, you line up for shoes. Sam hands over her sneakers and borrows size two climbing shoes. They are the opposite of elf shoes. They have long toes pointing down.

"Where to?" Mitchell asks.

There are walls and towers everywhere, but also lines. The shortest lines are for the little walls. These walls are so small you don't need ropes. If you fall, you land on blue gymnastics mats. "That's just for little kids," says Sam, but her dad tells her no. These are the bouldering walls.

The good thing about bouldering is when you fall off you can jump up and try again right away. You don't have to glide down and wait your turn to get strapped into a harness all over again.

It's weird. There are handholds, but the wall juts out at all angles, so you're never climbing straight. You hold on tight and use your fingers and your toes. You can see the floor, but if you touch the ground, you're out. Sam tries and tries one certain wall. It's like a puzzle. Actually, it's better than a puzzle, because you are the missing piece. She jumps and tries and jumps and tries until her arms start hurting and her fingers cramp. She is surprised, and then she starts getting upset, because she can't make it to the top.

She flops down on the mat.

"Okay." Her dad stands over her. "This is where you keep getting stuck. Think where to reach."

She skootches over on the mat and looks up at the spot. A green hold, a bumpy place, a ledge that's red.

One of the Boulders STAFF comes over. "Hi, Sam."

She is surprised the STAFF already know her name. Then she remembers her name tag.

The STAFF says, "My name is Toby. How's it going?"

"Good." She is still lying on her back. At first, she can't tell whether Toby is a boy or a girl. Toby's hair is short as a boy's, but her voice is like a girl's. Probably she is a girl. Her body is small, but she has muscles all over.

"Have you tried the other walls?"

"No."

"You might like those."

"No, I like this one."

"It's tricky."

"That's okay." Sam is afraid Toby will say this one is for older children, so she scrambles up again.

Toby offers her a bag. Sam thinks it's popcorn. Then she realizes it's white chalk.

Sam dunks her hands so that they're white, and then she tries and tries again.

Her dad and Toby watch together now.

"Almost!" her dad calls.

Toby says, "Push off with your left foot."

She's to the point where she can climb to the green hold in just two seconds. It's the red ledge she can't reach. She grazes the outcropping with her fingertips.

"Ohhh, almost!" Toby cries.

"You can do it," her dad says.

She falls, and they are both talking at once.

"Great effort," Toby says.

Her dad says, "It's okay, Sam."

It's not okay. Her arms are too short! She can touch the ledge, but she can't grab it. She wants to kick the wall, but Toby says, "We have a kids' team, Little Boulders. Eight and under."

The team meets on Saturdays, and there is a fee, but there are also scholarships. You should have your own shoes, but for now you can borrow from the gym. The team is for fun, but they also compete and train for higher levels. Toby started out that way and now she climbs in high school.

Mitchell says, "Wow, what do you think, Sam?"

She is still glaring at the wall.

"You'd really learn something on a team," Mitchell tells Sam in the car.

"Like what?"

"How to solve problems."

"What problems?"

"You'd learn how to climb that boulder."

"I *know* how to climb that boulder!"

"You'd learn strategy! You'd have coaching!"

"But you're already my coach."

"You'd have real coaching, so you'd know what you're doing."

"I already know what I'm doing." Sam frowns into the side mirror. Her eyes are annoyed, not pretty like her mom says, her forehead white under her short bangs.

Mitchell honks his horn, because a truck just cut them off. "Asshole!" He forgets to cover Sam's ears. They are running late to Jen's Halloween party and his phone is ringing. He flips it open and Sam hears her mom.

"Hello?"

"Good news!" says Mitchell. "They want Sam on a team!"

"Where are you?"

"They have scholarships. They meet on Saturdays."

"You're driving her to Newburyport every Saturday?"

"Sure!"

"Uh-huh. And what about when you're not here?"

Before he can answer, Courtney's words fill the car, because is he thinking she will do it? Did he forget she works on Saturdays? Jen cuts hair and Jen's husband Steve is at the shop, and Courtney watches their baby, Madi.

Mitchell hands Sam the phone and her mom is still talking. "You're an hour late."

Mitchell says, "Tell her we're on our way."

"We're on our way."

Sam holds up the phone and her dad grins, because even now, Courtney is still talking. But then he stops himself and puts on his serious look while he is listening.

"Your mom is one hardworking lady," he tells Sam after she hangs up. "I respect the heck out of her."

"Heck?" Sam giggles, because what's heck? She's never heard her dad say heck before.

"Hey," her dad warns, like don't get smart, but she knows he doesn't mean it. She can be as smart as she wants. The point is they have to work together.

Mitchell guns the engine and turns up the radio, while Sam reaches into the back seat for her black witch hat. She ties on a black salon kimono and pulls up her striped socks to look like witch's stockings.

They are speeding down the highway, and Sam can feel the music in her elbows and knees and even underneath her feet. Her dad shouts, "Great costume, by the way."

"I made it last night," Sam shouts back.

"What?"

"I woke up because I had a nightmare."

He turns down the music. "You know what's good for nightmares?"

"Staying at your house."

"You have a one-track mind."

"I can't sleep!"

"How come, Sam?" She doesn't answer, but he says, "What's going on?"

She thinks maybe she won't say, and then she thinks maybe she should—but she's afraid. "I started it," she says at last.

"Started what?"

Then she tells him how she's scared Jack will come back. She describes how Jack smoked and how she wouldn't move, and he picked her up and she fought him—but she doesn't say she bit his arm. She tells how Jack threw her out the door, and her dad turns the music lower and lower as she talks, until at last he turns it off.

She looks over at him and his eyes are bright and dark. He seems like someone else; his arms are tense.

"Dad?" she says, but he won't talk at all.

When they arrive, the yard smells like smoke and burgers and damp grass. Courtney is a cat with little black ears. Noah is a tiny lion. All the neighbors and relatives are there, including Noah's grandma and grandpa and even Jack.

"Hi, sweetie," Jen tells Sam. Jen's husband Steve did all the decorations. Fake cobwebs, tombstones, ghosts hanging on the porch—but Mitchell doesn't notice any of it. He walks straight through the yard.

"Fucking asshole!" He shoves Jack so hard that Jack staggers for just a second before he shoves Mitchell back.

"Whoa, whoa, what's happening!" Jen rushes over.

Grandma B. is holding Noah.

"What, are you drunk?" Courtney screams, but Mitchell doesn't hear.

Jack rises up like he will smash him, but Mitchell has an animal inside him too. He is a panther; he is so strong and fast.

The two of them are flying at each other and Noah is crying. Jen swears she'll call the police, and Steve tries to separate them. He grabs Mitchell's arm, but Mitchell throws him off.

Jack's lip is bleeding. Blood soaks his shirt. He doesn't care. He opens Jen's cooler and kicks it, so a waterfall of ice pours out. Then he grabs a beer and smashes it on Mitchell's face.

Sam's dad doubles over gasping. His nose is pouring blood, but he keeps punching, hitting, and Sam is screaming, "Dad, Dad!" because this is her fault. She told on Jack.

Courtney is begging them to stop, but they don't listen. They are on the ground, rolling in the grass. Jack is heavier and stronger, but Mitchell is wild. He's got his hands on Jack's face and his thumbs in Jack's eyes—and it takes Steve and his brother and his cousin to pull them apart.

7

Courtney holds Sam back. She won't let Sam help; she doesn't care if Mitchell bleeds to death. She yells at him. "What is wrong with you?"

"Nobody hurts my kid," Mitchell says, and Sam wants to say he didn't, because the truth is Jack didn't break her bones—but she is too scared to explain. "Nobody throws her out."

Only Sam and Courtney know what Mitchell means. Sam says nothing, and her mom is saying, Leave.

Grandma and Grandpa B. accuse Sam's dad. Everybody blames him because they saw him walk up and start the fight.

"You're a fool," Jack tells Mitchell. Jack's lip is swollen huge.

Mitchell's nose won't stop. All the blood is pouring out of him. Sam does not think he can stand up, but he does. He stumbles to his car and it starts right away, and he swerves around on the street in front of the house and he takes off, speeding down the street.

And then Sam doesn't see him, not for weeks. Jack comes around to play with Noah. Grandma and Grandpa B. take Noah to the playground or to their house, but where is Sam's dad? She asks her mom, and every time, her mom says he is busy, or he is away.

"But where?" Sam asks.

"Working."

"Where is he working?" Sam asks.

"On himself," says Courtney. "Or he should be."

"Is his nose better?"

Her mom says, "I guess so. Yeah."

"You saw him?"

Courtney won't answer—but why? How come she can see him, and Sam can't? "He has car trouble," Courtney says.

"Can he get it fixed?"

"I doubt it."

"Does he have a dead battery?"

Her mom thinks for a second. Then she says, "No, Sam, he totaled it."

Sam listens to her mom talk to Jen at the salon. She pretends that she can't overhear, but she listens to her mom say that Mitchell is unsafe. Unrealistic.

The next time Mitchell calls it is the day after Thanksgiving. Courtney says, "It's your dad," and Sam is almost afraid to take the phone.

In her mind he is still angry, but when he talks, his voice is light. He sounds like himself. "Hey, monkey."

"Hi," Sam answers softly.

"Happy birthday!" he tells her, even though he is five days late.

"Thanks."

"How does it feel to be EIGHT?"

"I don't know."

"The same?"

"The same."

"I got you something!"

"What?"

"It's a surprise!"

"Okay."

She thinks that he will come give her a present, but Courtney drives Sam to town instead. She drops Sam at the Atomic Bean and says, "I'll be right here in the car." She parks in front where Sam can see her through the window. "Here's money." She gives Sam a ten.

Sam says, "What's that for?" because wouldn't her dad pay? She is nervous, walking in alone. What if he doesn't come?

But Mitchell is right there waiting, and he is fine, even his nose. He is hugging Sam off the ground, and he is strong. He has a table and he has already ordered her hot chocolate and a glazed donut.

He laughs because he catches Sam looking for her present. "Hold on, hold on." He wants to know about school and reading and if she is still practicing the monkey bars.

"Not really."

"Okay," her dad says, like that's fine; everything is fine. "When you're ready, you'll get back to Boulders."

Sam frowns because he is unrealistic, just like her mom said.

But good news, her dad is back at work, which means gigging in New Hampshire, and he is driving a new car. Actually, it's his girlfriend's car. Her name is April.

"April?"

But that is her name, and she lives in Portsmouth. Sam can come up and meet her. They will all go to Strawbery Banke where you can ride a carriage through the old town and peek into the windows to see how people used to live. Sam says okay.

It's like listening to a story, hearing how it's going to be, the horses' hooves on cobblestones.

Her dad is sipping coffee, and she bends over her mug to lick the whipped cream. He tells her, "We'll have tea and scones."

"What are scones?"

"You don't know what a scone is? It's better than a muffin. It's buttery and flaky. Sometimes it's got currants. Sometimes you eat them with strawberries. The strawberries are tart and sweet at the same time."

"Yum," Sam says dreamily.

"Music is great at Strawbery Banke," he tells Sam. "And it's a great place for magicians."

Now Sam sits up straight. She knows what's going on. "You're moving!"

Her dad says, "Not permanently! I'll be back all the time!"

"When?"

"I'll come down, and you'll come up."

"How will I come up?" She looks through the café window, and there is her mom sitting in the car. Probably she already knows about this. It makes Sam mad because nobody tells her anything. "How far away is it?"

"Just forty miles."

"Forty miles!"

"It's not far at all!" He reaches to the floor and picks up a big cardboard box that wasn't even there before—but that doesn't surprise her. "Did you forget your present?"

She hardly wants her present anymore, but he says, Open it.

Slowly she lifts the top and finds a pair of pointy climbing shoes, bright blue and yellow with a little bit of black. He says try them on, so she slips her feet in, and they are way too big for her.

She just looks down at those big shoes, while her dad says, "Room to grow!"

If he were really magic, he would tap her shoes, and they would shrink to fit—but then he would know her size already, without looking. He would know her size and he would know what she is thinking—that she never wanted shoes or Boulders without him.

8

Sam stops climbing up the doorframes. Her mom says thank you. Then, later on, she says, Honey, don't be sad.

Sam says, "Honey?" because her mom never calls her that.

Courtney says, "You look so sad and tired."

"I'm not."

Courtney looks doubtful. She thinks Sam is pretending, but Sam is telling the truth. She is not tired. She is not honey either.

"We'll come down this summer," Mitchell tells Sam on the phone. Right now, he's on the road in Maine, Vermont, and Montreal. He is juggling, and conjuring, cutting April in half, but when school's out, they will take Sam to Crane Beach, and maybe camping, and maybe sailing to the islands—the little ones that you can see from shore. They'll get a boat!

Surprise, surprise, that summer nobody comes down. Her dad is up in Maine alone. Courtney says he has no boat, no money, and no April.

The day school lets out, Courtney says, "We'll go anyway." It will be the three of them, and maybe Grandma B.

Sam doesn't feel like swimming, but Noah says, Please, please? And so they go. Grandma B. drives, and she wants Jack to come, but he does not. He and Courtney are on and off again. That's what Courtney tells Jen at the salon. There are many fish in the sea, Jen says.

Mostly Sam finds dead horseshoe crabs. Grandma B. is setting up her beach chair and Noah is digging in the sand, but Sam and Courtney are walking along the wet sand where crabs wash ashore.

Sam wears a striped one-piece bathing suit, but Courtney is wearing a bikini the color of a nectarine. People turn and look at her as she walks by. Guys are throwing a Frisbee, and it lands right at her feet.

Courtney throws the Frisbee back, slicing the air, but she doesn't ask to play. She wades into the waves, instead. "Too cold!" says Courtney, but she keeps going, hip deep, then chest deep. She is standing in the water, and Sam is almost standing. On tiptoe she can touch the bottom.

"RIP second grade," says Courtney. "The older grades are better, and high school is the best!"

"Is that when you met Dad?"

"Not really."

"Didn't he go to your school?"

"Well, he did, and he didn't."

"What do you mean?"

"Don't try it."

The water is colder down by Sam's legs. Cold prickles her body. "How come you always say that?"

"You know what?" says Courtney. Sam thinks, Don't get smart, but Courtney doesn't say that. She says, "Your dad is an artist. Lots of people pretend they are, but he really is. His art isn't in museums. His songs aren't on the radio. His magic isn't in, like, the Magic Hall of Fame, but he's the real deal. He just—he puts ideas together you would never think of—and when he has his—" She interrupts herself. "He's unbelievable."

Sam asks, "In a good way, or a bad way?"

"I love you." Courtney laughs.

"What?" Sam hops to keep her head above the water.

"We met at the beach," Courtney says.

"Here?"

"No, Singing Beach. And you know what he was doing? Building sandcastles. I was sixteen and he was eighteen."

"Eighteen?" Sam says, because wasn't he too old to play in the sand?

But her dad's castles were fantastic. That's what Courtney says. He built her a castle three stories tall, and it had towers with scalloped shells on top and windows of sea glass, and a moat that filled with water when the tide came in.

Sometimes it's easier when he's far away. It's better when you aren't reminded of him.

When school starts again, Sam's dad is up in Canada, which is north of here. Her mom says, "Do you want to see it on the map?"

Sam says, "No thank you."

When Sam turns nine, Mitchell sends her fifty dollars. After Sam's party with the kids from school, Courtney cleans up the melted ice cream cake and says, Look at these beautiful markers. Why don't you write to Dad? Or draw a picture?

Sam stares at her new pad of art paper, and she has no idea what to draw. She doesn't have as many ideas as she did when she was younger. She tries to draw her mom, but then she rips the picture out.

"Hey, wait, I liked that!" Courtney says. She recognizes her green eyes and her long reddish hair. She is wearing her bikini top and she's got a mermaid tail. "But where's the rest? You didn't finish." It's true, Courtney is all alone on the white paper. Sam doesn't have all day, so she takes her dark blue and her light blue and her green-blue and quickly fills the whole page with squiggles for waves, so now Courtney is swimming in the ocean. "Sign it," Courtney says, "and write the date." Sam writes her name and then *11/21/99*. "I love it," Courtney says, but that's because she is Sam's mom. Sam isn't good at drawing anymore.

She is still good at hiding.

When Jack comes around, she climbs the beech to watch and listen. When his black truck pulls up, she waits for him to leave, and if he stays, she won't come in until it's dark and cold. Then she hides out in her room.

One night she hears Jack say, "What's *wrong* with her?"

Her mom says, "Leave her alone. She's having a hard time."

He says, "Just keep making excuses. Good parenting."

"You would know."

"What the fuck does that mean?"

"Think about it," Courtney says.

"Think about it," Jack echoes.

Courtney says, "Your mom is still making excuses for you."

That night Courtney and Jack start fighting for real.

Sam is sleeping in her bed, but she wakes up when her mom shouts, "No!"

There's a crashing sound and Noah wakes up too.

"While I live here, it's my house," Courtney screams.

"It's my house," he shouts back. "Nothing here is yours. You don't kick me out. I kick your ass out."

Sam hears the front door swing open. She feels the winter night through the thin walls. He's going to throw her mom out. That's all she knows. Noah is crying and she scrambles out of bed and gives him his teddy. "Hold Bill," she orders. "Don't move."

She rushes into the living room where her mom and Jack are struggling at the door. Her mom is strong, but Jack is turning back into the bear. He'll kick her if he can. He'll cover up her mouth and eat her head.

Sam launches herself at him. "Get off of her!"

"Sam. Stay back," her mom screams, but Sam is hitting Jack as hard as she can.

He turns on her and slams her to the couch. Before she can catch her breath, her mom says, "Get Noah. Find your boots."

Jack stands and watches as Courtney grabs Noah, who is holding Bill. Sam follows and they start the cold, cold car.

And that's how Jack wins. He gets the house.

9

The first night, Sam and Noah and Courtney sleep on Jen's couch under quilts.

The second night, they sleep down in the finished basement on new air mattresses.

Then Courtney finds an apartment in town.

It's for the best. They can walk to school, and Courtney can park under the building, so they won't have to shovel out the car.

Moving is gonna be great. Maybe. They collect empty cartons from the salon, the supermarket, the liquor store. After school, they drive back to the old house for their clothes and kitchen stuff. Every day they take a load to their new place.

The apartment is two bedrooms and one bath, and everything is pretty new. They have a dishwasher and that is huge. Sam has a tent. She sets it up on the carpet next to Noah's bed.

She got it when Jen was cleaning her garage to find them some chairs. "Look at all this camping stuff," said Jen.

"Can I have that?" Sam asked.

"Sam, that thing is filthy," Courtney said, but Sam brushed off the leaves. Then Steve helped Sam vacuum it.

The tent is olive green with white mesh windows. You can sleep there and then sit up and get dressed for school in privacy. It's like having your own house. Sam keeps her savings (seventy-

three dollars) in the tent, along with her good markers and expensive drawing paper, her lollipops from the salon, and her
china sheep, missing its front leg.

The apartment has wall-to-wall carpeting soft on your toes.
They take off their shoes to keep it clean. What's missing is a
beech tree. They have a balcony, but it's not big enough for anything. It's a trade-off. Another trade-off is that Courtney has to
take a second job to pay the rent. She works at Staples in the
shopping plaza, and that means Afterschool.

"Look at these classes at the Y," Courtney tells Sam.

"No way."

The Y is practically for babies. Sam says, No, don't make me
go there, but Courtney signs up Sam for the Y, anyway, because
who else can take Noah? "He can learn to swim," Courtney
says. "And look at all these classes for kids your age." Sam can
take photography or cooking or homework club—or climbing.
"They have a climbing wall!"

"I *know*," Sam says.

"You like climbing," Courtney reminds her.

Sam says, "Not really."

Courtney searches every box until she finds the climbing
shoes Mitchell gave Sam a year ago. "I knew I packed these!"

"Mom, stop!" Sam says. "They don't even fit."

"They've got to fit by now."

"No, they're too small."

"They can't be," Courtney says, but Sam is right. The shoes
that used to be too big now pinch Sam's toes. Sam throws them
in the trash.

"Sam! Those are brand-new shoes! Maybe some other kid
can use them."

"They're junk," Sam says.

"*Hey.*" Her mom is about to scream I've had enough of you.
But she does not. She just leans against the wall.

Sam doesn't tell anybody she's going to the Y. The first day of Afterschool, Sam picks up Noah from pre-K and rushes him outside so nobody her age will see them.

Noah says, "Ow! Sam!"

She slows down a tiny bit. It's not his fault for being born. His hair is black, but his eyes are green. When Sam tells him something, he believes her. Right now, she tells him to pretend he is a spy escaping from prison, and he has to walk as softly as possible, or gorillas will catch him. "Hurry," she whispers. "Don't let the gorillas see you. Here, I'll carry that." She grabs his little backpack and together they rush down the hall and out the door. "Okay, we're safe."

Noah asks, "What if they're hiding in the trees?"

He is a good brother, for his age.

At the Y, Sam takes Noah downstairs for lessons in the green chlorine pool where all the little kids are screaming. She hands him his bathing suit and towel, and she meets his teacher, and then she almost hides on the white bleachers, but everybody there is moms.

Slowly she walks up to the gym where more little kids are jumping, tumbling, and wrestling on gymnastics mats. There are only three big kids in climbing—a girl, a boy, and Sam.

The girl is tall with freckles and long, frizzy blond hair. Her jeans have a purple ink stain on the back pocket, and her name is Halle. The boy is her brother, Eric. He has red hair, and he wears glasses. Halle and Eric don't go to Sam's school. She has never seen them before, even though they also live in Beverly.

Eric looks around at the little kids. Then he asks Sam and Halle, "Are we the only people here?"

"I guess so." It seems like Halle really doesn't mind how babyish Afterschool is, even though she is nine and her brother is ten.

"Okay, everybody," announces a YMCA teacher. "Little Tumblers, follow me. Climbers, follow Kevin."

Halle, Sam, and Eric shuffle to the climbing wall. It's a relief that Halle and Eric wear sneakers. Nobody has climbing shoes.

As soon as Kevin takes attendance, he makes a big deal out of Sam. "Hey, kiddo. You got so big I didn't even recognize you. How's your dad?"

"Good."

"Say hi for me, okay? Who else we got here? Hailey?"

"Halle."

"Gotcha. And Eric. Apart from Sam, has anybody climbed before?"

They stretch their arms and roll their shoulders and lunge and practice jumping jacks and talk about how safety is their number one priority. Kevin shows them the ropes and clips that he will use and explains how he will belay them. Climbing, they take turns, and Eric goes up first.

He is so awkward! Kevin is holding the rope below, so nothing bad will happen, but Eric is afraid. On the first footholds, he just stands there with his legs splayed out and looks over his shoulder.

"Okay, reach," says Kevin. "Just reach over your head."

Eric's arms are long, but they won't stretch.

"One step at a time, buddy. Try moving your left foot closer."

"I can't."

"You won't fall," says Kevin. "I got you."

"He's afraid of heights," Halle tells Sam as they watch from the mats. Eric could step down, but he acts like he's hanging from a mountain by a thread.

"That's better," Kevin tells Eric. "A little more."

Eric inches his left foot over. He's getting ready to move that foot onto a new hold.

Halle rests her head on her knees and closes her eyes, but Sam keeps watching. He's like a bug caught in a spiderweb.

When Eric makes it up partway, Kevin allows him to come down. Instantly, Eric opens his book and starts to read.

"There's always a first time," Kevin says.

Halle is next, and it's her first time too, but she's way better.

"Steady as she goes," calls Kevin.

Halle is unafraid. She reaches with her long arms, and when she gets stuck, she listens to directions. Watching from below, Sam thinks, You're pretty good—but why did you take the long way? You can swing across!

By the time it's Sam's turn, she is stiff and grumpy. Then Kevin says, "Let's see if you remember what Dad taught you."

Sam's whole body tightens. She stares at Kevin's tattooed fingers—L.O.V.E.—but doesn't feel any.

"All set?"

She attacks the wall, jumping the first holds, climbing without stopping. She's been watching long enough to memorize the route, so she swings across and pulls up in two seconds. When she makes it to the top, she doesn't stop to enjoy it. She pushes off with both feet so she is dangling in midair.

"Whoa, whoa!" Kevin calls out, as Sam glides down.

Wide-eyed, Halle stares at her. Even Eric looks up from his book.

"You're on fire!" Kevin says. "Where have you been practicing?"

Sam tells the truth. "No place."

10

Every day, Sam and Noah walk to the Y. Sam takes Noah to the pool and then she goes to the gym where Kevin sets up new routes. Eric never climbs very high. He'll try just once to get it over with, and then he opens up his book. Halle is different. She tries hard and learns fast. Kevin says Halle is an athlete. Sam is quick, but Halle has longer arms. She is strong, and she doesn't worry about anything.

"Have you ever been to Boulders?" Sam asks Halle, after class.

"No, what is it?"

"A real gym." They are standing in front of the Y and Noah is pulling on Sam's arm to leave.

"Can kids go there?" Halle asks.

"Yeah, but it's too far."

"Where is it?"

"Newburyport."

Halle's dad pulls up in a huge black station wagon. Sam has never seen a car so big and black. "Dad," says Halle. "This is Sam."

"Hi, Sam. I'm Jim."

"I like your car," says Sam.

He smiles. "It's a hearse." He says he is a sculptor, and he bought the hearse to transport his work.

Halle and Eric squeeze into the front seat with Jim, and Halle asks, "Dad, can you take us to Boulders on Saturday?"

"Probably," says Jim. "Or Mom can." With Sam's dad, probably means no, but Jim makes it sound like yes.

"They can take me home on Friday and I can sleep over so we can go to Boulders," Sam tells her mom that night.

"What about Noah?" Courtney says.

"He can come with me to their house, and you can pick him up from there."

"Okay," says Courtney.

"I can go?"

"Sure," Courtney says. "Yes." She is lying on the couch with her feet up, and she is wearing her red shirt from Staples.

"Can I have two quarters?" Noah asks. He is on the floor with his homework, drawing things that start with G.

"For what?"

"Gum."

"You don't need gum."

Sam explains, "At the Y they have a gumball machine." She kind of wishes she could get some.

"Please?" Noah says.

"No way," says Courtney. "It's a good word, though. Gumball starts with G."

Halle lives in Beverly Farms and her house is old and full of books. There are even bookshelves in the bathroom. You can see where Eric gets it from. He has a giant bookcase in his room. Halle has a bookcase too. Her dad built it like a castle. She has her own room at the top of the house, and a secret staircase that leads up to it. The stairs are painted blue. All the rooms are different colors. The kitchen is bright yellow. The family room is green. Halle's room is white with a blue sky and clouds up on the ceiling.

At dinnertime, Jim cooks dinner while Halle's mom works late at the hospital. Jim's food is weird and spicy, cauliflower curry, but Sam tries to get used to it.

"I hear you're an amazing climber," Jim says.

"I'm okay."

"When did you start?" Jim looks old for a dad. He is bald and he wears squinty glasses like Noah's grandpa.

Sam says, "When I was seven, I was going to join a team."

"Why didn't you?" Eric asks.

Sam thinks for a second, and then she says, "Transportation."

On Saturday morning, Halle's mom, Lucy, drives the girls to Boulders. Lucy pays and signs a waiver for Halle. Then Sam hands over a waiver that Courtney got Boulders to fax to Staples so she could sign it in advance.

"Okay!" Lucy says. "Go for it!" And she heads off to find some coffee. She looks like Halle, except her eyes are tired and her hair is gray.

The girls borrow climbing shoes and take a lesson with a climbing teacher. It's the STAFF Sam saw that time with her dad, the one who said, My name is Toby. Now Sam is sure Toby is a girl, even though her hair is super short.

"Let's get started!" Toby says. Luckily, she doesn't remember Sam and ask about her father.

Sam and Halle take turns climbing with ropes while Toby belays them. Toby likes the way Halle does not give up. "Good effort!" she keeps telling her.

Halle picks her holds and tests them out. She is straightforward on the wall.

Sam can't be straightforward because she's not tall enough.

Also, she can't climb so slowly! She finds weird angles and cuts corners. She squinches her feet and crimps her fingers onto tiny handholds. When she sees a hold too high to reach, she lunges for it. More than once, she ends up dangling from the rope. She's frustrated, but Toby thinks she has potential. Both girls should come on Saturdays for 12 and Unders, Bigger Boulders. Halle's mom and dad can drive, if it's okay with Courtney.

"What comes after Bigger Boulders?" Sam asks Halle when they get back to Halle's house.

"Youth Competitions," Halle says.

Whenever you win a competition you get points. The top points go to regionals and then nationals and worlds and then you're famous. You're a prodigy! You wear patches on your sleeves and companies will send you shoes and water bottles.

11

When they start training to be famous, Kevin changes up the walls, switching handholds with his power screwdriver. The wall is like a giant pegboard and you can move the holds into a million different combinations. He is trying to challenge Sam and Halle now that it's just the two of them at Afterschool. Eric has decided he would rather walk over to the library.

On Saturdays, they practice with five other girls at Boulders. Usually, Sam sleeps over and Halle's mom or dad will do the driving.

They are pretty much the best in Bigger Boulders, except for one girl named Emily. Her legs are really long. She can do the splits, so she can stretch out and reach any hold—but she cries all the time. Her fingers hurt, or she stubs her toe, or she twists her ankle, or she doesn't fall right. She makes a big deal about everything.

She's always complaining, and she isn't *that* good. Halle is stronger than Emily. Sam is faster. Also, they're working on their splits at home. Halle can't get all the way down to the floor, but Sam can. Toby says she's bendy.

Toby is their teacher now. She has no fat on her entire body. She's streamlined, and she likes to treat the whole team equally. She doesn't give out many compliments, and when she does, they're small.

The lowest is okay.

Then after that, good effort.

Then nice.

Nice is as high as Toby goes, but once she says, What?

They are on the bouldering walls and everybody else goes vertical, then side to side. Sam goes vertical, but then she takes a chance and jumps, springing off black footholds to grab the purple ledge above.

"WHAT?" Toby exclaims, like Where did that come from?

Sam is climbing like a squirrel, stretching and leaping in a tree, and everyone below is quiet.

Halle looks a little glad, but a little jealous too. Then when it's her turn, she tries Sam's move and builds on it to climb even higher.

"Nice, Halle!" Toby calls out, and Sam wants to say I invented that.

Toby says, "We share beta." That means everybody should share information, like This is where to put your feet, or Don't do what I did.

Beta is annoying. It's like permission to steal your ideas. On the wall, Sam is like the scout. She will try stuff no one else will do. But Halle is always learning. She is always right behind.

At least Halle admits Sam is better than she is.

"You're smarter at climbing," Halle says after practice one day.

Sam nods. It's true—but Halle is smarter at other things. She has a hundred books, and she has read them all. She is always telling Sam, You should read this, and you should read that. She tries to get Sam to read *Black Beauty,* which is about an old horse explaining how he pulls wagons and coaches all his life—and that's all he ever does. Nothing happens to him, even though he knows how to write.

Halle gives Sam *Harry Potter* and a mini reading light for

her tenth birthday, but Sam likes the light better than the book, which is so long.

She likes everything quick. If she is climbing, she will scramble up as fast as possible. If she's got homework, she waits until the last second and scribbles down the answer. Her mom says, Slow down, but Sam likes being done. Her mom says, It's not a race. She also says, I was just like you.

Halle takes her time. On the wall she'll hang there, thinking about her next move. Sam just goes for it. For this reason, she falls a lot—but then sometimes she nails it.

Their first competition will be at their own gym. Everybody is going to wear Bigger Boulders T-shirts, which are blue with a drawing of a boulder and a kid standing on top. And you're supposed to wear your own climbing shoes. Sam wants blue shoes because those are team colors—and Courtney buys them.

They are the best things Sam has ever had. They are bright electric blue, extra narrow, and they smell so good. She loves the smell of new shoes.

"Okay, work hard," says Courtney, "and please don't grow."

But you can't help it. At the doctor's office, Pat, the nurse, says, Oh wow look at you, getting so tall.

"What grade are you in, Sam?"

"Fourth."

"How can that be?" Pat asks Courtney.

Courtney shakes her head. Nobody knows how it happens, but your feet keep growing, and your legs, and all the rest of you.

Sam's mom calls her skinny Minnie, and string bean. Sam's dad doesn't call at all, because he is having a rough time. Sam doesn't ask what that means. Her mom always says, You can talk to me about anything, but Sam doesn't want to talk about him.

Usually she only thinks of Mitchell when she is falling asleep. She dreams of him on the bus home from field trips. After the aquarium, her dad is swimming with sea turtles. After the zoo, he is in the woods with arctic foxes.

12

The day her dad does call, Sam almost drops the phone.

"Hey, monkey. How are you? Hey, Sam? Are you there?"

Her mom says, "Who is that? Dad?" She takes the phone. "Mitchell?" She is talking just like she always does to Sam's dad. What the hell? And where are you? Uh-huh. Oh my God. Courtney is scolding and arguing and finding out everything, but Sam can't talk, because she's crying. As soon as she hears his voice, all the tears start pouring out.

Her mom is trying to hug her. "Say something."

"Hi," Sam says finally. She is glad her dad can't see her crying face.

"Hi!" her dad says. "What's going on?"

Sam just says, "When are you coming back?"

"That's what I called to tell you! I'm coming in a few weeks."

"December ninth?" Sam wipes her face with her hand.

"What's December ninth?"

"My competition. Nine A.M. at Boulders."

"Oh wow."

"Write that down, Dad."

"Will do!"

She strains her ears, but she can't hear him writing. "Do you have a pen?"

"What do you mean, do I have a pen?"

"What color is it?"

"Green."

"Really?" She is afraid to trust him, and a little bit afraid to see him. How will he look next to all the other moms and dads? She is afraid for him to show up now, and, at the same time, she is afraid that he won't come.

She tells herself, Don't worry, he won't. Or if he does, he will not come in time. But then she has a feeling he will show up while she's climbing. Just as she reaches the top, she'll turn around and see him watching.

The competition is just local, but it's got tons of kids. There are prizes for every age, and Sam is glad Noah isn't climbing. She doesn't want to be related to a Baby Boulder.

Noah watches with Courtney and Halle's family while Sam gets a number pinned onto her shirt. She likes Halle's number better, but that's life. Halle gets 50. Sam gets 63.

All the parents have to stand back, because they're crowding. They stand behind a certain line.

It's confusing, because there are so many kids, and there is such a rush. Officials can't wait for you. They can't come looking for you. If you don't listen up, you'll miss your turn. Sam and Halle are in different groups for lead climbing, but they're in the same group for bouldering. The way it works is you have to sit in folding chairs while you wait your turn. The folding chairs are all in a row facing away from the wall. That's so you can't see the handholds or learn from what the other kids are doing. No sharing beta in a competition.

While Sam is waiting in her folding chair, she looks down at her blue shoes. She has a real chalk pouch too. It's belted on, so she can reach back and dip her fingers into the white powder.

Halle is sitting two chairs down, but all Sam can see is parents' faces, proud, happy, scared. First, the parents are excited; then they're crushed when their kid falls. They are so sad! But as soon as their kid comes running over, they pretend that everything is great. Good job!

A girl is crying, and her parents are hugging her, and they keep saying, It's okay. You tried your best! Sam hopes her mom won't do that. She doesn't want to try her best; she wants to win.

She kind of knows she will. She has a feeling that once she gets up there nothing will stop her—but how can you win if it's never your turn? Is she really on the list?

It's hard to sit in a chair when you want to twist around and stretch and hang upside down, but you can't even turn your head, because people might think you're peeking.

Halle goes up. All the other girls go up. Sam waits forever and while she's waiting, she keeps thinking he will be there. She will look down from the wall and he will be there—and he'll be done having a rough time.

When she hears 63, she jumps, and suddenly she's scared. It's like swallowing ice. Fear hurts when it goes down.

She takes one look at the bouldering wall and then she's climbing. The wall is angled, but it's got good footholds near the bottom. She looks up and she thinks Reach. She knows what to do. She is strong, and she is fast, but everyone is watching, and the ice inside her makes her slip. Her feet don't work in her new shoes. She climbs the wall, but barely.

She gets to try three routes for bouldering and three for lead, and each time she tries harder and each time she feels worse, because her dad was never holding a green pen.

In bouldering she falls onto the mat. In lead climbing, she slips and dangles from her rope in disbelief.

Halle gets ninth in bouldering and fifth in lead. Sam is seventeenth and twelfth. And Emily is on the podium. Emily who cries about everything is standing there in third place for boul-dering while her parents take her picture.

Sam's mom wants to take pictures too, but why? Sam did not do her best. She is not proud of herself, or anybody else. She wants to kick the wall and smash it with her fists. Her body is awake now. Hands, feet, toes.

13

"Sam, go to bed." It is midnight and Sam is sitting in her tent with her reading light, while her mom kneels outside the opening. Sam is writing out a chart in black. All the days until December twenty-second, which she circles in purple.

"What's December twenty-second?"

Sam doesn't answer because her mom should know that. December twenty-second is next time.

Next time she is going to win. She is going to climb the way she knows she can, because she won't be scared. She will know what to expect. She will know her dad's not coming.

On Saturday, when she and Halle go to practice, Sam doesn't smile or goof off with the other girls. She jumps up, attacking every problem. The handholds on the wall are like a maze or a connect-the-dots. They are a set of clues, if you can find a way to use them. A black hold, a pink hold, a boxy shape, a tilt, an angled triangle.

"Nice!" Toby calls from down below.

Sam leads the way, and Halle follows. Sometimes, Halle laughs at herself. She has a good attitude. She has good equipment too. Halle's dad installs a chin-up bar in the basement, so Halle can practice any time. She can hang from her fingertips all day.

"Mom, can I have a chin-up bar?" Sam asks.

"No."

"We could just stick it in the doorway here."

"No, we can't."

"Why not?"

"Because it will damage the apartment."

"No, it won't."

"Yes, it will. It'll mess up the doorframe."

"But it's suspension. You just wedge it in."

"It will ruin the paint."

"How do you know?"

"Stop it!"

Sam is jealous, but she tries not to let it show. When she sleeps over, she wakes up before Halle so she can slip down to the basement in her pajamas. Then she pulls up on the bar and drops to rest and tries again.

When she is done, Sam tries to take the secret stairs back up to Halle's room, but Halle's mom hears her. "Sam, is that you?"

Jim and Lucy are sipping coffee in the kitchen.

"How's it going?" Jim asks.

"Good."

"Were you practicing?"

Sam doesn't answer.

Lucy says, "Your mom says you're very serious."

Sam holds perfectly still, because moms aren't supposed to talk about their kids—not about their hearts.

"I think it's great," says Jim. "Set a goal and work for it."

When Halle wakes up, Sam practices again with her and then they eat chocolate chip muffins and mix weird smoothies in the blender. They try mixing bananas, coconut flakes and strawberries and almond milk and peanut butter. Courtney would come in yelling, Don't make such a mess! But Halle's mom is not so strict, and her dad just laughs when he walks in.

Halle says her dad used to analyze companies, but art was his dream, so he retired to do metalwork.

Sam says her dad has been an artist his whole life.

Halle tells Sam that a long time ago her dad was married to someone else, and he has two older daughters who are grown up in New York City. One is a stockbroker, and one is a lawyer.

Sam says her dad doesn't have any other children. She is the only one.

14

She knows she's going to win on December twenty-second. She can see it. She is standing on the podium in Danvers with first place in bouldering. Halle takes second, just one step down, and in the audience, Courtney and Jim and Lucy and Noah are all cheering. Sam's dad is missing but it doesn't matter, because winning is so good. Sam is famous; she is rich; she is standing far above. That's her dream. The problem is her mom won't let her compete.

Fourth grade is hard, but Courtney doesn't care. Sam has to catch up, or she can't climb. Courtney will be the bad guy. She will be that person if necessary, because she wants Sam to learn something get a job do better in her life.

Sam wants to win, and so she fills out a million worksheets. Math, social studies, biology.

My animal is the Ratel.
His scientific name is Mellivora capensis.
Some other animals in the same family are Weasels, Skunks, Badgers.
It lives in Africa and India.
It eats honey.
My animal's natural predators are? None.

My animal protects itself by spraying.
My animal poem:

Ratel, ratel,
Horrible smell.
Makes people run away.
Makes them run far away.
It can't get stung by honeybees.
It likes to climb up big tall trees.

Sam misses the trees at the old house. She misses when she was little, before homework.

Her mom sits next to her and says, "I *wish* I could go to school right now."

Then Sam makes a mistake. She asks, "Why don't you?"

BECAUSE I HAVE TO WORK! WHERE DO YOU THINK THIS FOOD COMES FROM? AND THIS FURNITURE AND THIS APARTMENT AND THE CLOTHES YOU KIDS WEAR? DO YOU THINK ANYBODY ELSE IS TAKING CARE OF YOU?

It's confusing, because you go to school to get a job, and Courtney only wishes she could go—but she has two jobs already.

Courtney says, That's the whole point. Then she says, "You think it's easy?"

Sam knows it's not. You have to work and work and pay and pay and even then, Jack comes around. He tries to take Noah out, but a lot of times Courtney won't let him. She trusts Jack around his mom and dad, but not by himself. He has too many friends and substances. Even his own parents are angry at him now.

Sometimes Sam hears her mom fighting with Jack on the phone. Jack tells Courtney she is keeping him away from his own son. Then Courtney says, That's right. She is out of patience; she is done. She says that, but Jack is still Noah's dad.

That's just the way it is. You pay your bills. You lock your door. You do your homework. Everybody's got a job. You don't have to like it. You just have to do it. And write neatly. And lose the attitude. Fractions and poems and maps of the world. Sam works nonstop, even at Halle's house.

Halle is reading a book about a girl named Jane who goes to a school with no food and no vacations. Jane only has one friend, and she dies in Jane's bed. "It's a really good book," Halle says.

"No thank you." Sam is sitting on the floor trying to write a story for her Language Arts teacher. She has been sitting there almost an hour, and she's got nothing.

"Just use your imagination." Halle thinks your imagination is something you can put on like a jacket or pick up like a spoon—but Sam's imagination is private! You don't use your actual imagination for homework. It's like telling wishes. She writes a paragraph about Halloween and making her own costume. She will not write a paragraph about winning, because then it won't come true.

After Courtney comes to get Sam and they drive home, Courtney asks, "Did you finish your homework?"

Sam says, "Yes."

"All of it?"

When they get home, Sam shows her.

Then her mom gives Sam her tightest hug, her mama boa constrictor. "You did that. Nobody else."

Sam looks at her because who else would do her homework? "Can I climb now?"

Her mom shouts, "Yes!" And she signs Sam's permission forms right that minute. *Boulders Ltd. will not be liable for . . .*

Then she says, "And I have a surprise for you."

Sam looks at her mom and groans. "Dad?"

"Sam!" Courtney thinks Sam should be jumping up and down like she did when she was little—but the surprise is always her dad, like the white rabbit. It's always the same white rabbit in his hat. "He's back."

Sam says, "I don't care. I'm done."

"You're ten! You aren't done with anything."

Courtney says Mitchell wants to come to Danvers, but Sam shakes her head.

On the phone, Mitchell says he is really back. He has a place to live, and he is getting a job at Roger's Garden Center. Sam thinks, Really? He says how glad he is and how he missed her, and he is sorry he got delayed before. He was planning on being there, but he got held up. He says I have so much to tell you.

Sam interrupts, "But, Dad, just please don't come to the gym."

"Okay."

For a second, she doesn't know what to say to that. She thought he would argue, but he is quiet, and so is she. "Thanks," she says at last.

He says, "No problem," and she knows she's hurt his feelings, but at the same time she's relieved.

She says, "Bye."

He says, "I'll see you later." And he does not come to Danvers. He does not distract or embarrass her or anything. She messes up on her own and ends up sixth in bouldering. Halle gets second and Sam is about to win, but on her last climb she takes a chance and falls.

"You tried your best," her mom says, in the car.

"No, I didn't," Sam says, because actually she tried her worst. She wasn't patient on the wall. She wasn't smart.

"Are you hungry?" Courtney asks.

"Yeah!" yells Noah from the back seat.

Sam says, "Not really."

"I was thinking maybe we could meet your dad for pizza. Do

you want to?" Courtney asks, but it is not really a question, since Sam only has one dad and she has got to see him sometime.

They park in front of Freeda's, and as soon as they get out, they see Mitchell waiting in the cold.

"Hey, monkey!"

He is pale and his eyes are dark. He is her dad, but Sam keeps walking.

"Give her a minute," her mom tells Mitchell. "We'll go inside and order."

Sam walks past Dress Barn and Mikado Chinese + Japanese all the way to the other side of the strip mall. This side is back doors of the stores and restaurants. It's just quiet. She leans against the cold cement so she can breathe.

But her dad is looking for her. She hears him coming, and he finds her. Now it's the two of them standing there, shivering.

He says, "Your mom says you were amazing on the wall."

"No, I wasn't."

"You got to semifinals."

"I got sixth."

"I thought you got second."

"No, that was Halle." She is staring at the asphalt parking lot. She can't think of anything else to say.

After a while, Mitchell lights a cigarette.

Sam says, "You know what kind of doctor Halle's mom is?"

"What kind?"

"Cancer."

"Nice."

"What do you mean, nice?"

"I don't know. I was just trying to make conversation." Her dad holds his cigarette down away from Sam. "Your mom says you're the most creative one."

"Are you going to stop smoking?"

"Now?" he says. "Or later?"

"Now."

He stubs out his cigarette. "Can I see your ribbon?"

"No."

He is thinking what to say that will be kind and understanding. "Are you mad your friend did better?"

"No."

"When I was your age, I never got a ribbon for anything."

"You never wanted a ribbon."

"How do you know?"

"Because that's how you are."

"It's true."

Her anger flares. "You never try for anything."

"I'm trying now."

II

Molecule

15

At first Sam thinks it's only temporary. Her dad is staying a short time before he leaves again. Her dad says no, but she does not believe him. Probably, he is practicing a new act.

"Nope," he says. He sold his unicycle in Montreal, along with his accordion. He gave up his magician clothes.

"Even your hat?" Sam is hanging from the metal bar in the basement of the Y.

"Hold on, monkey!" Her dad keeps talking to distract her from the pain. "No more hat. No wand. No rabbit."

Her dad doesn't miss the travel. He misses drinking, but he is committed. In the spring he does not disappear.

Sam almost thinks he will start traveling now that the weather is warmer, but no. He stays. In May, when Courtney says, Let Dad come and watch you compete, Sam says okay.

As soon as she walks in, she sees him standing with the other parents, and he looks brand-new. Courtney cut his hair, and it's still long, but it's not shaggy. He is thin but he's not pale. His eyes are dark but smart and happy. He looks like a rock star, compared to Halle's dad. Courtney is a mermaid next to him.

Halle says she's nervous, but Sam can't even talk. What would it be like to win and watch her parents jump for joy?

They would hug each other. They would say, Wow, that's our kid.

"Good luck! You can do it. Just believe!" says Halle.

Courtney always says Halle has a good heart, and it's true. You feel safe when you're around her, because Halle is not afraid of anything. She has no natural predators. At competitions, Halle climbs to win, but she is a good loser too.

Toby tells the team to just get up there and have fun, but Sam can't. She is too fierce and scared.

Sitting in her chair, she shuts her eyes and pretends no one is watching. She tells herself, Nothing matters. No one is looking at you. And then they call her number and her heart drops. She glances at the wall and she is so dizzy she can hardly stand. She feels faint, except she hears a long high whistle. Her dad is whistling with two fingers as she jumps.

Now. Now she will shake off all her sickness and her fear. She grabs the first hold and starts talking to herself again. Nobody is watching. Nobody is looking. Nobody is chasing you. Don't rush. But halfway up, she slips and falls.

"Sam," Toby tells her, "if you would just relax."

Other kids do great. A few are incredible. The best is a girl named Ayla from Vermont. She is only eight, but smart and tiny as a spider monkey.

Sam's arms are longer like she wanted. She is ten and a half now, and she is stronger, but she weighs more too. She feels her weight up on the wall.

Before her final round of bouldering, Sam sits in her folding chair, and she can't see the other girls climbing, but she knows how they are doing from their parents' faces. She looks at Jim and she can tell that Halle makes it almost to the top. Sam sees it in Jim's face. Oh . . . oh . . . almost! And then his smile. Oh well.

When Sam looks at the crowd, she can tell that Ayla is putting on a show. Everyone is smiling. Wow! Amazing! Even Sam's dad is standing there admiring Ayla, because she is so fast and graceful—and then, suddenly, everybody groans. Noooo! Even with her back to the wall, Sam knows that Ayla fell. Ayla messed up—and that means Sam has a chance. Sam realizes this, even though she is climbing badly. She could be the first to solve this problem—but there must be something weird about it, some trick question on the wall.

What is it? She can only turn and look up for one second when the judges call her. Then she has to start. She must climb upward with her clumsy arms and her big feet.

She wedges her right toe into a hold and reaches up above her head. What next? She dips her left hand into her chalk pouch, so her fingers are all white and dusty.

Where can she go?

She misses being eight. And seven! She didn't even understand that climbing hurt.

The wall juts out and what can you do? How do you leverage your whole body up there? This is the trick question, and Sam doesn't have an answer.

She isn't smart enough to figure it out, so she does something dumb. She lunges and grabs the ledge with her right hand, and now she's dangling. For just a second, she kicks and reaches with her left and now she's hanging by two hands, but her feet can find no landing place. She knows right away that this is where Ayla fell.

Sam will fall too. Her arms are straining. Her hands are claws. She can't hold on a second more, but she does hold as she berates herself. Stupid. Idiot. Hanging from the ledge, she hates her weight, but she starts pulling herself up, her body ripping. It hurts so much she can't hear anything except her dad whistling. Then she can't hear anything at all.

The wall seems to her the only person left. She is fighting the

wall with all her strength and all her pain, her fingers gripping
to the bone, her body curling under her and up. It's like a pull-
up, but so much slower, so much harder. It's life and death. It's
nothing she has done before. When she heaves herself over the
top, she is a castaway collapsing on dry land. Battered, broken,
saved.

16

Her parents are screaming. They don't hug each other, but they are jumping up and down. Her dad doesn't tell her, Climbing is falling. Her mom doesn't have to say, You tried.

After that day, Sam starts training for real. She squeezes rubber balls. She stays late at the Y. She climbs everything that she can find.

When she is eleven, she wins a Boulders scholarship. A full ride, her mom tells Cousin Jen and Steve, not just financial aid.

Steve tells Sam, You keep climbing like that and you can get into the Marines. Courtney says, No way. My kid is not going to the Persian Gulf. But Steve tells Sam, "You know what SAM stands for? Surface-to-air missile. You're exactly what they're looking for."

When Sam turns twelve, she almost makes the cut for regionals. At thirteen, she graduates from Bigger Boulders. She and Halle are advanced now and their shirts aren't blue but green. They practice Tuesdays, Fridays, and Saturdays.

That year Sam wins seventh place in bouldering at her new level, which is great for someone new. Then when she is fourteen, she wins fifth. She is as tall as Halle now and she is strong—not just a string bean.

Mitchell comes with Courtney and Noah and they all go out for sundaes to celebrate. "Life is good," Courtney says.

Mitchell says, "Amen to that."

"I'm proud of you," says Courtney, and she is talking to him, not Sam.

At that moment Sam looks up from her banana split and she wants to say Sh! Don't jinx it. She worries when everybody is so calm and happy. But her dad goes to meetings and he is working every day. Instead of going to the Y, Noah stays at school for Extended Day, and Sam walks to see Mitchell at the Garden Center.

"Let's see your hands," her dad says. "Okay, those are some calluses." He mists ferns in the greenhouse, and he shows her how to feed the orchids. He is good with plants. It's what he needs right now.

"I found a wall," she tells him.

"Where?"

"Behind St. Mary's."

"Is it dangerous?"

"Not really." The wall is actually the back of the brick church. It's got a good foothold, and then a concrete window-sill.

"Does your mom know?"

She shoots him a look, because what does he think? Then her dad mists her face. "Dad!"

"Be careful," Mitchell says. "Your mom's a stickler."

Sam says, "Next year is high school and that counts for college."

Mitchell smiles, but he says, "Hey, I had a strict mom too." Mitchell's mom, Samantha, passed on before Sam was born. She was a tough cookie and a teacher. Sam is named after her, but not exactly. Sam's whole name is Sam, because she is her own person. "But I appreciate Samantha now," says Mitchell. "She made me read, even though I didn't want to."

"How?" Sam is surprised. Mitchell hardly ever does some-

thing against his will—and he usually can't remember so far
back.

"She would read me a story and she would read and read,
until just at the most exciting part, she'd stop."

"And then what did you do?"

"I begged her! 'Keep going!' But she wouldn't listen. She
would leave the book there on my bed."

"And then what?"

"What do you think?"

"You threw it on the floor."

"Yeah, you know me."

"But then you read it?"

"Yup. She knew me too."

By now Sam's dad has read so many books, he is almost
like a book himself. He knows Greek and Roman history
and antique cars and the life of Houdini and World War II
and *The Lord of the Rings*. He knows other things too. He
can tie any kind of knot and play any kind of card game. He
can look at the sun and tell you what direction you are walking.

He'll look at a house and tell you when it was built. He has
a dream house by the ocean, and Sam has one too. Sam's is
Craftsman style with windows for the view. Mitchell's is Victorian with a widow's walk. "That's where I'll live," he tells Sam.
"When my ship comes in."

A ship is a metaphor. It's a dream. When your ship comes in
you can do anything. You can live in a tent. You can walk
around the world. You can climb mountains. Someday he and
Sam might climb the White Mountains. Money is one thing,
but you can be rich in other ways—like magic. Magic will show
you what's invisible; it will dissolve material things. "Magic is
dialectical," Mitchell tells Sam.

Sam says, "What does that mean?"

"Magic makes you question what you used to believe and believe what you were questioning."

"You're so crazy," Sam says, and he laughs.

He is a little crazy, but nothing is ordinary with him. A rock is not a rock just lying there. It traveled with the glaciers sliding over the earth and gouging out the valleys. Pick up that rock. Look closely. There are pieces of quartz and sparkling mica— but most people don't see them.

Every time they walk together, they collect rose quartz and white quartz. Someday Mitchell will get a rock tumbler to polish them for jewelry. This is just one of his ideas. He and Sam will learn to sail. They will also have a workshop for designing games and puzzles. When she was little, they started drawing a map of imaginary places. Right now, it's on notebook paper, but the real thing will be on vellum and they will use pigments from the earth like azurite, lead, gold, verdigris. It's going to be a one-of-a-kind artwork and they will sell prints—but it will take time because they keep adding countries, islands, and enchanted woods.

Middle-earth and Rivendell and Gondor.

Sherwood Forest where Robin Hood hides out with Little John and Friar Tuck, and Will Scarlet, the youngest, who fights with one sword in each hand.

Earthsea where you have to think about the consequences of every spell.

Ithaka where Odysseus arrives home and kills everybody who has been eating his food and stalking his wife. Everybody thought he was a beggar, but no. Don't judge by appearances.

In January, Mitchell and Sam go to the museum in Salem. There is a Chinese house, and art from India, and even feather capes from Polynesia.

"Hawaii. That's where I was born," says Mitchell.

"No way!"

"Yup."

"How were you born there?"

"The same way everybody else gets born."

"You're Hawaiian?"

"No, we just lived there."

"Did you go to the beach?"

"I guess so. I was just a baby. My dad was stationed there."

"You never told me that."

Her dad shrugs like it's not a big deal that he's from the other side of the world, just like the feather capes and fishhooks carved from bone.

"This is the end of the road," Mitchell tells Sam. It's like this. Connecting the oceans is a whale road. The whales started it, swimming back and forth. One end of the road is Salem and the other end is over in Lahaina.

"Can we go to Hawaii?" Sam asks, even though she knows the answer.

"Yeah! Probably."

The thing is—her dad would take her. She knows he would, and once they got there they could go camping on the beach. Sam could bring her tent, so they wouldn't have to pay for a hotel. "But you can't skip school," Mitchell says.

"You did!"

"And look where I am now."

"In a greenhouse?"

"In recovery."

"How long do you have to be in recovery?" Sam asks.

"Forever," her dad says cheerfully.

"You're never done?"

"Hopefully not."

"Do you like meetings?"

"Yeah."

"What do you talk about?"

"Well, people just take turns telling about their lives and what they're going through."

Sam feels bad for him. He is interested in the whole world, and now he is trapped forever listening. She tells her mom, "It sounds so boring."

"Yeah, well, boring is good," says Courtney. "With your dad, boring is exactly where you want to be."

17

Sam's mom has a lot of sayings like that. Boring is good. Also, just put one foot in front of the other. Sam disagrees. Boring is the worst. Boring is writing a report. Why does anybody want a report on the Battle of Vicksburg? Look it up! And putting one foot in front of the other? What does that mean? Just keep walking? Why would you walk when you can climb a wall or fence or tree?

Every chance she gets, she climbs the windowsill on the back wall of St. Mary's. The sill is concrete, the wall is brick, and she is learning all the fingerholds. She perches on the sill and imagines free climbing the whole thing and standing on the roof.

"Hey!" she hears from down below, but she doesn't turn her head. She's concentrating. "Hey. Get down from there."

She loses her balance; the voice startles her so much. She catches herself, heart pounding, hands spreading on the concrete window frame.

"Down. *Now.*"

She eases herself down and sees a policeman. He takes her name and her address and her whole body is shaking because what is happening? She knows who this cop is, and he knows her. He is related to Jen's husband Steve. Why does he ask her name? Why does he treat her like a stranger? He says,

For one thing, this is private property. For another, this is disrespectful and endangerment. He says all this, and Sam says nothing.

He says, I'm letting you off this time, but Courtney finds out right away, and then Sam is literally grounded. For one week, she can't climb anything or go anywhere, not even around the block.

That weekend instead of practice, she sits with her mom at the freezing rink to watch Noah play ice hockey. His team is called the Terminators. Their colors are black and gold, and they are small as gerbils. That's how it is with nine-year-olds.

Sam is shivering, but her mom won't even look at her. Courtney stares straight ahead, eyes on the game.

Sam says, "Why are you always mad at me?"

"I'm not always mad. I'm mad when you go out and try to break your neck."

"My neck is fine."

"Yeah, right. What happens when you climb up to the second story and fall into the parking lot? You're dead."

"But I didn't."

Courtney turns on Sam. "What were you thinking? Why would you climb a building? It's a three-story building, Sam."

"Because it's hard."

The other team scores. People are cheering on the other side. "What?"

"It's hard." Sam doesn't know any other way to say it. It's not the danger. It's that climbing is so hard. She loves how difficult it is.

"You know what's hard? Breaking your back is hard. So don't climb churches! Or anything else. Jesus."

"What if there's a fence and the gate is closed and that's the only way to get over?"

"If the gate is closed, it's closed for a reason, obviously!"

They watch the Terminators skating with their tiny little sticks. The coach praises Noah. "Good hustle!"

Courtney does not stop lecturing. "Do not climb buildings. Do not climb random fences, okay?"

"Okay," Sam says.

Sam does not climb churches anymore, but she can't stop climbing fences. Especially the metal ones. Cyclone fences are all footholds. It's like someone put them there for her. She could walk around them, but it's so much faster to climb over. As soon as she's ungrounded, she starts again. She climbs the tall back fence behind her building and then opens the gate for Noah when she walks him home. The problem is she rips her puffy winter coat. The fabric catches right in front, and she's got a nasty tear, so the stuffing starts coming out.

Sam holds her books and binders in front of her chest, and as soon as she and Noah get inside, she spreads the jacket on the table.

"Busted!" Noah says.

"Sh!" She is staring at the tear. It's not just the coat; it's that her mom will know she lied.

"Glue it?" Noah asks.

"No."

"Tape it!" He takes tape from the kitchen drawer, but the clear plastic is too flimsy. It won't stick.

The next morning, Sam pretends she's hot, and she's just going to carry her coat and wear a sweatshirt.

Her mom says, "What do you mean you're hot? It's twenty-eight degrees outside."

"I'm late," Sam says, which is always true. She rushes out the door with Noah close behind her.

———

The next day, Mitchell examines Sam's coat in the greenhouse. He does not ask, How did you rip this? He says, "It probably needs stitches, but they're gonna show."

"They can't!" Sam tells him. "They can't show."

"Okay, wait," her dad says. "Let's try something."

He gives Sam money from his wallet and sends her down the street to Family Dollar. When she comes back, she's got a sewing kit and a green Celtics patch.

He takes care of customers, and, in between, they sit together next to the mini waterfall. "Lick the thread like that." He squints his eyes and threads the needle.

He starts stitching and then Sam takes a turn, but his work is better. His fingers are long and white, his stitches quick as he sews on the patch.

"You're talented," Sam tells him.

"Sometimes," her dad says.

When Sam gets home, she hangs her coat on the hook near the door, so the patch faces the wall. She hopes her mom won't notice—at least not yet—but as soon as she walks in and hangs her own coat, Courtney sees Sam's jacket. "What's that?" She takes a good look at the Celtics logo. "Where did that come from?"

"I bought it."

"Really? Since when do you care so much about basketball?"

"We watch at Halle's house."

"Okay, who won Friday?"

"Us?"

"Sam, what happened to your coat?"

"I caught it on something, and it ripped, so Dad helped me fix it."

"Where were you when you caught it?"

"On the ground!"

"You better be telling me the truth," Courtney says. "I'm

not going to have any kids sneaking around climbing buildings and lying afterward."

Courtney is out of patience. She just doesn't have any left to give. They've got car trouble. They've got money trouble, and they've got Jack. He is taking Noah on the weekends and buying him stuff—for example, an ATV, which is a miniature Jeep for kids. Jack keeps it at his parents' property where there is lots of room and Noah gets to drive all over, which isn't safe! Kids crash and die all the time. You can hit a rock and just go flying. But Noah is too young to understand. All he wants to do is go off with Jack to his grandma and grandpa's house while they are in Florida. He is getting so spoiled with toys and candy that he actually has tantrums when he comes home.

Jack has his friends who come to drink and party. He has a job in construction, and he can't get fired because he is working for his dad. He gets whatever he wants, and now he wants Noah.

It's almost like Jack does it out of spite, because he knows Courtney is just getting by. Noah has a new ATV, while Courtney has no money to fix her real car.

Courtney has to ask Grandma Deirdre for help, and that takes a lot of phone calls.

The first phone call, Grandma D. has to tell Courtney how she didn't listen. She never listens. If she had listened, she would not be in this situation.

The second phone call, Grandma D. says she worked hard for everything she has, because if you work, you will succeed. She lives out in Western Mass and she is a retired bank teller—but don't treat her like a bank.

The third phone call, Courtney talks about the car and how she can't get to work without it. Sam covers her ears, because her mom's voice sounds so much like crying. I promise, Sam tells her mom silently. I won't make trouble. I won't cost anything.

18

Sometimes Courtney says, Don't be superstitious. There's no such thing as luck. Other times, she says you make your own luck, but Sam isn't sure. Mostly she feels that other people's luck can crush you.

She is at Halle's house and everyone is eating dinner when Lucy turns to Halle and says, "Aren't you going to tell Sam?"

Instantly, Sam knows it's bad. It's the kind of news that's supposed to be good, but actually, it's terrible.

Even Halle knows it's terrible for Sam. She mumbles, "I'm going to Andover in September." That's the school for gifted kids where Eric goes. The reason is Halle is bored in class.

I'm bored, Sam thinks. My school is boring. She tells her mom that all the time, and Courtney just says suck it up. Also, boring is good.

That night, lying in the trundle next to Halle's bed, Sam asks, "Do you really want to go?"

Halle says sort of yes, sort of no, because she's going to miss Sam—but it's not far. You can take a bus home.

Sam says, "Then why don't you just stay home and take the bus every day?"

"It's not *that* close, but you can take the bus home for weekends. I'll still see you."

Sam knows how it will be. At first Halle will come home on

Fridays, but then she'll make new friends and she'll just stay. Eric hardly ever comes home. The whole point of Andover is they keep the kids so busy. Halle says they have all these classes you can't take in regular school. Latin and Greek and number theory, and they have a theater and their own lake.

Sam says, "Aren't you forgetting climbing?"

But no. Andover has climbing.

When Sam hears that, she knows she will never see Halle again. Halle will start climbing on her school team, and Sam won't climb at all, because who will drive her? She can never get to all the practices and competitions without Jim and Lucy.

Courtney says, I'll find a way to drive you. We'll find a way!

Mitchell is different. He just listens to Sam's news and shakes his head.

She says, "I know."

They go to Cherry Hill Creamery and sit together on a picnic bench and lick their ice cream. Mint chip for Sam, strawberry for her dad.

"Does it help?" he asks.

At first she doesn't answer, because she doesn't want to be rude after he treated her. Then after a while, she says, "No."

"That's a good sign," he tells her. She looks at him in disbelief, but he says, "That means your friendship's real."

In the baking summer, Sam takes Noah to the Y, where she helps Kevin coach the little kids. You have to be sixteen to be a real day-camp counselor and Sam is fourteen, so Kevin pays her under the table. Under the table means fifty dollars. She finally gets her period, and her mom says, Oh, you're growing up, and that's exciting! But Sam isn't excited at all, just soggy.

It would be exciting to fly to California and then pack up for boarding school. It would be exciting to travel instead of just visiting Grandma D. in Amherst.

"Emily Dickinson lived in Amherst," her dad tells her at the Garden Center.

"Who?"

"She was a genius, and she didn't even leave the house."

"I'm not that kind of person."

"Not a genius?"

"Not the kind of person who stays inside the house."

"Me either," her dad admits. "That's why I used to move around so much—but I'm a different person now."

"What are you?"

Mitchell thinks about the question as he snips dead flowers off the plants. "A student," he says, finally.

"*Student?*" It's a weird answer, because he knows so many different things. Music. Illusions. Card tricks. Juggling. Unicycling. Poetry. "What are you studying?"

"Oh, you know. Living without magic. Not finding quarters in your ear. Shit!" He finds a quarter. "Staying here."

Right before Halle leaves for school, she comes to Sam's apartment. She stands there with Lucy and Courtney, and she offers Sam a present, which is a framed picture of the two of them. They are wearing their team shirts and the frame says FRIENDS FOREVER.

Sam just looks at it. After a while she remembers to say thank you, and then everybody hugs one another, especially the moms.

After Halle leaves, Sam stuffs the picture in her closet. Then she sits inside her tent.

Courtney kneels at the mesh window and says, "It's not like Halle's going to the moon."

Sam says, "I know."

"It's not like you won't see her again."

Sam says nothing, and Courtney sits there, until Sam says, "Mom."

"What?"

"I feel like an animal in the zoo."

"But you can come out," her mom says.

Sam doesn't answer. She just waits until finally, her mom takes the hint and leaves.

But the next day, Courtney says, "Okay, enough! You're going to high school too."

Courtney takes Sam to the Northshore Mall and makes her walk into every store. Some have shirts with *CALIFORNIA* on them; one shirt even has *HAWAII,* but it's pink, so no.

Sam won't buy anything with words, and she won't wear tight clothes. Also, she won't let her mom do anything about her hair, even though it's in her eyes and almost to her shoulders.

"Come on," says Jen. "Let's cut it so we can see your pretty face."

Jen and Courtney think hair and makeup and cute shirts will make a difference. They think a haircut changes you—but haircuts are like magic. They only work if you believe in them.

19

"Work hard," Courtney keeps telling Sam.

"Have an amazing time," says Jen.

"Tell me what it's like," Sam's dad says.

What is high school like?

It's big.

In the halls, you feel like a molecule. The bell rings and high school sucks you up into your classroom. Take a seat, pull out your book, and let's get started.

Sam has every kind of notebook and folder. Courtney bought her a value pack of mechanical pencils, a blue graphing calculator, and a geometry set with a ruler, three protractors, and a compass. Even with her mom's employee discount, it is a little bit ridiculous. "I just want you to have everything," Courtney says.

Sam has a new backpack with eleven pockets. She has her own phone, but no one calls her, except Halle.

She answers Halle's questions—*Yup. Nope. I'm fine.* She doesn't know what else to say.

You have to look where you are going in this school. Boys will ram you in the cafeteria, and they're not even trying to hurt you. They're just hungry.

Keep your head down. Girls stand together at the lockers with their arms around one another. After school, they walk together in their soccer uniforms, and as they walk, they toss their hair.

One says, *"What?"* when she catches Sam staring.

Another pushes Sam outside the science room. "I said *move*!" Sam doesn't play soccer or even volleyball. All her T-shirts are the kind a boy would wear. Also, her jeans are the wrong shade of blue.

If you wear jeans, they should be light or dark, not medium.

If you open your locker, do it fast. There are other people trying to open lockers all around you.

If you're going to eat lunch, don't sit down with people in the middle of a conversation. God.

If you're going to walk home, don't step onto the field. People are practicing. If you see a fence, it is there for a reason, not for you.

If you're going to exist, then wear your hair down your back or put it up and pierce your ears and wear a silver necklace with a tiny sparkling star.

If you disobey these rules, then run, don't walk to class. No one wants to look at you.

At dinner, Sam's mom says, "Oh, Sam, it's just the first day!"

Sam's mom loved high school. She got a couple of Cs because she didn't know how to work and plan ahead, which she regrets—but she was happy! She was in marching band! She thinks school spirit is a thing, like you can have it if you try, and she does not understand why Sam won't go to Homecoming. You can go with friends.

Sam says, "But I don't have any."

"Well, how will you make friends if you don't go?"

"Mom, that's circular," says Sam.

"Just go and meet new people."

Sam thinks of the girls standing by the lockers. "No."

"She doesn't want a friend," Noah points out. And Courtney sighs, like Yeah, you're right.

But they are wrong. Sam is a lonely molecule.

Every day she carries her books to school and each one weighs a hundred pounds. If you drop Literature, you'll break a toe.

In Physics she learns gravity, friction, tension. In History she's supposed to learn revolutions, like French, Industrial, American, but kids disrupt the class. In November, Sam turns fifteen, but nobody at school knows, and she is glad. It's safer to be anonymous.

A substitute arrives and writes *nationalism* on the board. It takes a while for people to realize the old history teacher Mr. Edwards is permanently gone. He quit to go into real estate.

Sam could do that. Her mom colors a real estate agent who says property values are going up, way up. You have to make an offer as soon as you step in the door, and if you don't, then the family behind you will say, We'll take it! "I'd just need a license and a bunch of signs and a car," Sam says.

Courtney says, "Uh-huh. You have to pass a test to get that license—so go to school."

There are tests and quizzes every day. You get tested all the time. There is homework every night, but the only subject Sam likes is geometry. You learn the rules for triangles and circles and it's like a map. You take those rules and step by step, you figure out what you should do.

Courtney looks at Sam's report card and says, "Well . . . math is good!" Sam can be an accountant. Then she'll always have a job.

"Oh great," Sam says.

Now that Sam is good at math, her mom is always asking, "Did you study? Did you finish all your math review?" Sam writes in her *Wordly Wise* workbook, *My mom is <u>tenacious</u>. She is also <u>pedantic</u>. Once she makes up her mind, she will not <u>digress</u> from her point of view.*

Courtney has this fantasy that Sam will come from behind and win at school. Sam will ace math and she will improve in everything else and she will have friends. She is always reminding Sam, Do your work! And don't forget your extracurriculars. She says that like Take your vitamins. She knows Sam will make friends, if she will join clubs.

What clubs? Sam asks. Some people go to dance team, and mock trial, and Model UN, where you pretend to be a country. Sam does not. The only thing she tries is the environmental club. It meets at lunch, and someone lectures about global warming, and the room is hot. Most days she eats lunch alone.

Now that Halle is away at Andover, Sam is alone at Boulders too. Her mom drives her, but she's always in a rush and they are late. Sam misses sleeping over with Halle and sharing pancakes in the morning and climbing together. The team is full of new girls. They aren't as strong as Sam, but they are tiny; they weigh nothing.

There is also a new coach named Declan and he is frustrated with Sam. She'll start out great and then drop off, or she'll do something stupid, right after a brilliant move.

He tells her she is not giving one hundred percent, and it is true. One day after practice, he takes Sam aside and asks, "Do you want to be here?"

She whispers, "Yes."

"What?"

"Yes."

He is dark-eyed, fierce, and strong. Sam loves to watch him climb. You can see every muscle in his arms and back. Now, on the ground, she is almost too shy to look at him. He has never talked to her alone before. He says, "You're smart. You have it in you."

She stands there holding still.

"Show me you can work."

What would that be like? To hear him shout out *Yes!*

"Show me that you're thinking. Show me that you actually care."

"Okay."

"And get your hair out of your eyes."

In the car, she looks at herself in the side mirror. The wind blows her hair into her face, then off again. She looks like a haystack. Then she looks like a girl.

Her mom is driving, and Noah is piled in back with all his hockey gear.

"How was it?"

Sam says, "What?"

Her mom is asking, "How was practice?"

Sam is remembering how Declan looked at her. His eyes were challenging and also curious. That was the strange part. Does he like her?

"Sam!" Courtney interrupts. "I am not your taxi. If I ask a question, I deserve an answer."

Sam can't think of anything to say aloud.

The next week before practice, she ties back her hair, and her mom pins it where it is too short for a ponytail. "I can braid it!" Courtney suggests in the parking lot, but Sam won't wait around for that.

She runs into the gym to study every route.

At practice she stops to think. Reach for the red hold near the top? Or swing left first and grab the blue?

She waits so long that Declan calls out from the floor where he is belaying her. "Come on, Sam."

Still she holds on, planning the next move and the next.

Declan has other kids to coach. "Go."

All at once, she swings left and pulls up with her right foot on a tiny foothold. One fast, decisive move. She's in position now and it feels so good. The younger girls are watching down below as she shows them how it's done, lunging for the red handhold.

"*Okay!*" Declan shouts. "That's what I'm talking about!"

Don't rush me then, she thinks, as she glides down.

20

At school Sam meets a few sad people in the cafeteria. They are girls who sit around talking about how tired they are and how much they hate everything. It's a relief, but it's depressing too.

Courtney says, "Why don't you get together and cheer each other up?" Meanwhile, Sam has physics lab.

Mr. Wood assigns trios to build roller coasters and Sam gets two deadweights. One is a basketball player who never even comes to class. The other is named Corey. He is in the juggling club, and always practicing.

He's juggling as he walks down the hall. He's juggling while waiting for the bus. He would juggle in class, but if he does it one more time, his balls will be confiscated. People say, ha ha, they're gonna confiscate your balls, but he keeps juggling. He is tall, and freckled. He's always got his face up in the air.

Apart from juggling, Corey is totally lazy, so they are already behind. They are supposed to work at lunchtime to cut up cardboard and wrapping-paper tubes, but Sam is the only one who shows up. She texts Corey, *your late.*

No response.

She texts, *whereru?*

No response.

By the time Corey wanders in, she is doing all the work herself. She is trying to cut cardboard tubes and he is walking around juggling three green balls.

"Hey," he says.

"*Hey?*"

He asks, "What do we have to do?"

"Everything."

"Okay." He is still juggling.

"How are you helping?"

"There's only one scissors."

"So, find the tape."

He starts hunting, while juggling. After a long time, he spots a roll of silver tape. Then he starts juggling the roll of tape along with the balls.

He works his way back to Sam at the workbench and he shows off, juggling three balls plus silver duct tape.

She swipes the tape, and all the balls come tumbling down. "Do something."

"I *was* doing something." When she doesn't answer, he says, "I can juggle five."

She demands, "Can you juggle knives?"

"No."

"Can you juggle fire?"

"You mean torches?"

"Yeah, lit torches on a unicycle."

"No." He sounds offended, but she doesn't care. She is the only one doing this project.

Welcome to my world, says Courtney.

One lab partner won't help, and the other isn't even there.

Tell me about it, says Courtney. She is <u>terse</u>. Also, <u>sardonic</u>. At the same time, she says rise above. Maybe you're <u>infuriated</u>. Maybe physics isn't fair. Your design is solid, but your supports aren't stable, and so you get a B, even though you spent all night trying to do the work of three people. Eventually, you'll see! You'll get your reward.

Yeah, right. Sam counts the days until the weekend.

The problem is getting to the gym. Courtney takes Sam on Tuesdays and Sam has a ride with Emily and her sister on Fridays, but Saturdays are not so good. Courtney is working and working, and she has a new boyfriend. He's really great. For one thing, he has a job. He is a fireman named Adam. And Courtney has not had a boyfriend in so long. She has been so tired all the time, raising Sam and Noah. She's done nothing for herself. The kids are old enough to babysit themselves now that Sam is fifteen and Noah is ten. Sam gets five dollars to watch Noah, and Noah gets one dollar to behave and go to bed.

Courtney is the one who doesn't go to bed. Sometimes she stays out all night. Sam hears her unlocking the door, early in the morning. Courtney will try to tiptoe through the living room and slip into the bathroom without bumping into anything. During the day, Courtney hums. Sometimes she even sings. She highlights her red-brown hair.

Adam lives in Peabody and his arms are like trees. If you come home with a carload of groceries, he can carry all the bags in one trip. Also, he's an EMT, so if you almost die, he can save you.

For now, the problem is the mornings. If Courtney goes out with Adam Friday night, then she can't wake up on Saturday. Actually, she does wake up, but she is sleepy and slow moving.

Sam starts brewing her mom coffee. She stands next to the bed, holding Courtney's travel mug. "Coffee? Coffee?" She hopes her mom will sniff and follow the scent to the car.

One time in December, Courtney can't get up at all. Her head is hurting. She just can't.

"Let her rest," says Mitchell, when Sam calls her dad. "She's tired out."

"Can you drive me then?"

"No car," he reminds her.

"Take ours!"

"No license. Sorry, monkey."

"You lost your license?"

"Yup."

"Can't you get a new one?"

"Not yet."

"Dad! What happened?"

"Nobody got hurt." Then Sam knows it's serious.

"No kidding," her mom says when she finally drags herself out of bed.

"What happened?"

"Not good."

That's how Sam's family is. Nobody tells the truth—not really. You're supposed to know, or guess, or just get older. Now Sam is older, and she can't get a ride, and still nobody will say what's going on.

At her next practice, Declan says, Where were you last week? You made a commitment to the team. She climbs badly and he looks at her like this isn't even worth it.

After practice, Courtney drives up with Noah and his hockey gear in back. "How did it go?" Courtney asks.

Sam doesn't answer. She gets into the passenger seat and slams the door.

Courtney says, "Hey, don't slam that door. This is the only car we've got. You think I can just go out and buy another one?"

She is already lecturing about every little thing, and Sam can't listen anymore. She bursts out, "When Halle went away, you said you'd take me to the gym."

"I *am* taking you. What do you call this? We are in the car driving home from the goddamn gym."

"Every week!"

"I missed *once*."

"And also, the time after Thanksgiving, and in September."

"Give me a break."

"I do give you a break." Sam glances at Noah in the back seat. "We give you a break every weekend when you're with Adam."

Courtney pulls over on 128. She stops on the shoulder like you do when you have a flat tire. "Do you want to walk home?" Cars are speeding past. Eighteen-wheel trucks are thundering, spraying slush and sand, but Courtney says, "Go ahead," like she doesn't even care it's dangerous.

Sam is so angry she opens her door.

"No, Sam!" Noah yells, and suddenly he's sobbing. "No, don't walk on the highway!"

Sam sinks back in her seat and her mom shouts, "Now look what you did!" Sam closes her door, but Noah is crying and crying, because he thinks she was about to kill herself.

Sam hugs her knees and buries her head and shuts her eyes. Her mom sits silent, with the engine running.

"It's okay, Noah. Stop it!" she orders, because he's too old to cry like that. But he won't stop until Courtney starts driving again.

That afternoon, Sam walks to the greenhouse and sits on the stone edge of the fountain.

"Hey." Mitchell sits next to her when the customers are gone. "Sorry I couldn't drive you."

"You mean sorry you lost your license?"

"Wow, you are tough." He almost tries to make a joke of it. She looks at him and says, "What did you do?"

"DUI."

At first, she doesn't know what that means. She knows DIY is Do It Yourself.

"Look it up."

"Just tell me."

He still won't say, so she does look it up on her phone, and then she has to read about it. "Dad!"

"It won't happen again."

"What if something else happens?"

"Well, I'm trying to prevent that."

"How?"

He opens his wallet and there is a picture of Sam with her change purse shaped like a cat. "This is what I look at."

Sam stares at the photo. She doesn't look like that anymore. She doesn't smile like that either.

Her dad says, "Don't be sad."

"I'm not."

"It happened a while back."

"Uh-huh."

Her dad jostles her, knocking her shoulder with his shoulder. "You know what?"

"What."

"The bus will take you anywhere."

21

Practice starts at nine and the bus takes fifty-three minutes to Newburyport and then you have to walk thirty-five minutes to the gym, so she leaves the house at seven-twenty.

It's windy and cold, but the sun is shining. She is afraid the bus won't come, but it does. There are only two other passengers, so she can sit up front by herself, with her jacket zipped and her backpack next to her. The ride is long, but she watches every minute, so she won't miss her stop.

From the bus, the trees look gray, but when she gets out and starts walking, the trees are reddish and dead leaves are blowing all around. She walks past houses and closed shops and a dry cleaner's and then an empty car wash and a bowling alley, and finally she gets to Boulders. Her hands are cold. The sky is white. She calls her dad from the gym. "I'm here."

"What? Where?" He sounds fuzzy, like he's afraid she's standing right outside his door.

"I took the bus to practice."

"Whoa!" Now he's awake. "Freedom!"

Meanwhile, Sam's mom is full of warnings. Don't talk to strangers or get in anybody's car, or lose your wallet, or your keys or phone. By the time Sam gets home, her mom has thought of new ones. Wear a hat and walk on the sidewalk. Don't walk on the street when the sidewalks are covered up with snow!

Sam knows all that, but if it's icy and people haven't shoveled yet, she does walk in the street. It's safe on Saturdays, because there are hardly any cars. Her mom would do it too.

The hard part is running to the bus stop after practice. The first week, she misses the bus. Then she has to wait almost an hour, and it starts sleeting. She stands under the shelter, but even though she's got her coat zipped and her hood up, the wind pelts her with tiny frozen bullets. By the time she makes it back to the apartment, her ears and cheeks and nose are raw. Her boots, which are supposed to be waterproof, are soaked through at the toes.

Her mom says, Don't be silly. She will come for Sam next week. Sam says, No, that's okay.

At the gym she keeps track of time. She watches the clock and she is torn. She hopes Declan won't keep her late, and at the same time, she wants to talk to him. She wants to know what he is thinking.

After practice, Sam hovers by the door for just a minute and he sees her. "Work on speed."

She thinks, But then I'll make mistakes. She says, "Okay."

"You can't just hang out forever wondering which way to go. You aren't even wondering. You're second-guessing."

"Okay."

"Make a decision and stick to it."

"Okay." Sam shoulders her backpack.

"The longer you hang, the tireder you get. And stop saying okay."

"I have to catch the bus to Beverly." Now she's surprised him. "If I miss it, I have to wait an hour."

He looks at her and says, "My girlfriend lives in Salem. I can drive you."

His car is old with one door dented. It's dingy white like dirty snow.

Inside it smells a little bit like beer. Sam buckles up and holds her backpack on her lap. Who is his girlfriend? Does he live with her?

"Your instincts are good," he tells her as they rattle down the road.

She doesn't know what to say, so she says, "Thank you." Then she says, "Sometimes they're not."

"You're frustrating," he says, "because you're doing great and then you get stuck, and it's like you're paralyzed."

"When I was younger, I climbed better."

"Younger, like seven?"

"Yeah."

"You know why? Because you weren't so nervous all the time."

His voice is challenging, his eyes amused. Sam thinks, You know what makes me nervous? You.

He tells her, Calm down. Be strategic. Attack the wall. "You know what I'm saying?"

She nods, even though she has no idea how to calm down while she attacks the wall.

He keeps talking about committing and being strong and being purposeful, and then he catches himself, almost laughing. "Okay, that's it. Any questions?"

These are her questions. How can I learn from you? How can I be you? Instead she says, "Did you climb in college?"

He says, "I'm in college now." He goes to Salem State, and climbs all over. He coaches at the gym but climbs in New Hampshire.

"My dad used to work there, at Strawbery Banke."

Declan is turning off the highway and he doesn't seem to hear.

"Thanks," she tells him when they pull up at her building. He touches her hand for just a second. Or maybe not. That's just what she hopes he'll do.

22

On winter break, Halle pretends she has not forgotten Sam, and Sam pretends she doesn't mind that Halle has abandoned her. She goes over to Halle's house and helps light candles for Hanukkah. Halle's mom and dad are Jewish, so they don't put up decorations. They don't even have a tree—but they do give one present per night for eight nights. Sam tells her dad about this, and he says, "Oh yeah, I know. I'm Jewish too."

"What?" They are eating burgers on Rantoul Street, and he is stealing Sam's fries. "You never told me that. You never gave me eight presents."

"I'm nonpracticing."

Mitchell never mentioned this before, but Sam asks her mom, and yes, it's true. He was born Jewish, but he had it easy because his mom and dad were not religious. Courtney's parents were the opposite. Her dad was a minister, so she had to listen to his sermons and memorize a gazillion Bible verses. Courtney would never put her kids through that—even though Noah's name is in the Bible, and Sam is partly in there too.

Courtney still knows her verses. *For you have created my inmost being. You have knit me together in my mother's womb . . . I have loved you with an everlasting love. I have drawn you with loving-kindness . . . And we know that in all things . . .* She makes Sam and Noah laugh; she is so fast.

Courtney says, "You think it's funny, because you never had to learn them." The truth is, religion causes wars, so they don't go to church, or synagogue either. The only holiday they celebrate is Christmas, because it's secular. Even that one is not Courtney's favorite, since that's when Jack appears. He wants Noah to come over, but his parents are in Florida, so Courtney says no.

Then he pressures Courtney. He comes over to the salon and to the apartment and he talks to Courtney on the phone. Sam can hear him pretending to be nice. He says, Why can't Noah just come over for the day? And he says, Why can't we all celebrate together? Courtney says no to everything.

Sam watches her do it. Her mom is standing in the kitchen with her phone and she says, "No. Just no." She also says, "Jack, I'm not going to say it again," but then she says it again anyway. "No." The way she says it, the word comes from deep inside her. She is like a weightlifter heaving up that word. She is so tough. But after she gets off the phone, she curls up on the couch under a blanket.

On Christmas Eve, Sam carries their bags and Courtney drags a half-sleeping Noah. It's like an escape. They pack the car and strap in Noah and drive off to Amherst. "It's easier this way," Courtney tells Sam. "We just won't have to deal with Jack."

But the next morning, at Grandma D.'s house, Courtney has to deal with him anyway. Jack is on the phone and Courtney takes it outside on the porch.

Noah is lying on the rug racing solar-powered cars while Sam looks out at the porch from the living room window.

Grandma says no feet on the couch. Then she says, "Noah, what are you learning in school?"

Sam can't hear, but she knows what Jack is shouting because she's listened to so many other fights. I'll go to court and take him from you. Fat lying bitch!

He always calls Courtney fat, stupid, and ugly, even though she is the opposite.

Courtney doesn't stay out long. She comes back inside and says, "Okay, that was nice."

Grandma D. is saying, "Noah, I asked you a question. Look at me when I am talking to you."

Noah does not look at Grandma D. or anyone else either. He is disappearing. All he sees is his two cars racing each other on the rug. Sam wishes she could do that.

For Christmas, Sam's dad gives her fifty dollars. Sam's mom gives her clothes, including a huge supersoft purple sweater that Sam can't ever wear to school.

"Why not?" Halle asks, when Sam sleeps over.

"Because I look like a grape. See?" She pulls the sweater over her T-shirt.

Halle sits up in bed and admits, "Yeah, you kind of do."

Halle still wears old jeans and long-sleeved shirts, but she's got shearling boots. She doesn't climb at Andover. She does theater instead. She is trying out for *Twelfth Night* to be Viola, who is a girl dressed as a boy.

She probably won't get the part, because she's only a ninth grader, but she has memorized a speech where Viola says what she'd do if she were in love—which she really is, but nobody knows. Halle recites it in the dark. *Make me a willow cabin at your gate, / And call upon my soul within the house; / Write loyal cantons of contemned love / And sing them loud even in the dead of night . . .*

"Wait. What's a willow cabin?" Sam says.

"Just a little hut where she'd camp out."

In college, Halle might go to England and study Shakespeare. She will go to libraries where the windows are diamond-paned, and the paintings are all kings and queens covered with jewels. She's got a poster of Queen Elizabeth I on the wall above her castle-bookcase. The queen's face is white. She has no neck, just a lace collar cut out like a snowflake. Her sleeves are so big that they fill the room.

This is what interests Halle. Velvet, silk, and diamond windows, kings, and queens. Plays full of poetry.

"Are you taking physics?" Sam asks.

Halle is not so interested in physics. She gets sleepy when Sam tells her about the roller coaster and how Corey juggled duct tape, but then she wakes up when Sam mentions Declan.

"Is he a good coach?"

"He's okay."

"Do you like him?"

Sam doesn't answer.

She does not tell Halle that Declan drives her home from practice. She never talks about that, even though it's fine. It's not like driving with a stranger.

Sam talks to Declan about ropes and speed and hanging from a bar. It's not really fair because the smaller you are, the longer you can hang there. In some ways it's better to be little, but as you grow, you get stronger in your arms and back and core.

In the car, Declan shows Sam where he broke his index finger. He jammed it in a crevice, so it's still bent. He holds it up for her.

At the gym, Sam tries to climb like he does. She stops dangling and wondering; she attacks the wall.

When she does something radical, Declan yells, "Yeah!" When she nearly makes a brilliant move and falls, he says, "Again!"

The crazier she climbs, the more he likes her. "Be *fierce*," he coaches. "Get up there!"

She's bruised all over. Tears start in her eyes, but she won't cry in front of him.

On the way home, they review her climbs, and he remembers where she swung right and where she went wrong. He remembers everything she does, and she remembers everything he says. Go, go, go. No, that's not it. Again! He has two voices. Harsh in the gym and gentle in the car. He always says, "I know you've got it in you." He tells her that like it's a secret between them.

"He thinks I can be good," Sam tells her dad on Sunday afternoon.

"You're good now," Mitchell answers.

They are running on the beach on New Year's Day. It was Mitchell's idea to run into the year.

They run on rocky sand, and wind whips their hair. Dream houses stand high up on the bank above, and the ocean spreads out to the sky. Gray and green up to the clouds.

"No, I'm not good yet," Sam pants.

"Hold on. Be patient, monkey."

"Be patient for what?"

"You're still young. You have lots of time."

She hates it when he talks this way. "I'm trying to get better."

"Why?"

"Dad!"

"No, really. What's the plan?"

"To win in Gloucester."

"And then what?"

"Top ten in Boston."

"And then what?"

She doesn't even want to say it. "Nationals?"

"And then what?"

She says, "I *know* winning isn't everything and if all you care about is winning, you'll feel empty—but I haven't won enough to feel empty yet."

He laughs, but then turns serious. "What do you want?"

"Prize money."

"Hey, wait a minute, Sam. You aren't climbing for money."

"You practiced magic," Sam reminds him. "You juggled for money."

They stop to rest in the gold winter light, and Mitchell says, "Juggling is not the easiest career."

Sam says, "Tell that to Corey."

"Who's Corey?" Her dad is sidetracked. "Girl or guy?"

"Guy."

"Does your mom know about him?"

"There's nothing to know!"

"Is he good news or bad news?"

"No news," Sam says, and that is sort of true.

23

She doesn't like Corey as much as Halle, but he is there. Halle goes back to school as soon as vacation ends. Corey sits with Sam in the cafeteria.

The first time he eats lunch with Sam, he apologizes for the roller coaster. "You were right. I did nothing."

She looks up from her terrible hot lunch, which is chili, and she says, "Well, it's too late to fix it now."

He says, "I know. That's why I'm apologizing."

He unzips his backpack and he's got a whole thing of cheese and crackers, plus beef jerky. He's also got a mini pack of cookies and a bag of sour cream and onion chips. And M&M's, and a container of blue pills, which are his meds.

"You keep them in your lunch?" Sam says as he offers her his chips and cookies.

"What's wrong with that?"

She shakes her head because can't he see Mr. Wood across the room? "You look like a dealer."

"I have a prescription."

He is druggy, but he's smart. In math, he does his homework in class. A lot of times he finds a shortcut and he'll show Sam. He likes to figure out proofs, but he doesn't care about world history or Spanish, or any of that stuff, so he has a lot of free time. When he was younger, he used to be destructive, and he went to a special middle school. That's where he started juggling. It's self-regulating. "You should try it," he tells Sam after physics, as they head down the stairs.

"Nah, I don't like it."

"How do you know?"

"My dad is a professional."

"You have his genes!"

"I don't think juggling is hereditary."

The bell is ringing. Huge crowds start thundering down on them, and Sam shrinks back into the elbow of the stairwell.

"What *do* you like?" Corey asks when the main crowd has passed.

Sam is sitting on the inner banister, the one near the wall. She wedges her body into the corner and stands up on the rail, just like you're not supposed to. "Climbing."

Corey does not look surprised. He does not think she is at all weird for perching on a banister. "You know what you should climb? St. Mary's."

"I did climb it! I used to climb it all the time."

"All the way up?"

She hesitates.

"I dare you."

"Yeah, right." She jumps down.

"I'll go with you."

"When have you ever been climbing?"

"I've been rappelling."

"Yeah, but we won't have ropes, so if you fall you die." He doesn't look concerned, so she explains, "Basically, you can kill yourself, and also the police could come any minute to arrest you."

His eyes brighten like he loves all of it—dying, and the police, and getting arrested. "Let's go tonight."

She already regrets this. "You can't see anything at night."

"Okay, before school. Tomorrow morning."

Luckily Noah is old enough to walk by himself, so Sam can sneak out alone. She just tells her mom she has to get to school early. Then, in the morning, she creeps out before her mom wakes up. Even Noah is still snoring.

January is a knife. The metal blade cuts through her.

She is wearing her jacket and her hat and gloves and running shoes and her feet are freezing, but you can't climb in snow boots. A few cars rumble past, but no one is out walking.

She wonders whether Corey will show up and kind of hopes he won't. He likes her, and she thinks less of him for that. She thinks less of herself too, because he's crazy.

She is standing in the parking lot behind the church and the sky is milky gray. He isn't there, and she feels stupid and relieved. It's way too cold to climb a church. There are massive icicles along the roof, so actually there are even more ways to die here than she realized. Any second, an icicle could fall and stab you through the heart.

It's still early for school, but she can't go home or her mom will ask what's going on. She tries to keep warm, walking around, stomping her feet, and then she heads up Cabot toward the sun, pink in the black trees, changing icy snow to shards of glass.

"Sam! Wait!" Corey is rushing after her. "Sorry I'm late."

She wants to say I knew you would be. You suck at dares, but her mouth is stiff and numb, too cold to speak.

He glances back at the church with its steeple, and its high brick walls, its arched windows, its pitched roof and icicles. "You really climb this?"

She nods like it's no big deal and actually she's already

climbed it twice that morning. "Now people will see us because it's light out," she tells him. "So, we'd better not."

"Okay."

They head for school, but the building doesn't open until 7:40, so they walk slowly.

24

Corey is a good friend, once you get to know him. He will share his lunch, his math homework, his money, just about anything. His downfall is rules. That is his tragic flaw. Mostly he ignores them. Also, deadlines. He does not worry about them. By the end of ninth grade he is on probation.

The best thing about Corey is he has no fear. He is not afraid of people looking at him. He is not afraid of failing. He's not afraid of getting hurt. If he sees a bike lying around, he'll ride it. If he sees a piece of fruit, he'll juggle it. If he sees a drink, he'll chug it. He keeps busy. His mom and dad share custody, so he is always moving. He has two of everything—two houses, two bedrooms, two computers, two sets of clothes, two tooth-brushes, and sometimes even two allowances when one parent loses track of what the other one is doing.

The worst thing is Corey wants to be Sam's boyfriend. When he tries to drape his arm around her, she feels weighted down, and hot. When he tries to kiss her, it's weird, because his eyes come so close together. She tries closing hers, but it doesn't help. She doesn't feel anything. Kissing is just wet.

She would ask Halle if she were around. She would talk to Halle for two hours, if she were still telling her anything. At school, kids are always making out in stairwells, but Sam can't figure out the point of kissing. Either she's gay, or the chemicals are wrong, or Corey is too weird, even for her.

Corey thinks she should get high first, and she tries that too, but no. Even after his blue pills, when she's half dreaming on the black leather couch in his dad's basement, she doesn't want to kiss him. She doesn't want to get undressed either. He's always licking and pawing her. It kind of tickles and it's embarrassing. Why does he want to? Her body is thin; her breasts are small, not like the ones you see online. She barely likes to look at herself, so why would he? She would rather let him touch her through her clothes and then sleep in all her layers, sweatshirt zipped up to her chin, legs curled under her, not a person, not a girl at all.

She does not want to be his actual girlfriend. She admits it to her mom, and Courtney says, "Then don't be!" She tells Sam, If you like him it's one thing, but if you don't, forget it. You don't have to do anything you don't want to.

Sam thinks, But what if you aren't sure? She doesn't want to be Corey's girlfriend, but she likes him. She doesn't want to kiss him, but sometimes she does—and she is always with him. She is in his dad's basement or at his mom's place in North Beverly. His mom is working, and his dad is out of town. His dad is a serial entrepreneur, which sounds criminal but no, he's just starting companies. Corey's only chore is feeding the fish in his dad's giant aquarium. Sam does it with him and it's her favorite thing. All the fish swim up to the surface; they are so excited.

"They have a good life," Corey says, which makes Sam laugh. She doesn't even know why she thinks he is so funny. He is so obvious and weird at the same time. He kisses her and she kisses him back, and it's okay. She almost likes it. When he lifts her shirt, she feels curious—but then he starts rushing, pulling off her clothes.

She says, "Wait, what if your dad comes home?"

He says, "My parents trust me."

Sam's mom is a little different. She says, "Let's be real here."

She takes Sam to Planned Parenthood to get a prescription for the pill. This is because Sam was a surprise, and Courtney never finished her degree. She started at Dean College, but she dropped out when she had Sam in sophomore year.

"But then you were glad you had me," Sam reminds her.

"I was glad, but I should have waited."

Sam points out, "Then it wouldn't have been me."

Her mom says, "Can you listen to what I'm saying? You go to college and you get a job and then you can decide everything."

In the clinic, Sam and her mom sit in the waiting room and Sam tells herself it's no big deal. It's like the dentist. When the RN talks to Sam alone, Sam acts very quiet and calm, but then the nurse puts on her stethoscope, and it's unfair, almost like spying, listening to Sam's pounding heart.

"Look," her mom says on the way home. "Better safe than sorry."

"I don't even *like* sex!" Sam blurts out.

Her mom is laughing.

"What?" Sam demands.

"Nothing!"

The most fun Sam has with Corey is outside. In the spring they work at North Beverly Car Wash. In the summer they climb trees.

They climb the oak behind the public library. Sam leads the way and Corey follows. Then they perch up in the leaves and look down at the hot bricks and the people carrying their books below.

There is a tree on Washington Street that's even better. When you climb high enough, you can see the ocean.
Sometimes the water is choppy. Sometimes it's so smooth
you can't tell where ocean turns into the sky. On sunny days
you can see boats, islands, and buoys, but if you climb up
on a gray morning, it's just mist. Then it's like sailing in a
cloud.

Corey asks, "Do you feel like you're in a ship?"

She is startled. "That's what I was going to say."

"Cool." They are leaning against a big heavy branch. Her
feet are braced in the crook of the tree; his feet are braced
against hers. "I can read your mind."

"No, you can't."

"I can."

"Okay, what am I thinking?"

"How you don't want me to guess."

That's true, but she won't admit it.

"So, you're annoyed."

That's true too, but she says, No, you're wrong, as she starts
climbing down.

"Wait!" He tries to follow, but she's too fast, and he crashes
through some smaller branches.

"Hey, don't fall." She is already standing on the sidewalk.
The fog is burning off and it's getting hot. "Just back yourself
down. Left foot first."

"Let's go swimming," Corey says, once he makes it to the
ground, but she has work.

That summer before tenth grade, Sam works at Family Dollar where she slits boxes and pulls out beach chairs and day-
dreams about Declan.

She waits all week for practice, and the ride home. They talk
about strength training and stretching and debate when you
should push yourself harder and when you should let up. Should

you try a shortcut that's more elegant, saving time and energy? How do you decide?

He says, "Climbing is half knowledge and half instinct— and a little bit experience."

She knows two halves make a whole, so experience doesn't fit, but she doesn't want to argue about math. Her instinct is to kiss him. Her instinct is to swim with him. There is no AC and her bare legs burn where they touch the seat. By the time they turn off 128, her shirt is sticking to her body. She is drenched in sweat.

He watches her push her hair off her neck and she half imagines what he does next. Half imagines and half knows this is his finger tracing her neck down to her collarbone down over her breast. She can't even breathe, but then his touch is gone, and his hands are on the wheel again.

Was that real?

She is shaky when she gets out of the car, because what just happened? She walks to the Garden Center instead of heading home.

On the lot, leaves shimmer in the heat. She follows the sound of running water. "Dad?"

He is spraying potted trees with water.

"What's wrong?"

She spreads her arms and he hoses her down. Cool water runs in rivulets over her hair, her shirt and shorts, her scorched legs. "Better?"

She nods yes.

He says, "You're okay, monkey."

They sit together on a redwood bench. They just sit until customers come, and then after her dad rings up their plants, they sit some more. Her dad can be very quiet. He is so quiet that talking is like thinking aloud. She asks, "Were you ever in love with the wrong person?"

Mitchell looks surprised. "Sam, what's going on?"

"Nothing!"

"Is no news bad news?"

"Dad, stop!"

No one else comes in. They sit alone there in the sun. "Usually I was the wrong person," her dad says.

25

The wrong person means her dad was wild. It means he was not dependable. He was bad news when he was young and even now, he's not so great. He makes you think that you can tell him anything, but he doesn't tell you what's happening to him.

All that summer he seems fine. On Labor Day he takes Sam out for sundaes to celebrate the start of school—and then she sees him in September and October at the Garden Center.

They talk about English class and reading Greek myths.

"The main thing is don't compete with gods," says Mitchell. "Don't steal their thunder." He is setting up the Halloween display with all the pumpkins and the gourds and he says, "I'll see you Saturday."

He is coming to watch Sam compete at Boulders. He has a ride and everything. Kevin is going to drive him but when Sam gets there, she doesn't see either of them. And when she calls, her dad doesn't answer.

"Dad," she tells his voicemail. "Where are you? Are you on your way? Dad?" She keeps talking, hoping he'll pick up, but it's time to pin her number to her shirt.

Courtney says, "Don't worry. He will be here." But she says that in her determined voice. "He's just late."

Jen shouts, "Love you, Sam!" She has a whole cheering section. Her mom and Noah and Jen and Steve and their little girls, Madi and Alex, and now Corey, looking tall and out of place—but not Adam, because Courtney broke up with him. And not Mitchell, because who knows?

The gym is packed with all the age groups and the different levels. The little kids have the silliest team names. For example, the ABCs, the Lemurs, the Rockers. Sam is wearing her green team shirt. The gym is all voices and shoes and bodies thumping on the mats, announcers and officials barking, parents clapping.

Declan is standing off to the side and he looks at her just once. It's a hard look. Not Go out there and have fun. Not Winning doesn't matter in the end, but I know what you can do.

She sits in her chair waiting and remembers the silver-gray leaves, and the dripping water. With Mitchell no news is definitely bad. She squeezes her eyes shut and tries to clear her mind, but she is not focused. She's just numb.

When it's her turn, she takes one sweeping glance at the bouldering wall and she climbs up, and it's strange. Her feet support her, and her hands don't slip. She can see the next hold and the next. Her body knows its length and force, where to reach and where to pause, where to lunge, and where to take a breath. She does not falter. She does not freeze up, second-guessing. There is nothing about this wall that scares her. She is climbing well because she doesn't care.

In the distance, she can hear her family cheering. Far away she hears her name. It doesn't help or hurt her. Even Declan seems distant, hoarse with shouting.

When it's over, she wins first place in bouldering and fourth in lead. Corey says she's awesome, and, luckily, he doesn't try to kiss her. Sam's mom cries. Jen says she can't believe it. Everybody says they can't believe it—except for Declan. He believes it, and at the same time, he isn't like himself at all. Not cool, not fierce, but goofy, happy, younger than anybody. He says she is at a new level now. She's got her head together. He says that because he doesn't know. He has no idea what is happening. Her dad is gone. Her heart is cold.

"I'm going to his house," Sam tells her mom that night as she takes out the kitchen garbage.

"You can't," says Courtney, because Mitchell's house does not take visitors.

"I'm going anyway." Sam stands there in the doorway of the apartment with the white trash bag in her hand.

Her mom says, "No, Sam."

"What do you mean, no?"

Her mom says, "I called them, and he's not there."

"Well, where did he go, then?" Sam demands, because her dad knew about her competition. He knew exactly when it was going to be and Kevin was driving him and everything. You don't make all those plans and vanish.

"He's sick. That's the way you have to look at it."

"He's not sick. He's an asshole."

"Watch your language."

"Why? You don't watch yours."

"Hey, I'm trying to help!"

"Tell the truth, then," Sam shouts. "Stop lying all the time."

"I'm not lying," Courtney says, and she is crying.

"I'm sorry." Sam is scared.

"I'm sorry too," says Courtney. "I don't want to say this, and I don't want to believe this, but some things can't be fixed." Her voice is so quiet and so sad, she doesn't even sound like herself. She sounds like she is talking about her whole life. She's talking about Sam's dad, and Jack, and Adam too. Adam is with someone else. That's why Courtney broke up with him. It turns out he was with this other person all along—but it doesn't matter. Courtney is over it. There are a lot of things she hated about him—like he is a Neanderthal and he has guns.

Sam clears the table, and her mom washes the dishes, and with the dish towel, Courtney dries her eyes.

"I'm going to find him," Sam says.

"And then what?" her mom asks.

III

Trouble

26

Sam takes the bus to her dad's group home. It's a big gray ranch house with red trim and a ramp next to the porch. Where the living room would be there is an office with a woman named Kristen at the desk. She calls Sam hon, but she can't show Sam her dad's room or let her look around because of privacy. All she can say is Mitchell is not there. She gives Sam brochures, and Sam stuffs them deep into her backpack.

She talks to Kevin at the Y after he's done teaching, so he can't avoid her. "Do you know where he is?"

"I do not," Kevin says slowly—but he was Mitchell's ride! He was going to drive Mitchell to the meet.

"I don't believe you."

"Well," Kevin says. "What you believe is up to you."

What does she believe? It changes.

She believes her dad is selfish.

She believes he's crazy.

She believes he's full of shit.

She believes he's magic.

All through tenth grade she wants him back, but at the same time no, because then he would disappear again.

She keeps calling, but he never answers, and then his voice-mail is full.

For a while she looks at a picture of her dad and mom when

they came together to her meet and he stood there like a rock
star, but after a few weeks she doesn't want to see him anymore.

She stops thinking about him—except when she's about to
fall asleep, and when she's daydreaming at school, and when
she's on the bus and she remembers climbing is falling.

She falls all the time. In Danvers, she makes a dumb mistake
right at the beginning, and then it's over. She knows that she
can't win.

Sam's mom says everybody has an off day sometimes, but
Sam disagrees. It's more like you have a great day sometimes
and then you can't repeat it.

"Where's the fire?" Declan demands. "Where's the focus?"
He says she has to bring that focus every time, not just occa-
sionally. Consistency is like a muscle. "Are you willing to practice? Are you going to work? Because if you're not, you shouldn't
be here."

They are standing in the gym and she thinks, No, I don't
want to be here. But she doesn't want to be anywhere else
either—not in school where other girls don't even see her, not at
home where her dad will never call. The wall seems like her best
option. Climbing hurts your body—but the pain is simpler. She
says, "I want to work."

She starts staying late with Declan after the main practice. It
starts with just a few minutes, but then, when walls are open,
they work longer. Some girls think it's unfair, but Declan gets
permission since Sam is earning points in competition, and she
represents the gym.

She knows she is getting stronger. She can feel weird little
muscles in her back and arms. She's getting smarter too. She
can almost trick her mind into staying calm. She takes a breath
and pretends she is the person she was before, the steady one,

the one who knows what she is doing. But it's not tricks or luck or magic that helps. It's time. During the week, she works with Kevin at the Y. He knows her mom can't pay him, but he is Mitchell's friend.

"Does my dad ever call you?" Sam asks casually.

She hates Kevin's answer. "I pray for him."

Usually when he's away, her dad sends cards, especially on Sam's birthday, but nothing comes in November, when she turns sixteen.

Her mom says, "Sixteen is big!" She wants to have a party.

"Don't you think I'm a little old for that?" Sam says.

But her mom won't let it rest. On the actual day, she says, "Sam, I got you something." It's one of those necklaces with a tiny star.

"Oh, wow," Sam says appreciatively.

"You can return it if you don't like it," her mom says.

"I do like it," Sam says.

"Here, put it on." Courtney clasps the chain. "I got the choker length so you can climb and it won't catch on anything."

"It's perfect," Sam says.

"And I got you these."

Courtney gives Sam a box and inside there's a pair of La Sportiva climbing shoes. Sam can't even speak. She just inhales the new leather.

"Whoa, how much did those cost?" Noah asks.

Sam thinks, More than the necklace, but she doesn't say that, because she doesn't want to show favoritism.

Her mom says, "I've got the receipt in case they don't fit." But they do fit because Courtney knows Sam's size.

Sometimes Sam is angry at her dad. Sometimes she's calm. At Christmas her mom gives her fifty dollars supposedly from him.

In February it snows so hard that there's hardly any school. Sam and Corey open his dad's liquor cabinet and search for Mitchell Kohl online.

Michelle Kohl. Mitch Kohl. There's nothing on Sam's dad.

Corey says, "Maybe he goes by an alias." They are drinking scotch and they keep trying his name all different ways, but they can't find him. "Maybe he's actually a spy."

"He is not a spy. He'd be a terrible spy."

"That's what you think. Maybe he's so good you'd never know."

They try drinking rum. It burns your tongue, but then it feels good.

Snow is piling up outside, so they lie down together on the couch. Corey's dad is at work, and they are all alone except for the two-hundred-gallon aquarium full of coral and little shrimp and tropical fish with spots and stripes and neon fins and bright black pinpoint eyes.

Corey is pulling off Sam's clothes. She kind of likes it, and she kind of doesn't. In the end she's just staring at the fish. How do she and Corey look to them? All tangled up and naked. It's awkward. It's actually ridiculous, humping on dry land.

She would rather glide under water. She would rather be a purple fish. She would rather be with Declan.

What does she like about Declan?

That he is strong and quick.

That he is older.

That he can see inside her.

That he is so critical.

That he is so hot.

That he teaches her.

That he can look at her and it's enough.

There are times he looks at her and she thinks she can do anything.

Then other times he looks at her the way he might caress

her. His eyes trace her body, like he wants her. Is that real, or is she just imagining?

One Saturday after practice, she and Declan take turns on the bouldering wall. First, she jumps up and tries the problem, and then he tries, and then she tries, and they both get stuck in the same place, a tricky angle where you have to switch feet. Over and over, they launch themselves and fall onto the mats. They are sweating, but they won't give up, and actually she gets it first. Maybe it takes thirty minutes, maybe it's an hour. She has no idea, but she figures out how to shift her weight just right and switch her feet and reach! Then she has it solved. She completes the route and drops off, happy.

"Yes!" Declan punches the mat next to her.

"Now you," she says, because she doesn't want to let him off so easy.

"I can't do it that way." He is stronger, but also bigger and much heavier. "That's your move."

Your move! He is just inches away from her and when she turns toward him, his expression is playful and admiring and tender. His fingertips tickle her bare arm, and she holds still, afraid he'll stop.

A minute later, they're sitting up and grabbing their coats and he is checking messages on his phone and he frowns and hardly talks as they drive home. She watches, but he barely glances at her.

That's the hard part, the way he switches over. He is in college and she is just a kid again. It makes her dizzy and a little sick. It's like coming off a ride where you were flying. Now suddenly, you're done. The music stops. You're standing on the ground.

27

The summer before junior year, Sam works every afternoon at Freeda's. The air-conditioning is so cold she wears a sweatshirt. Her legs are stiff from standing at the counter, so she switches off, standing on one and then the other.

"Yeah, that's why you need to go to college," Courtney says. Eighty-five percent of everything she says relates to college. It's because of Sam's last report card. B in English, B– in History, D+ in Chemistry, B+ in Spanish, A in Algebra II.

D+ in Chemistry? Courtney says. "What the hell?" It's like she doesn't even see the good grades. She barely even reads the comments about how Sam is bright and capable. "How did you fail chemistry? You *know* you can do science." She starts raving about how a B in History or English is one thing. At least you tried. A D+ is something else. It's a death wish.

"Oh my God," Sam says. "I didn't fail."

But no. With grade inflation a D+ is the new F. That's why Sam is taking summer school.

Every morning before work, Courtney drops off Sam at the high school and Sam goes to Earth Science in a stifling classroom. There are sixteen kids and if they are lucky their teacher, Mr. Dalton, will show them videos of molten lava devouring everything in its path. If they're not, they will take a chapter quiz.

"No trick questions," Mr. Dalton says. "I just want you to do the reading." That means you have to memorize every kind of rock there is. The book is boring, but he is funny, like *Okay, you guys, I am actually a biology teacher—help me out here.* The first day when he talks about the class and why we are all here, Mr. Dalton says, "What kind of rock do we have here in New England?"

Nobody answers.

"What kind of stones did all the farmers dig up every time they tried to plant anything?" Nobody says anything, so he answers his own question. "Okay, we have granite."

Oh yeah, Sam thinks. She knew that.

"Why do we have all that granite? Where did it come from? Anyone?" Mr. Dalton is very short. Probably that's why he rolls back on his heels and then up on his toes—so he'll look taller. He has reddish-brown hair and a beard. "Come on. You're killing me."

"Glaciers," Sam mutters, because she remembers when Mitchell told her glaciers dropped the boulders at Red Rocks.

"Yes!" Mr. Dalton pounces, as though she is a genius and she is on his team forever.

Wow, Sam thinks. That is probably the first and last time her dad helps her in school. She's in a bad mood after that, even though Mr. Dalton looks hopefully at her.

She is in a bad mood a lot, especially when her mom tries to understand her. Sam won't listen and instead of getting angry, her mom will say, "You're missing Dad."

Sam says, "No, I'm really not." But her mom thinks missing is the answer.

Courtney is always googling and taking books out from the library. Whenever she brings up Mitchell, she says, "It's not your fault." She probably got that online. Probably she looked up what to say when your kid's dad is the wrong person.

Courtney is so compassionate she makes Sam crazy. She will sit down next to Sam and say, "What are you thinking?"

Sam says, "Nothing."

Her mom says, "It's okay to be sad."

Sam echoes her mom's tender voice. "Thank you."

And then Courtney shoots Sam a look, because it's okay to be sad but not a smartass.

Usually in life it's better to be sad. Sad is more lovable—just like dying is more acceptable than, say, drinking full-time. Every once in a while, Sam thinks it would be easier if her dad died—especially if he would die of something you can sympathize with like cancer. This girl Kayla in Sam's math class lost her dad that way, and a large number of kids and even teachers went to his memorial. It was at St. Mary's and sitting in a pew, Sam could picture her dad's funeral like that, except in a Jewish temple.

People would get up and say how sweet and talented he was. He didn't care about money. He didn't care about winning. What a juggler. What a musician. He played twenty-seven instruments. Was it that many? Sam counts them up. Drums, piano, accordion, harmonica, guitar, ukulele, fiddle. That's just seven. Has she forgotten some? At his memorial, people would perform songs he used to cover in his one-man band. "The Boxer" by Simon & Garfunkel, "Creep" by Radiohead. And his favorite, Israel Kamakawiwo'ole's "Somewhere Over the Rainbow."

Then everyone would cry, because he is gone too soon. They would say, He's left us but he is in a better place and he was doing what he loved he touched so many.

But there is no cancer and no memorial, just Earth Science in the morning and Freeda's in the afternoon.

Noah goes to summer hockey, and Jack is in Gloucester fixing houses. Stay there, mutters Courtney. She is busy all day at Staples and the salon on weekends. Everybody has a job, even

Corey. He is up in Vermont, working as an assistant counselor at his summer camp.

He sends her pictures of charred marshmallows and cabins by the lake and campers juggling. You have to wake up early and watch the kids and break up fights and help the ones who cry, but you get free time too. He and other counselors stay up late patrolling after curfew. There are rules against counselors getting stoned anywhere near camp, but at night it's really dark.

At first, he sends her photos all the time, then just a few. Halle was the same way when she went to school. Sam is used to it, and she gives up too. It's not like she has any news. She is climbing Saturdays and sometimes Sundays at the Y. Declan is out in Colorado hiking in the Rockies with his girlfriend. She misses him, but that's a secret, and she has nothing else to tell. No news, no scenery. What pictures could Sam send? A slice of pepperoni pizza and a soda?

Courtney says that's the whole point. You want to go somewhere? You want to do something? She is talking about college, as usual.

It's one hundred degrees in August, the day Corey is supposed to come home from camp. The lunch rush is over, and only a few customers are left, and then they leave. Apart from the cook, Robbie, in the kitchen, Sam is all alone with Frank Sinatra on the sound system. "Fly Me to the Moon." She cleans the tables and then she leans against the counter with her book in front of her and she studies how the earth is always moving, shifting, breaking. She is studying a lot, because she has her final coming up and she is acing the course so far. To be honest it is not exactly hard. The last two quizzes she got 100.

She just gets it—the shifting continents, the molten mantle. Mr. Dalton shared her short answer with the class where she wrote that the earth's crust is like a hot pizza bubbling. "So good!" he said. "You're thinking like a scientist." She's not sure that's true—but geology makes sense, because it's all in flux. Mountains rising from the sea. Island chains stretching like beads on a string.

She is studying faults and fractures when the bell rings and this guy walks in and she looks up and he says, "Hey, monkey."

28

Her dad is thin and brown. His hair is long. He smells like nicotine. He looks like he has been living outside.

He says, "Sorry. I didn't mean to scare you!"

"What are you doing?" She is glad of the counter between them.

"Kevin told me you might be here."

Kevin? she thinks, because he is a hypocrite! He tells her dad where she might be, but he doesn't tell her anything. "When did you see him?"

"I should have called you first. I just wanted to talk to you in person."

She looks at the door, half-afraid, half-hoping someone will walk in. "Dad, I'm working."

"No problem," he tells her, and he reaches in his back pocket and pulls out a ratty roll of dollars. He counts out four and she's embarrassed, even though nobody is there except for Robbie, smoking out the back door.

Mitchell buys two slices of plain pizza and she heats them up while he fills a large cup with orange soda from the machine. It's the lunch special—two plain pieces, and the drink is free. "What are you reading?" he asks, like they are two people being friendly.

"It's just for summer school." She closes her book, *Dynamic Earth*.

"I missed you." He is probably hoping she will say I missed you too, but she does not. He says, "I'm starting a new job," but new customers come in. A mom pushing a double stroller with two little kids, one sleeping, one crying.

Mitchell sits down to eat while Sam waits on them. She brings out hot slices on white paper plates, and she avoids looking at her dad, because it hurts to see him eating there alone.

She wants more customers to fill the place. She wants to start rushing—but no new people come after the lady leaves with her two kids. Mitchell holds the door for the stroller, and Sam braces herself to hear about his job—but he surprises her. He throws away his plate and cup and says, "I know you've got a lot of work, so I'll head out and we'll talk soon."

She almost thanks him, because she is so glad that he is leaving—and then she thinks how obvious it is she doesn't want to see him. She thinks how she used to jump into his arms. Pennies rained down from her pockets—and now she's hurt him. But he made her! He made her do it. You can't go away for ten months and find your kid just the way you left them.

Nobody else comes in, but she can't study anymore. She can't do anything but stand behind the counter. At last she gets off work and steps into the heat. She takes the bus home and her phone lights up with messages. At first, she thinks it's Mitchell, but then she sees it's Corey. She had forgotten he was coming home from camp.

"What?" she says, calling Corey back.

"Can I see you?" Corey asks all in a rush. When she doesn't answer immediately, he says, "Can I just come over?"

"I'm on the bus."

"Can I meet you?"

"Why?" The whole thing is weird; she is so distracted, and Corey hasn't texted her in weeks. "To say you're sorry?"

There is a long pause, like How did you know? And she didn't know until that moment. She hadn't thought of it at all, but now she knows exactly what he wants to do.

"Sam?" He sounds shaky. Maybe he thinks she can read his mind—even though it's not like that at all. She can't read anybody, and she doesn't want to. He says, "Can I meet you at the church?"

"Okay." She is staring out the bus window.

So, they stand behind St. Mary's, and he hugs her and then he looks at her and says, "I think you're an amazing person." And she thinks, You memorized this. He probably memorized a whole speech on his way back from Vermont. "The thing is something happened." He is talking fast, and she is translating silently. Something happened means he hooked up with someone else. "We've been apart so long."

She says, "It's true."

"I just think . . ."

"Me too."

"Really?"

She says, "Yeah, we should break up."

He is shocked because she's jumped ahead of him. Confused and relieved, he says, "I always want to be your friend."

She nods, even though she knows they won't be. They won't hang out in his dad's basement with their clothes on. That's not how their friendship worked. She says, "Yeah, definitely."

He looks like he wants to hug her again, but she steps back. "That's okay." She doesn't know exactly what she means by that. It's okay, you don't have to keep hugging me? Or it's okay, I don't mind you slept with someone else? It's more like it's okay, you didn't break my heart. Try knives. Try torches. My dad is a professional.

29

At home when Sam's dad calls, she says she can't talk because she is studying for her final. Even after the exam, she carries her Earth Science book everywhere. It's like a shield.

At Freeda's, she turns the pages and stares at all the diagrams and photographs—but mostly she reads about the Rockies. They are the result of plates colliding. They are igneous, and they are ancient—what's left of prehistoric islands.

Whenever the door opens, she is afraid her dad is back to order pizza, but it's never him. He felt bad for barging in. That's what he tells Courtney. He wants to see Sam—but he doesn't want to put her on the spot.

Courtney sits with Sam on the couch and says, Just hear him out. He wants to tell Sam how he missed her.

Sam says he already did.

He wants to tell her how much he regrets losing so much time with her.

Sam says, Uh-huh.

He is working on a farm.

Sam says, That's nice. She imagines little pigs with corkscrew tails.

Courtney says she can see how Sam might be upset.

Sam says, "I'm not," but she doesn't want to talk, or see her dad for any reason. She doesn't really want to see anyone. Not

Halle. Definitely not Kevin. Instead of climbing at the Y, she sits at home in air-conditioning. She gets a 92 and *very good!* on her exam, but she doesn't show it to Courtney.

Her mom says, Let me cut your hair, but Sam says no.

Her mom says, You're starting junior year and that's the most important year.

Sam says, Thank you for reminding me.

School starts, and Sam walks to class, and she walks home, alone.

Corey is off with new people, so she hardly sees him juggling in the halls. Halle is away at Andover. Even Noah plays hockey every afternoon. Courtney works until six, so Sam is alone with her thoughts, which are not about her dad or Corey or school or really anything around her. They are all about the people she can't see—Declan and his girlfriend.

On Facebook Declan's girlfriend is beautiful with dimples and her name is Ashley. She goes to the University of New Hampshire and she skis. Does she climb too? Sam isn't jealous. How could she be? She is just wondering.

Practice starts two weeks after school begins. What will it be like this time? Will Declan critique her, the way he did before? Will he drive her? Sam is taller and stronger. Her arms are hard. Her eyes are sad. What will he think when she climbs for him again?

Her dad sends her a letter in the mail. It's on lined notebook paper and the writing is thick black print. *Sam I still owe you an apology actually a lot of them. If I could just talk to you if you would let me. You are my*— At this point, there is a tiny drawing of the sun, the moon, and stars—and maybe a comet. It could also be a spaceship. It is hard to tell.

Sam leaves the note at the bottom of her locker, and her textbooks crush it down. Precalculus and U.S. History and

Spanish and American Literature and Biology. She likes the weight of all those books. She likes the way people ignore her, because it gives her time to count the days and hours until she can climb again.

She sees Declan as soon as she walks in. Even though he is at the far end of the gym, she recognizes his stance, his legs apart. The gym is giant, crawling with climbers, but everywhere he goes, she senses him.

When he gathers everyone, he picks up right where he left off, except that this year he divides the team into two practice groups because there are so many kids. It's not like one group will be better or worse. They are still one team, and the groups are equal, and they will switch off drills. Declan takes one group and Toby takes the other.

Sam holds still as Declan calls names from a list. She doesn't want Toby's group. It's true Toby has been at the gym for longer, but she coaches all the younger kids. How can the groups be equal? Nobody believes that, and nobody believes the groups will switch off either.

When Declan calls her name for Toby's group, she looks at him in shock and silent protest, but he ignores her.

She climbs with ten other girls and Toby, and he doesn't even glance in her direction.

As soon as practice is over, she packs up and changes shoes. She is never coming back. She is never going through that again. She is almost out the door when he asks if she wants a ride.

"Okay," she says, as though her heart's not racing.

There is sand on the floor of his white car and all between the seats. It's still summer weather in September. They are both wearing shorts and T-shirts. The sun is beating down, and she brushes sand off her bare legs.

He starts driving, and the wind is whipping through the

open windows, and they don't speak. It would be embarrassing to whine about Toby's group. And she would feel dumb asking, How were the Rockies? She doesn't know what to say, and so she tells him, "My dad came back."

She has no idea why she said that. Her dad is the last thing she wants to talk about. She wants to start over, but she can't, because she's crying.

"Sam!" He takes the next exit and pulls off onto Cherry Hill Road and parks the car in a crunch of gravel. "What happened?"

It's very still. The air is hot. She is afraid to say more, but she does anyway, because it turns out Declan is the only one she wants to tell. She has been waiting and waiting. "He was gone almost a year and now he's back."

"Your dad who used to whistle at the meets?"

She is watching his face. His dark eyes can be hard or mischievous or playful. Now they're just surprised. He doesn't seem so much in his twenties. He's more like a kid now, and she's the older one. She is the one with more experience, or at least, more pain. "He has a new job."

"That's good, right?"

She tries to explain. "No, because he does this every time and it won't work! He starts out good and then he disappears."

They sit there together, and she thinks, Do you know what I mean? Do you have any idea what I mean? It helps to tell him, but she can't read his face, and she can't have anything she really wants, a kiss, a caress, a return to what happened when he looked at her for real and touched her. She can't ask about that either. They never spoke about it then, and they can't start now. Everything is unsaid between them.

30

At school Sam's first class is gym, at 7:50. It's called conditioning, but all that means is sit-ups, pull-ups, and sprints between orange traffic cones. Sometimes Sam runs; sometimes she is too sleepy.

The teacher is a pregnant lady named Mrs. Keith, who stands and watches everybody. Her last baby was premature, so she waves her hands and blows her whistle, but she can't actually do anything. On the day they take turns climbing ropes, Sam watches Mrs. Keith's round astonished face below. She can't believe how fast Sam climbs to the gym ceiling.

Sam hangs out there, swinging a little.

"Okay, come down now," Mrs. Keith calls nervously.

Sam pretends that she can't hear. Down below, the other kids don't want to climb, so they are happy for Sam to run out the clock.

"Come on down. Safely."

The rafters are covered with thick dust. Sam writes with her finger. *SCHOOL SUCKS*. Also, *CLEAN ME*.

Her class sits on the polished floor like kindergartners, and Sam is nicely balanced, gripping with her hands, clamping with her legs and knees.

"Sam!" Mrs. Keith is starting to freak out a little bit. Sam knows how teachers think. What if something happens? What if there's an incident? It's not like Mrs. Keith can climb up after her.

The bell is ringing, and Sam is on the floor in just an instant, jumping the last few feet. Mrs. Keith almost laughs with relief. Everyone is staring.

Too bad her other classes are so hard. English is terrible, especially *The Scarlet Letter.*

"Just try!" her mom says. Also, "Enjoy school, because real life is so much harder."

Sam already knows life is hard, but Courtney's new thing is letting go of anger. She thinks it would be good for Sam to see Mitchell on her birthday. Her mom says, "Seventeen is big."

Sam points out, "You say that every year."

"But your dad's here now. He's here for it! We could celebrate together."

Sam just shakes her head, and so she turns seventeen without him.

But even after that, her mom will not give up. She says, "How about in a week—or when you're ready—you just call him?"

Sam chooses the second option—when she's ready—which is never.

Her mom says, It's not good for you. It's not good to carry so much sadness and so much pain.

"Yeah, that's why I'm not calling him," Sam tells her. It's not like she holds a grudge. It's self-defense, because the sadness and the pain come from seeing him.

Courtney says, "It's hard to be so unforgiving."

Not true. It's easier. And anyway, Sam does forgive her father. She gets it: He is sick, he can't help screwing up. She just doesn't want to watch it happen anymore.

What's hard is going to school each day and sitting there, then going to the gym and climbing in Toby's group where Declan can't even see her.

Sometimes Declan drives her home, sometimes he doesn't. When he does, she wants to ask him why she's in the lower group, but she knows what he will say. There is no lower group. He'll talk like any other teacher.

In December Toby is out of town, so Declan coaches both groups together. He says, "Okay, let's see what you can do."

Like you care, Sam thinks, but on the wall, she feels alert and smart and curious. What will I do? What will I try? I'll show you.

There are three separate bouldering problems set up, and the girls rotate between them. Sam tries the first and solves it fast. She attacks the second, and it's harder. She has to work at it, but she knows what to do. Wedge yourself in. Leverage yourself, so you're like one side of a triangle.

"Okay!" Declan compliments her.

But the third problem kills. It's weirdly tricky, because the holds you think will work don't work at all. Your route looks right but then you're stranded, and there's nowhere to go.

"Think," Declan says, when she falls. "No," he tells her when she falls again, and then she has to stop because other girls are waiting, but she can't give up. She almost sees the answer, but he yells, "Hey! Get down."

She reaches anyway. She lunges, and she's swinging by one hand.

He isn't interested. She is taking time from everybody else. "I said get down!"

She drops to the mat and her face burns.

"Over there." He points her to the sidelines. The other girls are watching, hushed, as she draws her knees up to her chest. "Which part of that don't you understand?" he says. "Over. There."

She will not move.

He takes her by the arm and slides her off. He actually yanks her off the mat, and she thinks, What's happening?

She glares at him. He just turns his back.

The other girls pretend they are not looking at her, and she pretends she doesn't see them pretending not to look. They think she is about to cry—because they don't know her.

She zips up her jacket and pulls her hood up and runs all the way to the bus stop.

Cold cramps her toes inside her shoes. She stamps her feet. She stuffs her gloved hands into her pockets. She could call her mom, but then she would have to talk to her.

She looks far down the road, watching. It's been an hour, but the bus doesn't come. A white car pulls up instead. It's Declan.

Slowly she opens the door and feels a blast of warm air.

They sit there in the car by the side of the road and she knows he feels bad, even though he won't apologize. He looks at her almost softly. "Are you okay?" He takes her hands and blows on them.

She is afraid he'll hear her pounding heart. He is so close. The ice inside her melts away. The windows fog over. He unzips her jacket, and she feels him under her shirt, against her skin, inside her pants. His palm, his fingers, the heat radiating from his hands.

She can't see anything outside. She can't feel anything but his hand against her. He is pressing, and she is coming to meet him, throbbing harder and harder until she breaks apart like hard candy smashing into the tiniest sweetest pieces.

Again, again, her body pleads, even as he wipes mist from the windows and the world shines in.

He avoids her eyes as he starts driving. He doesn't speak; he doesn't look at her. Together they watch the stripy road. White black white. Sun trees sun.

31

Sometimes he kisses her; sometimes he doesn't. Sometimes they park near snowbanks and she warms her hands inside his jacket and his pockets and his pants. And then, instead of taking her home, he drives her to his place in Salem. She says, What about your girlfriend?

He says, I don't have a girlfriend, and that might be true. There are no new pictures of Ashley online when she looks for them.

They only go to his place when his roommates are away. It's quiet and his sheets are dark and tangled. They lie down, and she pulls her shirt over her head and when he kisses her, she thinks, This is kissing. When he strokes her body, she thinks, This is why people like it so much. This is what they mean.

She also knows she can't tell anyone. He even says it when they are together. He whispers, and it's like a spell. "You were never here."

It is strange but magic in his apartment. It is wrong but delicious, like all the things not good for you.

It is a dreamworld; it is underwater where everything looks larger and more beautiful. Other people shrink to half their size, then half again. She can barely hear their voices in the distance. School is tiny, almost off the map.

She is always thinking and then wondering about him. What

if she grows up all at once? What if she turns eighteen next year and then . . . ? She has no idea. She is confused, and she is also calm. She is mixed up and at the same time smooth as glass.

They are so secret; they are almost secret from themselves, almost dreaming when they lie down together. They do not speak. They do not text each other. Just once she sends a message *Hi* and a few question marks.

> ?
>
> ?
>
> ?

He does not reply, and when he sees her next, he's angry.

He tells her in the car, "Don't text me," and it stings, and at the same time, she knows he's right. Texts would be evidence if they get caught. But they won't get caught. They will be too secret, and too fast. They will be too quiet in the dark.

They are thieves. They steal time—not just hours, but the years between seventeen and twenty-two. They hide those years under their coats, and when they are together they leave those years on the floor with their boots, and socks, and clothes.

"When did you start liking me?" she whispers.

"How do you know I like you?" he asks, but he is stroking her bare skin.

"Was it the first time you drove me home?"

"No."

"Was it when I solved that problem you couldn't do?"

"No."

"When was it?"

He says, "When you kept climbing, after I said stop."

"Even though you were angry?"

"Yeah."

She looks at him and says, "That doesn't make sense."

It's strange because he is almost shy when she looks at him like that. "I'm confused about you," he says at last.

"I'm in love with you," she whispers back.

But as soon as she says those words, the spell is broken. He pulls away, sits up, and gets dressed.

At practice, she is glad she's in the other group. She keeps her eyes on the wall, glances at her choices, and climbs decisively.

At school, she doesn't worry about math tests or history. At the gym she doesn't think about points or competitions. She thinks about Declan and what he said. *I'm confused about you.* She repeats those words because they're real. That is how Declan really is—and she waits and waits to see him, because she wants him to be like that again.

Her mom thinks Sam is coming down with something. Then she thinks she is depressed, because she goes to bed so early, especially on weekends. Then she is afraid Sam is cutting class or taking drugs. "I'm not," Sam tells her, because she is not taking anything, and she is not depressed at all. Mostly she is surprised to see her mom. It's surprising to come home from Declan's place and think, Oh, this is where I live. She feels light-headed—still dreaming—until one day he drops off Sam, and Courtney is standing there.

It's not like they are holding hands or kissing in the car. Sam is leaning slightly toward Declan, but she's not touching him. And then suddenly she sees her mom, holding the empty recycling bin.

For a second, Sam freezes. Then she ducks her head and gets out fast.

"What do you think you're doing?" Courtney demands. Declan is already backing out, and Sam's heart jumps. "What is going on, Sam?"

"Nothing."

"What were you doing in that car?"

"Nothing!"

"Oh really?"

"He was just giving me a ride."

"I thought you take the bus home."

"I do. Just today he gave me a ride."

"Since when are you getting in his car? Why didn't he stay to talk to me?"

"Oh my God. It's not like I'm hitchhiking." Sam starts walking toward the building, but now her mom can tell she's nervous.

"Don't walk away from me."

"I'm not walking away. I'm walking inside."

They are standing in the lobby, and Sam would rather take the stairs; she would rather do anything than take the elevator with her mom and that recycling bin.

"What's happening?"

The doors open and Sam steps in. "Stop freaking out because I got a ride!"

Her mom crowds in after her. "Which you weren't ever going to tell me."

Sam leans against the elevator walls.

"He's your coach. Let's just be clear on that, okay? He is an adult. You're just a kid. He is not your friend."

The elevator arrives at the fourth floor and Sam says, "Nothing is happening."

"I don't want you in his car again. I'll pick you up next Saturday."

"Then I won't go." Instantly, Sam realizes her mistake. Why would she care who drives her if nothing's happening?

"I'll call him now."

"No! Mom, listen!"

She tells her mom she will never drive with Declan again. It was just a one-time thing and from now on she will take the bus. She promises. She also says she wouldn't have done it if she had known her mom would be so upset.

"I just don't want you to get hurt," her mom says at last.

"I *am* hurt," Sam confesses, because her mom wants her to confess something.

"Oh, sweetie," her mom says, because she assumes Sam is thinking of her dad.

"It's okay. It's okay," Sam soothes her mom, and she means it, but she is not thinking of her dad at all. She is only thinking about Declan. She is mixed up and calm and bad, and she will say anything to see him.

32

Lying is like everything else. Practice every day, and you get better.

Sam tells her mom that she and Corey are friends again. She says that's where she is on weekends, and she swears she never drives anywhere with Declan. In fact, he drives her to his place, and then she takes the bus home from Salem. That way her mom can't catch her.

She is careful, and Declan is even more careful than she is—so careful that a lot of times he won't even see her. He has a whole complicated life with roommates and part-time jobs and college classes and weekend bouldering trips. He is always rushing, and she's always waiting.

Then when they're together, she forgets how hard it was to wait. When they are alone, he can't stop touching her. His hands caress her, and he lifts her up to look at her. You are beautiful, he whispers, almost reluctantly. You are amazing, he says, as if he wishes that it weren't true.

As careful as he is, as distant as he becomes away from her, when they finally meet, he wants her more and more. They hide out at his place for hours; they spend entire afternoons, and Sam tells her mom that she was with Corey studying.

"Yeah, right," Sam's mom says, because she knows studying

is the last thing Sam and Corey would do. Studying with Corey is the kind of lie Courtney can handle.

Sam's mom is working. Her brother is off skating, trying to outscore all the other sixth graders. Her dad leaves her a voicemail. *Hey, monkey, I was just thinking about you.*

But she is not thinking about him. She does not wonder why he's back or where he's living, because she is gone now. She is somewhere else at home, and on the bus and on the street, and in biology at school. Finally, she has learned to disappear.

In math she tucks her feet under her chair and feels a warmth, a hidden glow. It's in her pockets, and in the lining of her coat, and in her boots, and all inside her clothes, against her skin.

For days after she sees Declan, she walks collar up, hands in pockets, to keep her secret in. Then another day passes, and another, and she can't talk to him or feel his breath, and loneliness creeps up on her. She feels the ice, and her mom's words haunt her. *He is not your friend.*

"What will happen?" she whispers when they are together.

"Sh." He is kissing her, muffling her words.

They are so quiet. They will never give themselves away. They are an island, and when they are together, nothing worries them. Only rarely does she get scared or sad. It happens at odd times—for example, watching Noah at the hockey rink, or hearing her mom come home exhausted, with the groceries. Then all the warmth and light inside her dims.

Her mom says, "Could you at least put these away?"

And Sam feels the chill of the refrigerator and the milk, and she knows how it will be. Declan's roommates will walk in on them. Her mom will find out and she will tell the gym and he will lose his job and Sam will be the reason.

He already snaps at her, even though she only wants to talk to him. She says, "Can't I call you?" But it's impossible. He will not answer.

She wants to know him. She wants to ask, What did you do today? Where did you go? She wants him to look at her like he did that time and say what he is really thinking. But when she speaks, he pulls away, and she is afraid of that. So she is quiet, alert, fearful—and at the same time, she knows he has been waiting for her too. They are both under a spell.

Nothing is dangerous.

Nothing is wrong.

Nothing is right.

There is no limit to what they'll do.

There is no end.

She dreams she is asleep with him.

Then outside, the cold air slaps her face. Saturday morning, the wind whips her hair into her mouth as she walks from the bus stop to the gym. It's early, but she senses that he's in the building. She hears his voice and follows the sound down the hall to where the staff have offices and locker rooms, and she finds him there, in the cold passageway with Toby.

Toby has her hands on Declan's shoulders. Her cropped shirt is riding up, and his hands span her bare waist.

Sam is staring, and Toby stops flirting for just a second, but not really, because why would she? She would never think of Sam and Declan.

When Declan sees Sam, he is not embarrassed. He pulls Toby closer; he's got his arm around her now and Toby looks just right with him. She is small, but strong, a coach, a climber. They both teach annoying girls. They laugh together all the time. Sam can tell. They kiss and laugh and take off their clothes.

"Hey, back in the gym," Declan tells Sam.

She searches his face, but his eyes are hard, not even a glimpse of recognition. You do have a girlfriend, she tells him silently. You have Toby. You have lots of people.

He is getting angry. He doesn't even want her looking at him.

You lied to me, she's thinking, because she can't ever talk to him.

He sees she isn't moving, so he takes Toby's hand and they brush past her, instead.

You were never here, she tells herself, just as he once told her. But there she is, standing in the cement block hallway at the gym. There she is with her bag and her climbing shoes. Practice is starting, and she stands there alone.

33

He is glad. He's glad she caught him, because he doesn't want her so in love with him. She is trouble. He'll get in trouble with her, so he pushes her away. Back off, Sam. Get back to the gym. I don't know you. I don't see you—except when it's dark and we're alone.

She doesn't decide this all at once, but gradually as she walks out. Slowly, as she rides the bus home.

It's raining lightly, and the big snowbanks are melting. If she blinks, she can forget for just a moment, but then she sees him again with his hands on Toby. He got his wish; nobody ever caught him and Sam together. Sam was the one intruding, opening the door.

She hates herself for finding him there.

How did this happen? How did she fall for him?

She remembers climbing is half knowledge and half instinct—and a little bit experience.

He never added up. She knew that before. She always knew, but she still wanted him.

34

The next Saturday her mom says, "Did they cancel practice?"

"No." Sam is curled up on the couch.

"Are you sick?"

"No."

"You missed the bus!"

"That's okay."

"I'll drive you."

"No, that's okay."

"What do you mean?"

"I'm not going."

"What do you mean?"

"I mean I'm not going."

"But why?"

"I don't want to."

"You're skipping?"

"I'm quitting." The word stings—and not just Sam.

Her mom stands there demanding, "What about the team?"

Sam says, "I don't like the team."

"Yes, you do."

"Not really."

"Not really? Sam, you made a commitment. They gave you a scholarship. What's going on?"

"Nothing," Sam says, but of course her mom does not believe her.

"It's Declan."

"No."

"What happened with him?"

"Nothing." Sam is a mouse hiding in a box. Her mom is a cat pawing and clawing, but she can't get in.

"I'm going to call him."

Sam doesn't say it, but so what? It doesn't matter. Her mom can't force her to go back, and Declan can be all coachlike and professional. He can act concerned; he can act any way he wants. He has nothing to worry about because Sam won't tell. She won't ever talk about him, or see him, or think of him again. She says, "It isn't Declan."

At school she hugs her books, so no one will even brush against her in the halls.

At night she lies awake. She has a bed now, not a tent, and there is a wardrobe-partition thing separating her from Noah. She waits until Noah is asleep on his side of the partition. Then she stands on her bed and pulls ribbons from the bulletin board on the wardrobe door. They are blue and white and royal purple. 1st place, 3rd place, 5th place. Emerald green, and printed gold. She loses a few tacks behind the bed, and a couple fall onto the floor. Hopefully she'll find them all before she steps on them. Right now, she takes her ribbons to the kitchen and stuffs them in the recycling bin.

"No! Sam!" The next morning, Courtney pulls out those satin scraps, even though Sam won't have anything to do with them.

She won't set foot inside the Y. Walls don't tempt her. She doesn't even glance at fences.

Every night, Courtney tries to talk to her. Sometimes she scolds. Sometimes she sympathizes. She says, "Why don't you call Dad?"

"No thanks."

"You're just so down."

Sam shrugs because yes. True.

Every morning, her mom chases Sam out of the apartment, but she gets to school late. In class she takes out her notebook and writes nothing.

Her mom says, "You can't hold a grudge forever. Dad's working and he's trying to do good."

Courtney won't let up, and Sam knows it's her own fault. After all, she made her mom think it's her dad who upset her. "Just call him," her mom keeps telling her, and then when Sam does not, her mom calls instead. She arranges for Mitchell to come over, just for an hour Sunday morning.

Sam doesn't even argue. What's the point? If her mom invites him, there is nothing Sam can do.

When the morning comes, Sam sits on the couch and watches her dad walk through the door. He looks cleaner than he did before, but she is glad he doesn't try to hug her.

He sits on the couch near Sam while Courtney says she is driving Noah to hockey practice. Don't go, Sam thinks, but they take off.

The room is quiet. There is nowhere to hide.

"It's good to see you," Mitchell says.

Sam says nothing. Then she says, "Thanks."

"Can I tell you something?"

"What?"

He starts telling her a long story about how this is his home and Sam is his family and he is never going anywhere again. "I went to Montreal," he says. "I was in Toronto. I was busking down in Santa Fe. I did some stupid shit you probably don't want to hear about—but now I'm taking care of horses. I'm starting over—from the beginning." He shows her pictures on his phone. There is a white horse named Daisy and a gray one named Archer. They are both rescues. "Your mom tells me you're not climbing."

"Yeah, I quit."

"Why?" he asks, carefully, as though he knows it's not his business.

"I just don't want to do it anymore."

He doesn't say, But you were good! Or you made a commitment! He just says, "And how is it?"

"How is what?"

"Not climbing."

"It's great."

Of course, that doesn't fool him for a second. "You'll get back there. I know you."

"Not really."

He flinches but he takes it. "I've missed a lot."

She swallows. "Well, I'm seventeen."

He turns up his palms, as if to say, What can I do? except he's got a card in each hand, a red and a black queen.

He brushes his hands together and both cards disappear. "I'm not going to bother you. I'm not going to come around unless you want me to." He tells her he is working on himself. Each day he concentrates on what's in front of him. He sticks around. He cleans the stalls. He isn't performing anymore.

She says, "How is it?"

He says, Hard. He says he will be going; he won't keep her. He will let her decide when she wants to see him. He will be at Windy Hill Farm, so whenever she is ready. And he only hugs her for one second.

After he leaves, she finds the red queen in her back pocket.

35

She is grateful he is not always coming around, but at the same time it's weird. He calls and he is careful on the phone. It's like being strangers. He is so timid, nothing like her dad.

Courtney says maybe you can't control what happens, but you can control how you respond. She always says that when she is miserable. She is convinced quitting Boulders symbolizes something terrible—like Sam is giving up on life. That isn't why Sam quit, but she can't explain the real reason when her mom was already suspecting, and Sam lied so much to reassure her. Her mom has enough to worry about, especially with Noah.

When he was little, he was just curious, and then when he got bigger, Noah was quiet, playing with his cars, but now he's twelve and he is angry. At home he breaks stuff. At school he will hit and kick and punch whichever kid is bothering him. He's had detention. He's had team meetings. He has written out his point of view.

My point of view is that it's not my fault he started it. He poked me with a pencil. I rettaliated.

He writes that nicely with good handwriting, but then he fights again. He'll smash things. A plate. A mug. "Noah, please," Courtney begs him. "Goddammit, Noah." But you can't stop him. He breaks stuff and then afterward, he cries.

"I'm sorry! I'm sorry!" he sobs.

Once, Sam asks him, "If you're sorry, why do you destroy everything?" He is facedown on the couch, so when he answers, his voice is muffled. She bends over him. "What? I can't hear you. Sit up."

He doesn't sit up, but he turns his head. "Something happens to me."

"But what happens?"

"I turn into someone else."

"Well, don't do that!" She sounds like their mom, half scolding, half begging.

One night he can't figure out history, and he rips it up. First, he tears his homework down the middle and then he tears it again, and Courtney says, "Noah, stop!" She tries to lecture him. "You can't just tear up the assignment!"

He slides open the glass door to the balcony to throw the pieces out there, but Courtney won't let him, and she fights him, and for a minute Sam thinks the glass will break, and the landlady will come and make them pay for it—and how will they find the money?

By the time the fight ends, both Courtney and Noah are crying. Noah is curled up on the kitchen floor.

Maybe Noah needs a different school. Maybe he needs more time with his dad—except his dad is Jack. He still wants to go over to Jack's house and Courtney won't let him—but sometimes she does. When Noah comes back, he is tired and spoiled and he can't remember if he had dinner. One time he comes back and says Jack hit him, but then he changes his mind. He never has any bruises or scratches, but he won't go to sleep or follow any rules.

Courtney says he can't go back. Then she says Jack's house is like Six Flags. You wouldn't go there every day but if Noah's grandparents are there, she's okay with it.

Jack is still family, even if Courtney doesn't trust him. He helps with money. He never used to, but now he will pay for Noah's clothes and even groceries. He will say to Courtney, "I'll take care of it," and she accepts. That's how he wins. Little by little, he buys everybody.

Noah might need medication. He definitely needs more space. Courtney says, "We have to rearrange the bedrooms."

Sam and her mom take the bigger double room, so Noah has the smaller bedroom to himself.

It's not great. They should probably move.

"Good idea," Courtney says. "Now tell me where with one car and two jobs we can afford to live." They can hardly afford where they are now—even with help from Jack.

Sam is tired all the time because her mom has allergies. When Courtney starts snoring, Sam wakes up and can't get back to sleep. She lies there worrying about Noah because what if he gets kicked out of school? Who will watch him? And what if Jack comes for him? She drifts into those shallow dreams you get when you are barely sleeping. She dreams that Jack kidnaps Noah, and Courtney doesn't have the money for his ransom. One time she dreams she is calling her own dad and he comes over and fights Jack right in their apartment. It's like the fight at Jen's Halloween party, except this time they are bleeding on the rug. The beige carpeting is soaking red.

Then she wakes up and walks to school and she is tired. Her eyes keep closing.

Sam's history teacher nabs her after class. "Is everything all right?"

"Yup."

"I noticed you were sleeping."

"When?" Sam asks, as if she's never heard of such a thing.

"In my class."

"I'm a little bit under the weather." Sam is careful and polite, because her mom can't have two kids failing.

She tries to stay awake during the day. She tries to memorize U.S. history and raise her grades, but it's hard, because she didn't learn much the first half of junior year.

Other kids are doing amazing stuff. Not just Halle, who was already gifted, but people you would not expect, like Emily who used to cry at practice and is now in student government. Corey is on the robotics team. He is obsessed with building an autonomous vehicle that scoots around eating Ping-Pong balls and then barfs them into a container. Sam knows, because he posts videos everywhere. Corey calls his robot THE REGUR-GITATOR.

Sam doesn't build autonomous vehicles or govern anything. She just sits around trying to learn biology like mitochondria and DNA, and she no longer counts the hours, because she's not expecting anything.

36

Courtney says, We can turn this around. In April the snow melts and Noah gets a 90 on his vocabulary test. Courtney says, You see? He's gonna be okay. Everything will be fine and more than that, it will be great. Also, choose joy. Sam looks at her, like Make me.

Then Courtney says, "I've had enough out of you."

"What did I do?"

"That's the whole point. You don't do anything!"

A lot of times after work, Courtney just lies down on the couch, but if Sam lies down, her mom says, What are you hoping to do with your life? What's your plan? Please tell me.

Saturday, when Courtney and Noah come home from hockey, Courtney looks at Sam, who is just sitting in a chair. "It's a beautiful day, Sam. What are you doing?" Then when Sam doesn't answer, her mom says, "Okay, come with me."

"Where?" Sam says distrustfully.

"Nowhere," Courtney says. "I'm teaching you to drive."

"*What?*" shouts Noah, because Sam doesn't have a learner's permit, even though she's seventeen. The reason is her mom has been too stressed to teach her.

But now Sam hurries after Courtney and her brother is jumping around the living room and cheering. It's like the old days; he thinks she's a celebrity.

Even when they get down to the parking lot beneath the building, Sam can't believe her mom is letting her sit in the driver's seat. Courtney hands her the keys.

"First lesson. A car is a lethal weapon. One false move. One. Just *one* second you don't pay attention, and you've murdered someone, or you're dead. Okay?"

"Okay."

"Second of all, this is the brake. Put your foot on it. Go ahead. Now turn the key."

Sam inserts the car key and turns it gently, so the old car sputters.

"No, turn it like you mean it!"

Sam turns the key and the engine roars, extra loud in the belowground parking area. "Now what?"

"Turn it off."

It takes Sam a second to realize it, but the lesson is over. No way is her mom going to let her pull out, because she would hit the other parked cars and they would all need body work.

For Sam's next lesson, they go to a big empty parking lot by the old middle school where she can't hit anything. Then Sam inches forward slowly and backs up while she's looking behind her. It's weird and scary and amazing, operating a lethal weapon, even if her mom barely lets her move. "Slowly, slowly, turn the wheel hand over hand. Little movements, Sam. WHOA! Be GRADUAL."

"Are you okay?" Sam asks her mom.

Every weekend, her mom takes her out and sometimes during the week as well. In May, Courtney lets Sam ease onto the road, where Sam learns to wait for traffic and then turn.

"This is a stop sign, that means STOP," her mom yells as Sam hits the brakes. "Jesus, Sam. Never do that! You stop gradually."

"I didn't see the sign."

"You always have to see the sign!"

"Okay, okay."

"Now, here's what you do if you want to turn. Full stop and then you creep forward a tiny bit, so you can see cars coming. You know why I'm teaching you all this?"

"Why?" Sam asks as she drives slowly, slowly up Washington Street.

"Because driving is freedom. Turn on Cabot AFTER the stop."

Even though Sam practices for hours, she pisses off the guy testing her. His badge says Trent Dickson, and he is small with glasses, and he fastens his seatbelt and adjusts his chair like he's in the cockpit of a fighter jet and he might not come back alive. He says, "When it's safe, pull out and merge."

He's got a Staples clipboard in his lap, and Sam says, "That's the exact same one my mom has." She is just nervous, thinking aloud. Big mistake.

"It's not the *exact* same," Dickson explodes. "Either it's the same or it's different. It's not the exact same."

Sam grips the wheel.

"It's an absolute, so don't try to augment it! The same or not. The exact same is incorrect. Unique or not. Very unique is incorrect. When it's safe, turn left onto Rantoul."

Instantly, Sam turns left.

"STOP," screams Dickson.

They are in the intersection and oncoming cars are honking.

"I said when it's safe. Left turn yields."

Sam knew that! She knew it perfectly, but he scared her.

They return to testing headquarters.

"You would have caused an accident," Dickson informs her as he fills out her test report *FAILED*.

After the test, Sam won't drive home. She lets her mom take her.

When they get there Noah nearly jumps on them as they open the door. "Did you get it?"

Sam doesn't answer.

"He's just an asshole," Courtney tells Sam on the couch that night. "He looked like a pervert. Seriously. Even his name. Dickson? People like that correct everybody's grammar, but they're always watching porn. We'll go to Salem next time, so you won't get him."

"Noooo."

"Oh, stop," her mom says. "Get back on the horse! Take a good look at all the morons on the road. At some point they passed their road test."

37

"Believe you're gonna pass," Courtney tells Sam on the way to Salem. Sam's mom is all about believing and manifesting, as in you have to manifest your vision.

Meanwhile, Sam is thinking, What if Dickson works in Salem too? He'll take one look at her and say, "You're the one who says exact same AND you almost killed me."

She barely speaks when she meets her examiner. His badge says Jeff Zuluaga and he is pretty laid-back, sitting in the car. He tells her, "Just take your time."

Slowly, she pulls away from the curb. When she turns, she yields so long at the intersection that she misses her light altogether. She is so cautious that every time she stops, she grinds to a halt. Then Zuluaga says, "Yeah, but keep moving."

Now she's going to fail because she's driving too carefully. Also, she messes up parallel parking, even though the whole test is set up to make it easy. All you have to do is park between some orange cones—but she gets confused, because the way her mom taught her, you pull forward to the other car's mirror, and then back up exactly to the other car's passenger door—and with cones there are no landmarks. She's not sure when to start cutting her wheel.

"Gotta work on that," Zuluaga says as he fills out her test report.

She's afraid to look at it when she gets out of the car.

Her mom is the one snatching the paper. "You passed."

"What? Seriously?"

"You believed!"

Sam tells the truth. "I didn't."

Even so, she has a license, so Sam and her mom and Noah stay up late celebrating with popcorn and the Bruins on television. They take a sheet and drape it over the couch, and then it doesn't matter when your fingers get all buttery.

They aren't just celebrating Sam's license. They are celebrating Noah's new school. Courtney appealed to the district that Noah was not being educated. Then Noah interviewed in a button-down shirt and he got into a special school. It's private, but the state will pay for it.

"Kids, here's what I want you to remember," Courtney says. "You don't give up and you will get somewhere."

Nobody is listening, because the score is tied.

"You've gotta have goals like . . ."

"College," Sam and Noah intone, eyes on the TV.

"And you've gotta have . . ."

"Money," Noah says.

"Values!"

"Sh," Noah says.

Sam asks her mom, "Are you even watching this?"

They are glad when the phone starts ringing, and Courtney takes it in the bedroom.

At first, it's quiet. Then Sam can hear her mom half pleading, half shouting. Probably Grandma D. is lecturing.

By the time Courtney returns, the game is over. She sinks down on the couch and tells them Grandma had a fall. She didn't break anything, but Courtney has to drive out tomorrow and stay for a few days to help her.

"She hardly ever helps us," Noah points out.

"That's not true," says Courtney. "She sends money."

Noah mutters, "She's nasty!"

"You can be helpful and nasty at the same time." Courtney says a lot of things, but Sam thinks this one might be true. The Bruins and the Kings are fighting. Referees are skating now to break it up, and Sam thinks maybe there is such a thing as good and nasty, the way some people can be bad and sweet. She is pretty bad. So is her dad. Noah is violent sometimes, but he's still sweet.

38

"The days are labeled." Before she drives to Amherst, Courtney gives Sam Noah's medication in a pillbox with dividers. "Make sure you watch him take them."

The reason is that Noah hates his medication. There are pills to calm him down, but he says they make him sleepy. There are other pills to help him focus, but he says they're gross. "You have to concentrate all the time."

Sam holds out a glass of water. "But that's what they're for."

"Yeah, but it's depressing!"

"What do you mean?"

"It's like you're a TV, but you're stuck on the homework channel. You get no sports or shows or anything."

"So, finish your homework and then you can concentrate on something else."

But no, your brain is stuck until the pills wear off. He says, "It's like you're paralyzed."

She looks at him and all of a sudden she thinks, You're smart. It's not that she thought he was stupid before—but her brother has opinions, and ideas. What if he is right? He does get sleepy, and he does look paralyzed, staring at his home-work. What if Sam is poisoning him? But the doctor says he needs the pills. Her mom says Noah needs them—so Sam hands them over and she stands there while he swallows—and then for the rest of the day, he won't talk to her.

He has his own phone now and Jack sends him messages, so the two of them are making plans.

"We're going camping," Noah tells Sam on Friday afternoon.

"You can't do that," Sam says. "Mom isn't even here."

"Why does she have to be here?"

"Because she has to keep an eye on you."

He looks at her, like I am twelve, what are you talking about, even though he knows what Sam means. He's not supposed to go anywhere alone with Jack. "He's free this weekend."

"Yeah, but you're not," says Sam. There was a whole agreement Courtney figured out and Jack said yes. Why is Jack changing it up now? Because I'm home alone with you, thinks Sam.

"I said I could go," Noah tells her.

"But I say you can't." Sam is already calling Courtney.

"No, absolutely not," Courtney says on the phone. She tells Noah no. Then she says she's calling Jack. Camping is not happening.

But what if Jack tries something anyway? And what if Noah runs out the door? He's big, almost as tall as Sam, and strong. She has seen him outskate other kids and block them at the rink. He can rush opponents and send them flying. At the same time, he is just little.

She says, "I never went camping with my dad."

"He was never here."

"Yes, he was. We just didn't go. I never even slept over."

"He never wanted you to sleep over."

"Because he respects Mom's judgment," Sam shoots back, because how can Noah even start comparing his dad to hers? Both fight and drink and do a million stupid things, but Jack doesn't respect anyone.

"I'm going," Noah tells her.

Sam says, "No you're not."

"He's picking me up in the morning."

"Mom said no. Please, Noah! I'm responsible for you."

She is afraid Noah will run out, or Jack will get inside the building. She keeps listening to every sound, and so she's scared to go to bed. Finally, she lies down on the couch, drifting in and out of dreams. Birds singing, boats sailing, buzzer ringing.

She jumps up, because it's the real buzzer, and it's morning.

"Who is it?" she asks into the intercom.

"Jack."

She throws on a shirt and jeans. She waits for the elevator, but then she runs down the three flights of stairs. She is wearing shoes without socks.

"Hey, Sam," says Jack, all nice and casual standing outside in the entryway. When she closes the inner door behind her, he says, "How are you?"

She hasn't seen him up close in years. His neck is thick; his arms are massive. His black hair is cropped short. Sam does not say hi. She does not say, I'm fine. She says, "He's not coming."

Jack stops smiling. "I want to see my son."

"You can see him later. Mom says it's not on the schedule."

It's strange the way he looks at her. His eyes travel over her body. Not curious, like Corey, or hungry, like Declan, but like he's measuring her. Like he could take her. "He told me he would come."

He reaches for the intercom and she tries to block him, but he reaches around her and starts buzzing and she is scared Noah will wake up and let him in. Jack is buzzing over and over again, but Noah doesn't answer.

Jack could force past her, but Sam keeps standing there. She is holding her phone and almost daring him. Silently she's telling him, Go ahead and try to push me or pick me up and throw me. Just go ahead. I'll call the cops. I'll scream. She stands there staring Jack down. It seems like a million hours pass, and then suddenly, Jack turns around and leaves.

And then she has to face Noah when he wakes up, and he is the one who yells and screams and calls her names. He throws his medication on the floor and smashes his glass. And she is begging, "Sh. Noah. Please!" because the neighbors will hear. They will complain. And finally, all she can do is grab him by the shoulders, half hugging him, half smothering him. "I'll take you somewhere. I promise we'll go hiking. As soon as I can." She keeps talking and holding him until he starts to cry. Then he is exhausted, and he lies down on the couch and won't do anything.

All day, she guards Noah. Her heart pounds whenever the phone rings. She jumps that evening when she hears a key turning in the lock—but it's her mom.

"God, I am so tired." Courtney sinks down on the couch next to Noah and hugs him whether he likes it or not. She spent three days talking to Grandma D., who might move into assisted living in Holyoke but then again might not. She might sell her house, but she might not. She might make plans, but she might not. Courtney says, "Don't let me get that way."

They eat fish sticks for dinner and Courtney says she won't get old.

"Mom," Sam whispers at night, across the wardrobe-closet partition. "What if Jack takes Noah for real?"

"He won't."

"But what if he did?"

"He'd have to kill me first."

"Would you do the same for me?"

"Yup. Go to sleep."

"Mom?"

"What?"

"How do you know what to do?"

"I don't always know."

"Yes, you do."

"Yeah, that's how you can tell you're an adult," her mom says. "People start thinking you know what you are doing."

39

No one thinks Mitchell knows what he is doing, but he is still family. In the fall when Sam starts her senior year, her mom calls Mitchell and they talk and talk and he tells her about the horse farm where he works.

When Courtney gets off the phone she says, "I really want to see that place."

Sam looks at her, like Go ahead.

"I love horses," Courtney says.

"Aren't you allergic?" Noah asks.

"Not to horses." Courtney is looking at Sam. "Just once," she tells her. "Just go there once. He sounds really good."

She drives Sam and Noah to Windy Hill Farm, and they pass through a wooden gate onto a dirt road. There are two horses standing in the field.

The barn smells like wet straw. Eight horses live there, and Mitchell is mucking out the stalls. The horses shuffle and sniffle and nibble their oats. Some are shy, but some peek out through bars. Mitchell says, "This is Roxy. This is our pony, Frodo. This is Daisy." He introduces them to a tall white horse with nervous eyes. "She had a hard life, didn't you, girl?"

He breaks a carrot and when Noah holds out a piece, Daisy snuffles up his whole hand.

"This is Archer. He was starving when we got him. You could see his ribs. His owners abandoned him."

Mitchell leads Archer out of his stall, and the horse stands quietly so they can take turns currying him. His coat is gray, but silver when you brush it. Mitchell lifts up each foot in turn and scrapes out dried mud with a metal tool. "You are so patient," he keeps telling Archer, and Courtney says, Oh wow, you are so beautiful, but Noah just leans against Archer's flank and closes his eyes.

Mitchell says, "Yeah, it feels good."

Windy Hill trains horses for equine therapy. That's the whole idea of the farm. There is an indoor ring and outdoor paddock and kids come to ride. Therapists boost the kids up into the saddle and slowly lead the horse around. It helps everybody. Maybe next time Sam and Noah can ride.

Noah says, "Yeah!"

Sam says nothing. Her dad has that light in his eyes he gets when he's performing. Some people tell lies about the past. Her dad tells lies about the future. He is always telling a new story.

"It takes time for them to trust you," Mitchell says. "They've had a lot of bad experiences, so it takes a lot of patience."

He is talking about the horses, but Sam knows what he means. She looks at him like Stop. Don't put me in your metaphor.

Courtney is so happy about the farm that she thinks they should go there for Sam's birthday. They can all go riding.

"Sweet," says Noah.

"Take him for *his* birthday," Sam says.

"Let's just invite Dad here, then," says Courtney. "It doesn't have to be a big deal or anything. Just ask him to stop by."

"No thanks," says Sam.

Her mom does not tell her to lose the attitude. She stays positive. "Just think about it, okay? You only turn eighteen once!"

Sam says, "That's true of all the other years too."

Courtney says eighteen is different. You can vote—but Sam's birthday is after the election.

She and Noah can't figure out what Courtney is so happy about. It's not just positivity. It's not history, even though Courtney is celebrating President Obama. Something else is going on with her.

When Sam asks for no party with all her quote friends from school, Courtney doesn't even argue.

Jen and Steve come with their girls, Madi and Alex, and they sit around the table eating cake and opening presents. Jen gives Sam a professional hair dryer diffuser thing, which is charcoal gray. The girls give her rainbow cards with *HAPPY B-DAY 18!!* in bubble letters. Then Courtney tells Steve, "Okay, go get it." And she turns to Sam and says in a funny voice, "We have to go downstairs."

"It's a puppy!" Noah whispers as they cram into the elevator.

"Ha," says Courtney.

The doors open, and they head out to the sidewalk in front of the building and there's Steve standing in front of a car.

It's not new; it's not cool. It's not sporty or all-wheel drive or anything, but it's parked right in front with four wheels and four doors and an engine. The car has 161,000 miles on it, which is even more than Courtney's Subaru, but Steve checked it out and it's okay. It's Grandma D.'s baby blue Buick.

The story is, Grandma D. is finally moving to assisted living—and also, she doesn't like driving anymore.

Sam just stands there because she never thought she'd get a car so soon. And it's so big! It's so old and fancy, and now she really will be free. She can drive anywhere—like Montreal or Maine or to a job or to go camping. She will never have to wait two hours for the bus again.

"Open the door," Courtney says.

"Open it!" Jen tells her.

Sam opens the driver's door, and the whole car is crammed with helium balloons. They are blue and green and gold, and they are clear with little balloons floating inside them. They are tied together in huge bouquets, one in the front and one in the back seat.

Now Sam is standing on the sidewalk holding enough balloons to float away. There is a gold number 1 and a gold number 8 and they twist in the breeze.

"Look," says Noah. "You're 81."

"Here, I'll take them." Her mom holds one bunch and Jen holds another as Sam peeks into her new car and sits in the driver's seat.

"Pull that to open up the gas tank," Steve says. "Press that to pop the trunk."

As soon as Sam pops the trunk, more balloons fly up into the air. Noah catches some and some escape—a whole trunkful of purple and red and fancy silver.

Courtney says, "You know who thought of that."

40

Now that she has a car, Sam can run errands. Best present ever, Courtney says. Sam can pick up groceries, and drive Noah to hockey, and transport herself anywhere she needs to go. Courtney even says, Sam you can go back to the gym—as though Sam quit because she didn't want to take the bus. You can go anytime you want.

Courtney also says, You can drive out to the farm. You can see your dad, and maybe you can ride the horses. They are so beautiful. It's true, Sam could drive out to the farm. Sometimes she almost thinks she will, but then she never does.

Her mom says, At least see Halle, and Sam thinks about it. She would like to drive up to Halle's house and surprise her— but Halle does not come home for winter break. She and her whole family fly out to California. Everybody leaves. Jen and Steve take their girls to Disney, and Jack flies to a Caribbean island with his new girlfriend, Nicole. It is a package deal, all-inclusive. Courtney says, Good, but Noah doesn't feel that way.

He is fighting, even at his new school, and Courtney talks to him and meets with teachers, and then he cries at home, because he hates his classes—but where else can he go?

Winter break is pretty bad. Noah does nothing. Sam works part-time at the Atomic Bean, and Courtney works more than full-time at Staples and the hair salon. On top of that, she has a cold.

Sunday morning, Courtney tells Noah to do the laundry, but he just plays on his computer, building walls and cities brick by brick. At lunchtime, Courtney says, "I told you, do the laundry. Did you hear me?" He says no, and she says, You had one job. He looks straight at Courtney and says no. Then instead of yelling at him, Courtney slams the bedroom door. She is not positive; she is exhausted. She needs to sleep, but she keeps coughing.

"Do it," Sam tells him, but he doesn't listen. "What is wrong with you?" she yells, even though yelling doesn't work. Finally, she tells Noah, "Remember I said I'd take you hiking?" But he is not the kind of person you can bribe. Or if you can bribe him, it's with stuff, not with an activity. Apart from hockey, he doesn't like activities until he is already doing them. And he doesn't like going anywhere until he is already there.

Sam sits at the table and Noah keeps playing his computer game and Sam wants to get out of the apartment, except she can't leave Noah when their mom is sick in bed. "Let's go," she tells him again, and once again he ignores her—except she has a secret weapon. There is no food in the house, because nobody went shopping.

Around one o'clock he gets up and hunts in the refrigerator. He looks in the cabinet, but he ate all the cereal the day before. Sam says, "I'll buy you lunch, but carry down the laundry."

"We're getting food," she calls out to Courtney, but she tells Noah, Take your real coat. Wear boots.

"Where are we going?" Noah asks, after he carries down the laundry.

"Subway."

"Yes." He cheers softly.

"And then somewhere else."

Sam buys him his favorite sub, smoked brisket. Her own sub

is roast beef, and she is taking bites as she drives to Gloucester. They drive past town and the Fisherman's Memorial *They that go down to the sea in ships* and Sam gets lost, but she keeps driving through the marshes to the trees, until she finds the parking lot for Red Rocks Conservation.

No other cars are parked there. The light is dim and cloudy and it's cold, even for December.

"Remember I said I'd take you hiking?"

Noah looks at the thick trees and the whole place is deserted and mysterious and they are probably not allowed to be here, so he's like, Yeah! Let's go!

Sam gets out of her car and he zips up his coat and follows her.

Trees swallow up the trail. The only sounds are twigs and branches rustling. The only creatures they can see are chipmunks streaking across the path. They climb over roots and stumps. They scramble over a fallen birch tree and they are all alone—except people must come here, because there's broken glass. "Careful!"

You can cut yourself, and you can trip, but Noah loves the slippery path, the thick wet leaves, the mud that sucks your shoes.

Sam pulls branches out of the way. "We're searching."

"For what?" Noah asks, and then he sees them. Boulders, gray and towering.

Noah wades through piles of dead leaves and Sam follows in his wake. Together they look up at the rocks looming over them. Sam touches the cold stone and feels moss and lichen, rough edges, and crazy geometric planes. "They're metamorphic," she tells Noah. "They were under a lot of pressure and that's how they ended up like this."

"What are these for?" Noah points to metal loops bolted to the rock.

"They're for ropes," Sam says. "For climbing."

"Can you climb these rocks?"

"Yeah. Probably."

Noah grabs one metal loop and pulls himself up a little bit, but he falls back. "I dare you."

For a minute Sam gazes at the boulder with its metal loops. The granite is icy. It's only four o'clock, but it's almost too dark to see. Suddenly she remembers the walk back. "We've gotta find the car."

They start hurrying to the place where they left the trail, but they can't see white blazes on the trees.

They take out their phones to see if they can call someone. Noah says, "Look, Mom left a message," but when he tries to listen, there is no service.

Sam stops walking. They can't be far from the lot, but how will they get there? Should they listen for the sound of running water? Noah's eyes are bright; he is awake in the cold air, and he is not afraid yet.

They stumble into muddy bogs they cannot see. They trip over tree roots. Noah says, "Could we dig a burrow?" He is thinking what to do if they have to spend the night.

But they can't. It's too cold. Their boots are wet. They have no food. They don't have anything. Sam closes her eyes and tries to feel which way her feet are drawing her. "Let's go."

Close together, she and Noah push forward through the trees, looking for the trail in the mud, some sign, any sign that they are back on the path.

"What if we're walking in the wrong direction?" Noah asks.

Sam doesn't answer, because she doesn't know. Maybe she did pick wrong—but she had to pick something. They can't stand still. Without the sun, it's just too cold. "I'm so stupid," she whispers to herself. "How dumb can I be?"

"You're not dumb," says Noah, even though his teeth are chattering.

"I am if we're stuck here all night."

He says, "We can just keep walking." It's scary how much he trusts her. She touches his shoulder. "Do you think I know what I'm doing?"

Noah trips. "This is where you said careful."

"It was?"

He feels down at his feet.

"Here's the fallen tree."

"There's lots of fallen trees," she tells him, but together they climb over the fallen birch tree with its long branches trailing the ground. "Listen!" Noah says, and Sam hears traffic. They creep back through the mud, and the path starts broadening and they can hear the highway, louder and louder. They race to the parking lot and to Sam's car.

They sit together and Noah is shivering while Sam runs the engine. "Just a few minutes," she says, as they wait for the heat to warm up.

Noah holds his fingers over the vents. "That was so fun."

"Sh." Sam's phone is full of messages. "She's gonna kill us. Get ready," she tells Noah as she returns Courtney's last call.

"Sam?"

Immediately, Sam says, I'm sorry, Mom. We're fine. We're okay, but Courtney is crying. "Mom, stop," Sam says. "We got lost in Gloucester. It was my fault, but we're good."

Now her mom is going to say, What the hell did you think you were doing? What were you doing taking your brother to Gloucester without telling me? But she doesn't. Sam puts the phone on speaker as she starts driving.

"We were just looking at rocks," Noah explains.

Courtney sobs, "Sam."

"What's wrong?"

Her mom says, "Just come home."

In silence, Sam and Noah drive back to Beverly. They don't even listen to the radio. They don't try to guess; they are afraid to know.

Covered in mud, they step inside the door to their apartment and Courtney doesn't even say take off your shoes. She is standing there to meet them.

"Sam," Courtney says, and sensing danger, Noah hovers behind Sam in the open doorway. "Sam," Courtney tries again, but she can't even get the words out.

It's Mitchell. Of course it is. Sam knows immediately what happened, and at the same time, she does not believe it.

Courtney holds out her arms, but Sam does not come to her. "He's gone."

"He's dead," Sam says.

"He really tried."

A cold anger fills Sam's heart, because *really tried?* How does that help anything? Try harder!

"He loved you," her mom says. "Your dad loved you more than anything. He wanted to get better, but he couldn't." She keeps talking, but Sam turns around and pushes past Noah into the hall. She doesn't even know where she is going, just down the stairs and out. It's freezing, but Sam heads back to the garage underneath the building.

Her mom is calling for her. She rushes after Sam and she keeps saying, I'm sorry, I'm sorry. She is probably afraid Sam will do something like crash her car.

They are standing there in the garage, and Courtney keeps trying to talk, but she can't stop crying.

Sam doesn't cry at all. Her mom cries enough for everyone. It's strange how sad her mom is, even though she split up with Mitchell so many years ago. Could she still love him a little bit? No. That's not why she is upset. She is afraid Sam is blaming herself and feeling guilty, and she is right. Sam does blame herself.

"Come inside," her mom pleads.

"Leave me alone," Sam tells her. Courtney doesn't want to leave, but Sam says, "I just want to sit in my car. I'm not going anywhere."

As soon as her mom leaves, she drives to the beach. She parks on Washington Street and takes the stairs down to the water's edge, where the wind whips sand around. Her teeth are chattering as she dips her hand into the freezing ocean. The wind is so harsh that if you were crying, it would dry your tears.

It's too cold to stay, so she climbs back to the street and sits in her car with the engine running. She is parked right near the dream houses, but she doesn't look at them. She just sits and stares out at the night.

She should have called him, but she did not. She should have talked to him, invited him, forgiven him, but she did not. She treated him like he was dead—but she did not understand what dead meant. She knows now because it is too late. That's what dead means. Too late for everything.

Her dad is dead, and all his ideas are dead too. All the plans they had when she was little—now they're over. He is gone, and so his view of her is gone as well. She was smart with him. She was a climber. She was famous in his eyes—but in real life, she will not be famous, any more than he was. He is nothing now, and she is nothing. No one will remember her.

IV

Woods

41

Death puts high school in perspective. People in the halls are yelling, laughing, acting important, but they are not. Girls turn away like they can't stand the sight of her, and Sam thinks, You will die—not because she wants them to, but because everybody will.

She keeps her head down. At lunch she sits with the sad people in the cafeteria who complain about their weight and physics homework, their parents, their college applications. Sam was supposed to apply too, but why?

The depressing girls talk about what they did on winter break. Sam does not say, I went to my dad's memorial. Everyone would look at her. She does not say, He overdosed; police found him.

The memorial was at Windy Hill and there was a scattering of ashes in the trees. Kevin was there and people from Mitchell's house and Jen and Steve. Everyone wore black and Sam had a black dress from Dress Barn. It came with a black patent leather belt too big on her. Sam's mom asked if she wanted to say something and she said no. Other people said her dad was in a better place.

"You know what my dream school is?" one girl says in the cafeteria. "Northeastern."

Sam thinks about her dad and the dream houses by the ocean.

She doesn't go down there anymore. She just walks to school, and she walks home, and she is like a regular person. She is just quiet. She is self-contained. She walks with an invisible bubble protecting her. It's like those bubble umbrellas you have when you are little. They come down to your shoulders and you can look out at the rain through the clear plastic. She has that protection because no one really knows her.

Only when she gets home, she has no umbrella. Noah is suspended and he sits on the couch. Sam gets a 3 percent on her math test and her mom doesn't even yell. She says, But why? And Sam doesn't know, except the problems looked strange to her. She squinted at the numbers and she had no idea what they meant. Her mom says, But you were good at math. Sam says, Not really.

They eat dinner together and Sam takes out the trash and washes dishes, and she tries to clean the living room just to make her mom feel a little better. Her mom blinks back tears, and the silence grows like a tree. A boulder. You have to walk around it.

In the middle of the night, Sam comes out to the living room with her blanket wrapped around her shoulders, and she finds her mom sitting there.

Courtney is taking an online business course and she is always sitting at the table. Sam sits next to her and she says, "Do you ever sleep?"

Her mom takes off her headphones. "Sam, go to bed. You have school tomorrow."

Sam says, "And you have work! What are you doing?"

"I'm just learning how to . . . trying to figure out a way."

"To do what?"

"Switch careers and earn some money."

"You do earn money."

"I've never earned any money," Courtney says. "I've never done anything."

Courtney keeps saying this, and Sam can't tell what she means. She is a good mom. What else could she have done? Saved Mitchell's life? Saved Sam from having Mitchell as a father? She never used to talk this way. "Mom," Sam whispers, "I would do anything if you would just be happy again."

"Go to college and get a great job," her mom says, immediately.

Then Sam almost laughs. "You're funny."

"I'm serious."

"I know." Sam rests her head on the table.

"Go to sleep."

"I will if you will."

"Promise." Courtney is still talking about college.

"I don't have the grades," Sam says. "You have to believe me."

"Okay," her mom says. It's incredible how fast she can switch dreams. "But there are accounting programs at North Shore. And it's just two years!"

"I want to work."

"Selling pizza?" her mom says. "Selling printer paper?"

"Something."

"I don't want you to do *something*."

"Yeah, but."

"If this wouldn't have happened," Courtney begins.

"It wasn't Dad."

Courtney's voice breaks. "That's when your grades got worse."

"Not really," Sam tries to comfort her. "They were bad before."

"Oh, great. Wonderful."

"I never liked school."

"That's not true. You used to!"

"When?"

"You said you would do anything for me." Sam's mom is a stickler, even late at night in tears.

"I mean anything within reason!"

Sam's mom thinks Mitchell is the reason for everything. She goes ahead and tells the school counselors he has died, and now they are always reaching out to Sam. No thank you. Courtney also tells Halle's mom and dad—so then once Jim and Lucy know, they tell Halle, and she calls.

"Hello? Sam? Oh my God, Sam!" Halle says, and Sam can hear wind whipping around. Sam is just sitting on her bed at home, but Halle must be out there at Andover on a hill or in a field. "I'm so sorry!" Halle shouts above the wind.

"It's okay."

"I'm sorry it took me so long to call you."

"It's fine."

"No, it's not," says Halle. "I should have called before."

Sam says, "I'm glad you didn't call. People were making such a big deal about everything."

"But it is a big deal."

"Can I tell you something?" Sam says. "I'm fine. It's not like I spent so much time with him before, or he was taking care of me, or anything . . ." Her voice trails off as she whispers, "So what's the difference?"

She doesn't want condolences. She doesn't want her mom to cry because she is so tired. Sam just wants to get her family back to where they were before.

Saturday night she makes popcorn in the microwave and spreads the sheet over the couch so she and Noah and her mom can watch the Bruins and she cooks dinner (macaroni). Sunday night she helps Noah draw an ancient Greek trireme for history. The boat has twenty-five oars, and they draw it on one long piece of butcher paper. When the paper rips, Noah wants to crumple up the whole thing and throw it away, but Sam says, "No, wait. Let's try something." She shows him how to tape it underneath, so the repair won't show.

42

Even in spring of senior year, Courtney has a vision of high school. Sam could love it if she tried. She could work on yearbook! She could go to prom and dress up and be pretty. In Courtney's prom pictures she is wearing a long green gown and her hair is long too, swept over one shoulder. "I could do yours." She smooths and gathers Sam's brown hair.

"But I'm not going," Sam reminds her.

"What about Corey?" her mom says, as though the problem is finding a date. Somehow, even after all this time, Courtney can't move on from Corey. Meanwhile, he has a new girlfriend named Darci. "What about a bunch of girls?"

"A bunch?"

Sam's depressing friends are not a bunch, and they will never go to prom. They won't even go to the anti-prom, which someone is having at a house where parents are away. It's one of the things Sam likes about them.

"At least think about it."

"But why?"

Her mom says, "I just want you to be okay."

"I am," Sam tells her. "Why don't you believe me?"

"I want you to enjoy something."

"I do!"

Sam enjoys watching everyone at school get so obsessed

with one expensive party. They are frenzied, voting for a king and queen. Sam writes on her ballot *ANYBODY*.

On Friday, the day of prom, she works at the Atomic Bean. She serves toasted bagels and tuna melts, corn muffins, and donuts. The donuts are stale by the afternoon, but people eat them anyway.

Her manager lets her off early. "You go ahead," he tells her, and she thinks, Wow. He's letting me off to have my hair and nails done—but she doesn't argue. She gets in her car and starts driving to Gloucester.

She drives past the town and through the marshes and the trees to a dirt parking lot. This is where she and Noah hiked in the winter. This is where they sat in the car together in the dark. Why does she come back? Because it hurts. Because it scares her.

The trail is different now. Everything is growing and blooming and the day is long. There are the tangled trees and there are the boulders, massive as walls. There are the metal loops Noah asked about. There is the broken glass.

She hears birds and rustling in the leaves, and every sound is delicate.

"Pull!"

"Got it."

For a second the voices scare her, because she thought she was alone. A shaking jingling noise. Somebody's dog.

"Whooh, nice," she hears a woman calling.

She can't see them. They can't see her, but the dog comes running. He is shaggy brown with matted fur, like I'm happy, don't ever wash me. She can't tell what kind he is but he's up on her knees and licking her hands.

"Bolt!"

The dog turns his head.

"Bolt." The dog's owner appears, and he is so tall and huge he snaps branches as he walks. He clears his own path without even noticing. "Come here, boy!"

Bolt keeps licking Sam, but she says, "It's okay."

"Are you lost?" the huge guy asks.

"No."

"Hungry?"

"Not really."

"Thirsty?"

"Yes."

Even though Sam remembers Don't talk to strangers, don't take candy, she gives him her name and where she lives and where she goes to school. He says his name is Kyle and he climbs here with friends.

"I used to climb," Sam tells him.

"You came to the right place. Follow me!" says Kyle. "We have beer."

Kyle's friends are Justin, Sean, and Amber. The first thing Sam notices about them is their hair. Amber's hair is pink and spiky. Justin's is shoulder-length and dirty-blond. Kyle and Sean have beards. Everyone looks shaggy, like they live out here.

A giant boulder looms above their blue tarp and their snacks and bags. Metal anchors stud the granite.

Justin is climbing, with Sean belaying him. "Sit," says Amber, and she shows Sam the cooler filled with drinks. There is beer and soda and there are bags of corn chips and there are green grapes, and also apples.

Up on the wall, Justin has amazing reach. He wears a battered brown fedora, which is strange, but also kind of cool, like Here's my hat. You think I'll lose it?

Sam can't see his face, but she knows he's wondering where to go. He eases over with his foot, searching for a hold. No. Not there.

He braces with his knees and explores with his hands, check-

ing out the rock above. From where Sam sits, it's hard to tell
what he should do. It's not like the gym where there are colored
handholds. The route is cracked and overgrown with lichen,
roots, and brambles.

He inches up with his right foot and tests a new hold—
but no.

"Try your left," Sam blurts out, thinking aloud.

Her voice startles him, and he half turns to look at her.

Already, Justin's got his left toes in. He's pulling up with his
arms and clipping his rope. Slowly, steadily, he zigzags upward.
"Yeah," he says, when he pulls himself atop the boulder.

"You should try," Amber tells Sam, as Justin zips down and
unclips himself.

"I don't have shoes."

"Wear mine," Amber offers, and Kyle says he will belay her.

"Go for it," Sean says.

Sam doesn't want to. She doesn't even know if she can
climb real rock like this, but you can't say that. It's like being
a fish and admitting you grew up in an aquarium. "It's been a
while."

Justin says, "Okay, now you really have to."

She tries Amber's shoes, and they're too big, but she doesn't
want to disappoint her.

"Good?" Kyle asks Sam as she straps up and clips the rope
onto her harness.

"Yeah." She is rusty; she thinks this is going to hurt, but she
knows half the route from watching Justin.

The rock is rough and damp, and sometimes slippery. They
are subtle, but she finds the cracks, and when she gets halfway,
she feels along with her left foot and finds the hold she spotted
for Justin. Her arms are weak from lack of practice, but there
are no mean angles. She remembers how her dad said, You'll
get back there, and she bangs her knee. Fuck, she breathes, because she's not back to it. She's not back to anything, but Kyle

and his friends are watching, and she keeps moving, clipping her rope to each cold metal loop.

You can do it! she hears the others calling from the ground. She pulls herself up and for a second she feels light-headed. It's not the route that's hard; it's forcing herself to climb again. She bends over, almost sick, but she's standing at the top.

"She's faster than you," Kyle tells Justin as Sam descends.

"Where did you come from?" Amber cleans up Sam's knee and tapes on gauze from a first-aid kit.

Justin is protesting, "It's not a race!" At first Sam thinks he's annoyed, but then not really. He raises a can of beer and tells her, "You were better."

They sit together in the shelter of the boulder, and eat and drink, while Bolt lies at their feet. They finish off the chips, and smoke some dope, and it's so peaceful Sam almost forgets she has to drive home or go to school or graduate or help her mom or anything. She forgets her knee and her nausea on the wall. It feels so good just sitting on the ground again.

She leans back against the rock and it's like entering an imaginary place. She murmurs, "Just like Robin Hood."

She does not expect anyone to answer, but Justin says, "Yeah, totally. Kyle is Little John, and Amber is Maid Marian."

Amber says, "Who's Sam, then?"

Justin studies Sam and says, "Will Scarlet."

"Really?" Apart from her dad, and maybe Halle, Sam has never met anyone who knows Will Scarlet.

"There he goes," says Amber.

"He's trying to impress you," Kyle tells Sam.

Justin sounds serious. "Will Scarlet in the version where he fights with two swords at once."

"Whoa."

"See," says Amber.

Then everybody laughs, and they say, You're flirting, but Justin says, I'm not.

"What do you say?" Amber asks Sam.

She says not.

Justin says thank you.

Amber says stop.

The light is fading, but nobody bothers to get up.

Only Amber says, "Hey, I've got work tomorrow." She is a mechanic, starting at seven A.M., so they start walking down the trail to the parking lot.

When they get to the cars Kyle asks Sam, "You know your way home, right?"

"Pretty much."

"You can follow me to the ramp," Justin offers, so she drives along behind his station wagon.

She can feel the climb between her shoulders, but the first stars are shining. Her knee is bleeding through the gauze, but nothing serious. People help you. When they get to the highway, Justin's rear wiper waves goodbye.

43

At Red Rocks no one is in school, and nobody is in college either. People just have jobs like Amber and Sean, who are mechanics. Kyle works for Gentle Giant moving, and Justin is a gardener. Everybody works, and so they climb for fun on Fridays and some Sundays, and there are no points or ribbons. Sometimes Sam climbs well, and sometimes she climbs badly. Sometimes she can't climb at all, because she has to stay home and watch Noah. Then people will say, Where were you? But it's not like a team where you made a commitment, what were you thinking?

Her mom is afraid that Sam won't get her diploma, because sometimes she does not make it to class—but it's not just Sam. A lot of seniors skip, since the district is making up for snow days, and nobody can learn in June.

Sam tells her mom, "I think as long as you don't do anything really bad, you graduate."

"Uh-huh."

"Like something criminal."

"Great," Courtney says. "Go ahead. Give up on everything."

This is their never-ending fight. Sam says, I'm not giving up, and Courtney says, Oh yeah, prove it to me. Show me that I'm wrong! You didn't even apply to North Shore. Sam says, It's rolling admissions. Her mom says, Just do it. Sam says, I will.

Her mom says, When? Sam says, When I have time. Her mom says, Yeah, time is not the problem. You don't even want to think about the future. And she starts talking about her own life and how this is her fault, and Sam says it's not. Then finally, Courtney stops talking altogether. She is silent, and that's when Sam drives off in her car.

You can disappear into the trees. You can take a boulder and map it in your mind, and that rock becomes your entire world, like your own asteroid. You might get scratched and bruised. You might have bug bites all up and down your arms, and on your ankles, but it doesn't matter. If you find and solve a new problem, you can name it. You are a discoverer.

In the evenings, Sam and Kyle and Sean and Amber and Justin kick back to smoke and laugh about their falls.

"Look at this," says Amber, and she pulls down the waistband of her shorts to show a giant bruise on her left hip.

Sam says, "It's like the colors of the rainbow."

Kyle holds a cold beer up to it and Amber says, "Don't freeze me!"

"It's for your own good," he tells her.

Then Sam says, "Nobody ever does anything when it's for their own good."

"Deep," says Amber.

Justin says, "But true."

"So why does anyone do anything?" Amber challenges them.

Justin says, "For fun."

Sean takes a deep drag and says, "For money."

Sam runs her fingers over thick moss. Her body is tired, but she feels light. "The reason anyone does anything is because they want to."

You can be a new person in the trees. You can have a reputation—like, you are fearless. You climb the hardest, even though you

are the youngest. You can be a legend when no one knows you
from before.

That's why it startles her when they have visitors. Bolt hears
them first, and he starts barking.

Sam is studying a boulder with a couple of different routes.
The main one is called Little Bear and it is not little, and it
hurts when you drop off. She is crouching on a mat when Bolt
runs out to the trail to lick and snuffle the newcomers.

Kyle says, "Don't ever ask this dog to guard anything."

A moment later, Bolt comes running up with Declan and a
new girl—not Toby.

Sam's face is burning, but she was hot already. Probably no
one can tell. Nobody knows. And what does it matter anyway?
It happened a year ago. More. She never thinks about Declan—
except now, because he's looking at her. For just one second he
looks surprised, and almost a little upset to see her—and then
he says, "Hi, Sam," like he's being friendly. He's being *kind* to
her. He tells the new girl, "Sam used to be on my team at Boulders."

"You guys must've been good," says Kyle.

Meanwhile, Sam scrambles off the mat. Anger, confusion,
shame—it all comes back to her. The new girl's name is Gina
and they are here for Little Bear. Declan and Gina and the guys
are all discussing what to do, but Sam takes her water bottle
and sits with Amber in the shade.

"Hey, it happens," says Amber, and it takes Sam a second to
realize she's talking about her frustration with the rock. "You
can't always solve a problem in one day."

"I could solve it now," Sam mutters, because she isn't giving
up. She is waiting for Declan to leave.

But Declan and Gina climb all afternoon. Sam takes off her
muddy shoes, and peels off her sweaty socks, and watches.

Gina's skin is very white. She has long legs and arms, and

she climbs lightly. She's not fast, and she's not creative, but the guys are all right there giving her beta whether she needs it or not.

As for Declan, he is still amazing, unfortunately. He's so quick and strong and smooth. He could power his way up, except he doesn't need to.

"Hey, Sam, get up here," Kyle says.

"Yeah," Sean says. "Why aren't you even trying?"

And she realizes they want to show her off—but she's done with that. She won't climb in front of Declan.

When everyone gets tired, Declan and Gina share wine in a screw-top bottle. They've got cheese and crackers, and a huge bag of jelly beans, which they pass around. Sam doesn't take any.

"We're going up to Maine," says Declan.

"You guys should go there," Gina tells them.

"Acadia," says Declan.

They are like married people, finishing each other's thoughts. They are together, but invisibly. They don't touch. They don't kiss—but they don't need to. Just looking at them, you can imagine. As for Sam, she never happened. Maybe Toby didn't happen either. Sam looks at Declan and she thinks, This is what it's like to be you. You turn the page, and, nothing personal, but you keep turning. Or you rip the pages out.

It's fine. She doesn't care. She doesn't even know him anymore. She just hates him in general.

She sits in silence as the conversation floats around her. When someone turns to talk to her, she barely answers. It's fine, she tells herself again. They're going to Acadia and they won't come back. Also, nothing happened.

What did happen was mostly because she'd wanted him so much. If he took advantage of her, it was because she let him. Actually, she encouraged him.

She was in love with him, but that was her fault.

No, it wasn't. She remembers what her mom said. *He is not your friend.*

Yeah, that was true, but she was a bad kid. She lied about him to her mom. She lied about him to herself. She pretended she meant something to him.

The evening light begins to fade, and everyone starts gathering their stuff and walking together down the trail to the parking lot. Declan takes the lead with Gina. Kyle, Amber, and Sean follow—but Sam lags behind. She leaves so slowly that Justin circles back to check on her. "What's wrong?"

"Nothing."

"You don't like him."

She is carrying a rolled-up mat strapped to her back, and Justin has one too, so it's awkward to turn toward each other. "Does it show?"

He smiles. "No, not at all."

"I don't really know him."

"But he was your coach, right?"

"No." Sam isn't giving Declan credit for anything. "My dad was my coach."

"Oh wow. Does he still climb?"

"Not here."

"Where is he?"

Wait, Sam thinks, because what is she doing? Now she will have to keep on lying or explain everything. And she can't explain. She can't say my dad passed away, because then Justin will say, I'm sorry. She'll say, That's okay, and Justin will stand there looking at his shoes. Then what? She makes up a disease? And Justin is like, Aww, you poor girl, you must miss him. No way. "He's off the grid."

"I want to do that! I want to build my own house and grow my own food."

"It's harder than it looks," Sam says, and she keeps walking.

"How long has he been gone?"

"Five and a half months."

She is trying to figure out what to say next, and in the pause Justin says, "He's dead, isn't he?"

"What?" She is startled and relieved and also scared to hear him say it. She stops short on the trail to face him. "Don't say you're sorry."

"Okay."

"And don't feel bad for me."

"I won't."

"You can't really feel bad for people you don't know."

He says, "I'll wait."

44

Sam's mom has a new linen dress, but it wrinkles if you look at it. She steams it in the morning with a portable steamer, but it still creases on the way to graduation. Courtney wanted Sam to dress up too, but what's the point if she is wearing a cap and gown? It's hot, so Sam wears shorts and a T-shirt underneath, and Noah is angry because he has to wear a button-down shirt.

"You know what?" says Courtney, but she is too jittery to finish her thought. They drive to the high school and there are people directing traffic. The big field is full of cars, and it takes a while to find Jen and Steve and the girls. There are so many families swarming.

Jen tries to take pictures during the ceremony where Sam is a speck in a sea of graduation hats.

She takes the real pictures after, when Sam and Noah stand on either side of Courtney.

"Smile," Courtney orders Noah, and when he doesn't, she squeezes his hand and threatens him, which makes him laugh and come out blurry. But they are good pictures, and everybody is relieved, especially Sam, because she is done with school and all the people there. They celebrate with Chinese takeout at Jen's house and there are fortune cookies. Sam gets WHAT IS NOT STARTED WILL NEVER GET FINISH.

"There you go," says Courtney.

Steve still thinks Sam could enlist. She would do great. Jen thinks Sam could go into construction. She's good with heights! But Courtney made up her mind when Sam was born that she would go to college and that will never change. "Well, sweetie, your mom is stubborn," Jen says.

And it's true. Courtney won't rest until Sam registers for classes. She was happy about graduation but that was temporary. Even in the car, on the way home from Jen's house, Sam can see her mom's good mood evaporating. Courtney parks and as soon as Sam and Noah get out, she snaps, "How many times do I have to tell you don't slam the door?"

Then as soon as they get inside, she says, "Why are there dishes on the table?" And she walks into the bedroom.

Noah takes the couch and starts playing his game, while Sam sits at the table and scrolls through Jen's pictures on her phone. She knows what her mom wants, but why? If Sam gets a job she could actually help with rent, or at least groceries, since Noah is an eating machine, and he is still growing.

She looks at him and thinks, If I were a better sister, I would show him an example. She could do it even now. She could just take out her computer and register for accounting. That would cure Courtney's headache. It would cure a lot of things. What's holding Sam back? Only herself. Only her craving to earn money now, not later.

She works at the Atomic Bean and at the UPS store. Then on Fridays and sometimes Sundays she drives to Gloucester.

She buys a new phone and shoes and a better mat to fall on, so she doesn't have to borrow.

Amber says independence is the best. She left home the second she turned eighteen because she hated her stepmother. She fell in love with auto repair and the rest is history.

Kyle says the day he bought his truck was the best day of his life.

Sam says that's kind of how she feels about her car.

Only Justin says, "Come on. The best day of your life can't be about a vehicle."

"Why not?" Amber is down-to-earth. It's in her climbing too. Amber is practical. She doesn't try routes that she can't handle. Justin is the opposite. He is out there. He will try something, and everybody will say no. Then he will keep working and falling until people say, Okay, Justin, this is boring now.

One day in July they are climbing a route called Old Bones. There is a long fissure in the rock that looks easy, but it's not. You can just barely squeeze your fingers in, and there are no good places for your feet. Kyle and Sean give up first because their hands are too big. Amber gets farther, but she says it hurts. The rock scrapes her knuckles and she can't get her feet under her. So, then it's Sam and Justin.

He is up first, and he tries a thousand times, leveraging his weight with feet and fingertips.

"Let me!" Sam says. "Let me!"

"Hold on," Justin tells her, and she remembers how her dad always said *Be patient, monkey*—as if she knew nothing about waiting.

She's glad when Justin falls the thousandth time. He falls so many times that he has to let Sam try, so he can catch his breath.

At first, she does better than he did. She is lighter, and she has practiced in her mind how to leverage her feet on either side of the fissure. Then she understands what's tricky. The crack narrows as you go. At first there is space around your hand and thumb, but after that you hold on with your fingertips. Each time she tries, she falls six feet to the mat.

"Try reversing?" Kyle says. "Left hand first?"

Everybody has an opinion, but she doesn't listen. She stands there staring down that boulder, and her shirt is soaked with sweat, her face streaked with dirt.

"You got farther than I did," Justin says, thinking she is done.

She glances at him for just a second, because does he think she's weak? Or stupid? Does he think she'll wait for him *again*?

"Hey, have a beer," says Amber in a voice that sounds like You need to calm down. That's the last thing Sam hears before she jumps up again.

Her feet know where to go. Her fingers find their holds, but just before the fissure narrows, she starts to lose her grip. Her left hand slips and snags the sharp edge of the crevice. She can hear a gasp. Is that her? And is that blood? She's cut herself but she holds on anyway with feet and knees. Her bloody hand now free, she holds on with her right again.

Her hand is throbbing, her body straining, but there is no way she will let go. She is too strong, too stubborn, too angry. She feels it happening, that change coming over her, because she cannot, and she will not stop. This climb is life or death. It's truth or dare, and she chooses the dare.

She's got her balance now, as she climbs upward. Pain is like a shadow. It is hard to see. Her hand and arm are slick with blood. The shadow blackens for a second and then clears. And she has done it. She is standing high above.

A second later, she hears Bolt barking, and she is looking up at him. She is sprawled on the ground, and she is not sure how she got there. Did she jump, or fall?

Everyone is talking at once, like What the hell? What did you just do?

"Shut up shut up." Amber is wrapping Sam in gauze, applying pressure.

"I'm fine," says Sam.

"Hold your hand up," Justin tells her.

"Hold it high." Amber's voice is scolding, but also awe-struck. "What were you doing climbing like that?"

Sam can't even answer.

45

"What happened?" Courtney demands as soon as Sam walks in with her bloody hand.

"I'm okay."

Noah comes over to take a look, and she can tell he is impressed, but Courtney is already grabbing her keys to drive to urgent care and she is asking, Why didn't you go already?

"They were going to take me."

"Who's they?'

"Justin and Amber."

"So why didn't you go?"

"I didn't want to."

"And they let you drive home?" Courtney is hustling Sam into the elevator.

Sam wants to defend them, but her mom has that steely glare she gets when you can't tell her anything.

It's a quiet Sunday night, and they hardly have to wait. The nurse takes them inside and Sam sits on an examining table while her mom stands next to her. The room is white as a light box and there is Sam in her bloody shorts and shirt while the nurse takes her temperature and asks what happened.

The doctor is tall and lighthearted, like You will be just fine. He says, "Mom, why don't you take the chair for just a sec?"

The good news is that Sam didn't slice anything, but she's

not going to get away with glue or Steri-Strips. The doctor is going to stitch her up. He gives her some numbing medicine and he says, You will feel a little pinch.

She looks away, because she doesn't want to see the needle and thread.

"Hold on to me." Her mom is hovering next to her.

Sam holds on hard with her uninjured hand.

"It's okay, Mom," says the doctor, because Courtney is crying. It's as if the pain flows straight through Sam to her. "You're doing great," the doctor tells both of them, but the stitches hurt worse than the cut did. Maybe it's just that Sam is not distracted. She is shivering with pain and adrenaline but this time she is trying not to move. The doctor keeps talking in his light cheerful voice. "So, you were climbing?"

"Yes."

"And you know what you are not going to be doing the next few weeks?"

"Climbing."

"Bingo."

"Ow."

"Sorry," the doctor says more gently. "You're a champ." Maybe he is impressed Sam isn't crying, except for a couple small involuntary tears.

Her mom is the one who's scared. Sam hugs her around the shoulders when they finally get out and walk back to the car in the warm summer night. "I'm fine. I'm fine," Sam tries to reassure her.

"I'm not going to tell you what to do," Courtney says. "I'm not going to lecture you."

"Okay," Sam says hopefully.

"But what are you doing ripping up your hand?"

"It's not like I was trying to hurt myself," says Sam.

"And why are you climbing with people who won't take you to the emergency room?"

"It wasn't their fault."

"Oh really?"

"I won't do anything until my hand is better," Sam promises. The doctor already explained that if she climbs too soon her stitches will open and her hand will get infected, and she will have to come back and get sewn up all over again. "I won't even try," she promises, but she does not say she will stay home.

It's weird when she comes back to Red Rocks. The others respected her before, but now she is like their teacher. Even standing on the ground, she gives advice like I don't think that way is doable or Try your other foot. They say, What do you think? and trust her judgment if the rock is slippery. They also treat her like You know what, you're a little crazy.

"I still don't know how you did that," Sean says after he tries to climb Sam's route and fails.

"While bleeding," Justin reminds him.

"You have a high tolerance for pain," says Amber.

Sam says, "Not really."

"It was like you couldn't even feel it," Kyle tells her.

"I felt it." Sam looks at her stitched-up hand. The thread is black and gunky; it's an ugly seam across her palm.

For now, Justin carries all her stuff—even her backpack. She says, "It's not like I've broken all my bones."

"But it's easy." Justin carries her mat and bags all the way down to the parking lot and they plan what they will climb once she gets her stitches out. He knows this boulder that nobody else likes.

"Can I see it?" Sam says, as they reach the cars.

He looks up at the sky. It's almost dark. "Come early next time."

Kyle teases as he gets into his truck, "Watch out for him."

Sam and Justin look at each other and start laughing. "I want to see it now," Sam says.

It's dusk. The air is still. At first Sam can't make out the whole boulder in the shadows, but then she touches it and she looks up and it is so big it blocks her view, a highball leaning sharply like a sinking ship.

Justin says, "The upper part is easy."

"Yeah."

"But this part." They walk around and feel the underside of that great boulder and it's like the flank of a gigantic animal. How could you ever climb up and over? You would have to cling and scramble all across like a spider in a cave.

"How would you even start?" she says.

"Oh, I've started," he tells her, and she can imagine how many times he's tried. "I saw this boulder when I first started climbing."

The rock face is comforting; it shields you. "How did you learn?" Sam asks.

"Climbing?"

"Yeah."

"Not from my dad."

She confesses, "I didn't learn from my dad either. He never took me here. He just talked about it."

She waits for Justin to ask, Then why did you say he taught you everything? But he says, "My dad doesn't talk to me at all."

"Why?"

"Because a long time ago he was angry at my mom—and I took her side."

"What was he angry for?"

"She left him for Jesus."

"Oh." In the twilight, she can't read his face. "Did you leave for Jesus too?"

"No, just for my mom."

Does she seem confused? Too solemn? He takes off his brown hat and claps it on her head. Instinctively, she touches the brim. The hat is so old and battered. It's like a relic. She almost can't believe he lets her wear it, even for a second. She asks, "How old are you?"

"Twenty-four."

So, he is six years older—but it doesn't matter. She's just as good as he is on the wall, and maybe better. He touches the tipped boulder, and he says, "You're probably the only person I know who would try this one."

"I would try," she tells him. "I doubt I would get anywhere."

"Yes, you would."

"Nah."

He looks at her in the hat. "You know exactly what you're doing."

"No, I don't know anything."

"But you climb like you do. You believe in yourself."

"No, I don't. It's not like that."

"Then what's it like?"

She struggles for the words because it's harder and also simpler than he imagines. "I don't know anything, and I don't believe anything, but I keep going anyway."

46

Despite her stitches, she works long hours. Her mom says go to school go to school go to school, but Sam is earning good money. Her mom says, Sam, just register, but Sam takes Noah out and buys him hockey skates instead. Courtney won't let her pay the bills, but she can't stop Sam from taking Noah to Dick's Sporting Goods.

When they get there and the guy is measuring Noah's feet, he asks, "New or used?"

Noah practically falls off the bench when Sam says, "New."

They never buy new skates. Noah is always growing, so they buy used skates in good condition, but they're broken in and scuffed. Not today. The salesman carries out boxes of black skates and they are stiff and perfect. They cost twice as much, but they were never even laced before. When Noah stands up in them, he looks gigantic, and also shy. Under his breath he says, "Aren't they too expensive?"

Sam says no, because she has money in the bank. She can go ahead and buy the skates and also a new helmet and new pads.

Noah doesn't say a word as they walk out to the parking lot with their Dick's shopping bags. The sun is beating down on their shoulders and he doesn't say thank you and she doesn't say you're welcome. They just look at each other and they are both thinking the same thing. Did we just spend four hundred dollars?

"This is your reward," Sam says, as they drive home.

"For what?"

"For how hard you're gonna work this year and how you will behave."

"It's a reward for what I'm going to do?"

"Yeah."

"Isn't that backward?"

She looks at him and she thinks, probably. But he needs skates now, not at the end of the season.

He opens up the box and his blades are mirrors in the sun. "I didn't need new ones," he says, but he is glowing, and she is too.

But when they get home their mom is serious. She smiles when Noah shows off his new gear, and then she says, "Okay, Noah, can you get all those boxes into the recycling?"

All through dinner Courtney hardly says anything.

"What?" Sam asks at last, when she is clearing the table and her mom is washing dishes.

"Nothing," Courtney says.

"What's wrong?" Sam presses. "What's wrong with buying new?"

"Nothing."

They are standing together in the galley kitchen and the only way you can go in or out is by turning sideways. "Why are you annoyed at me?"

"I'm not," says Courtney.

"Then what is it?"

"You know what."

Sam looks at her mom and says, "You're the one who wants to go to school. Not me."

"I have to work!"

"I'll work for you," says Sam. "I'll work and you go back for accounting."

"No, that's not realistic," her mom says.

"Why not?"

"It's just not going to happen."

"But why?"

"First of all, I'm not good at it."

"You would be if you didn't have to do other things."

"You would crush accounting," Courtney says. "If you would just decide."

"I did decide." Sam is trying to squeeze between her mom and the counter, but Courtney won't move. There is no way around her.

Sam knows something then. She will do what her mom wants. It's because her mom has done so much that Sam can't say no. She can't slip past so much sacrifice. She will register. Except every day she puts it off.

Every day her mom says, Did you? and Sam says, I will, and her mom says, When? And then Courtney says, What if you missed the deadline?

By the end of August, Sam can hear her mom's voice everywhere she goes. Home and car, the UPS store, the Atomic Bean. Red Rocks is the only place that's out of range.

As soon as Sam gets her stitches out, she and Justin start meeting at the big tipped boulder. They come evenings, because it is still light. Even before Sam's hand is strong again, they keep working on the project.

One Friday they try for three hours straight. They work and work, climbing, scrambling, falling, strategizing. Then they gobble up some trail mix and drink some water and keep going, but it's no use. They collapse onto Justin's mat and they are bitten up and bruised. Sam says, "We're not gonna solve this in our lifetime."

"Yes, we will," says Justin. "You will, at least."

"Why do you keep saying that?"

"Because I know what you can do."

"You sound like my mom."

"Well then she's right."

"She wants me to be an accountant."

"She can't make you," Justin points out.

Sam rolls on her side to look at him. "How did you get out of going to college?"

"I did go for a year."

"Really?"

"I went to UNH."

She looks at him all scraped up and tries to picture him in a classroom. "What did you go for?"

"Writing."

"But now you're a gardener."

"Yeah, writing was a waste of money."

Bugs are swarming, so she scrambles to her feet. "That's the thing. I think accounting might be a waste too."

"Nah, it's practical."

"Not if you're unmotivated."

He gets up too, and they roll up their mats. When they're done and they start walking, he says, "Life is short."

"My mom doesn't think so."

He turns to her and asks, "Why would you study for something you don't even want to do?"

She slaps him hard across the face.

He is startled, his cheek streaked with a dead mosquito and his own blood.

"Sorry! I had to kill it. Did I hurt you?"

"No," he says, half laughing.

"What?"

"You sounded kind of hopeful."

"Why would I want to hurt you?"

"Just because you can."

"That's weird."

"I think you're a little warlike," he tells her.

"I am not."

"See, you're still fighting with me."

"Is that what we're doing?"

"No."

She wants to say, What are we doing then? But she does not. She wants to say, What's happening, but if she speaks, then it will stop.

47

Justin has a journal he carries with him. The cover is black, the pages are pure white. When he was younger, his mom gave him fine-line pens for Bible study. Now he uses them to write about plants. He writes in block print THE HYDRANGEA IS CHANGING FROM LIGHT PINK TO DARK and then he will draw the flowers. He will draw a fern just starting to unfurl, and outline oak leaves.

One Friday it starts drizzling, and he seals his journal in a plastic bag and stuffs it in his backpack, so it won't get wet. "This book is my Bible," he tells Sam.

They are sheltering in the lee of the tipped boulder and she says, "Does that mean you're writing your own religion?"

"I think I'd have to be more detail oriented for that."

"Like write down all the things you aren't allowed to do."

"Yeah, I'm not into rules."

Sam frowns. "Well, you're lucky you can live that way."

"It's not luck. You can too."

"Not really."

"You mean you have to listen to your mom."

"Well." Sam looks out at the fine rain.

"You decided that she's right."

She can't say that. She doesn't think her mom is right about her and accounting. She just says, "She's done a lot."

"So, you registered."

"Yeah."

"What if you try a bunch of things?" he says. "Like a bunch of different classes."

"I'm actually good at math," she tells him. "I don't think accounting will be hard."

"Just boring."

"How do you know?" she demands. "Have you ever taken bookkeeping?"

"No."

"So, don't be prejudiced."

"Okay. Don't be angry."

"I'm not. I'm jealous!" He smiles, but she is serious. "You climb all day. You work in people's yards and write in your journal about ferns. You do whatever you want."

"Not always."

She doesn't know what to say to that. They are standing so close in the slight shelter of the rock. Slowly, she asks, "What would you do in my place?"

"You know what I would do."

"Study something else?"

"Yeah. You could do a million things. That's all I'm saying."

She says, "But I don't want to do a million things."

"Neither do I."

The rain is so light that you can't see it, but they are both wet. His hat is dripping, but he keeps his eyes on her when he takes it off. She says, "What do you want to do, then?"

He shakes his head.

"Tell me."

"No."

She thinks, Show me then, but he is waiting. When he touches her cheek, he brushes the rain off. When he looks at her, she can see he does not know what will happen. He does not take her in his arms. There's no forcing everything at once. No rush, except for her own heart.

48

His hat is on the ground. His hands are on her shoulders and he feels so good, his mouth, his tongue. His breath is in her ears. They are both slippery with rain and sweat. They pull up their soaked shirts, and then they take them off, and he is salty when she licks him. He whispers, "Wait, wait, let me look at you."

Probably someone will come embarrass them. Probably, but it doesn't happen, and then they start forgetting. They lie down on his climbing mat, and gradually they pull themselves under the tilting bolder. His hands slip over her breasts, and her bare waist, and then underneath her shorts, until her heels dig into the ground, ripping up the moss.

And even then, she reminds herself, This isn't serious. This isn't dangerous. It's like swimming because the water is warm. It's not like you have to drown yourself in him.

It's weird, how they understand each other. He says, Let's take it slow, and she says, Yeah. But even as they say that, they both know that nothing slow is going to happen. They are filthy wet, but they don't want to leave.

Only when they hear hikers and dogs do they sit up and collect their stuff. They head back to their cars, and then they drive to Justin's place in Gloucester.

He leads the way and Sam drives after him. The road turns to gravel. Then to dirt.

By the time they arrive and park their cars, she is getting cold. Her hair is wet and tangled, her arms streaked with mud.

She says, "This is where you live?"

He lives all the way at the end of the dirt road near the marshes. The house belongs to his great-grandma Ann and it's Victorian, painted the darkest green. The house has a steep roof, and bay windows, and a wraparound porch.

Justin says, "Come in."

"Is it all right?"

The floor creaks, and the paint is peeling. "Ann?" he calls softly as he opens the door. "She's sleeping," he whispers.

"Where?" There are so many doors and hallways.

"Sh. Come upstairs."

He has the whole third floor, which is a bunch of little rooms and a half bath. His bedroom has a window like a porthole. If you stand on the desk, you can see the ocean.

To take a shower you go downstairs to the bathroom on the second floor. Quietly, quietly, so you don't wake Ann.

In the shower, they are half whispering, half laughing. The water pressure isn't strong, so they take turns standing under and then shivering. Sam asks, "How long have you lived here?"

"Since high school." Justin is lathering Sam's whole body, front and back. "Ann let me live here when my mom kicked me out."

"How old is she?" Sam asks, light-headed.

"Ann? She's ninety."

"Whoa."

"But she's like a young ninety."

Somewhere in the distance, Sam's phone is ringing, but they keep soaping each other slippery. They are washing away the mud, and when they lie down together, they are clean.

The phone rings again. Sam's mom calls her three times, and then the fourth time Sam sits up in Justin's bed and answers. "What?"

"Where were you?" her mom asks, and for a second Sam thinks, Shit, where was I supposed to be? Her mom says, "Remember you said you would drive Noah?"

"I'm sorry."

"Well, he missed practice."

"I'm sorry. I forgot the time."

"What are you doing?" her mom asks.

Sam looks at Justin lying back against his pillow. "Just climbing."

"Uh-huh."

"I'm just sleeping over with a friend."

"What's his name?"

"I'll be home tomorrow."

"Tomorrow's Saturday." Sam thinks, Really? Her mom says, "Sam, I need you at nine. Remember I open up on Saturdays?"

"Okay, okay. Stop." Sam is too happy for this conversation.

"Just say you'll be there," Justin whispers. "We'll get up early."

49

When Sam opens her eyes, she sees the sloped roof and the porthole window.

Then she sees Justin lying in bed watching her and he says, "It's morning." But it's late, not early. It's already nine o'clock.

"Why didn't you wake me up?" She scrambles out of bed.

"You were so peaceful."

"But I'm supposed to be there now!" She is hunting for her clothes on the floor, but they are too dirty.

"I'll wash them," he promises.

"You don't understand." She is checking her phone, reading her mom's messages. "I'm supposed to be watching Noah."

"Just let me get you breakfast."

She is hungry, but she says, "I have to go, or he won't do his homework before hockey."

"Wear this." Justin gives her one of his clean shirts. "I'll make you coffee."

Following him downstairs, she sees worn wooden floors and dusty windows. One room has an old black sewing machine and a dressmaker's dummy. Another room is lined with drawers and shelves and that is just for linen.

Justin says there used to be servants and there were bells, but in the 1930s, a modern kitchen was installed. The cabinets are metal painted white, the floor is checkerboard, tiled with linoleum. There is a white oven and also a black pot-bellied stove. And there is Ann, a tiny person sitting at the table. Her eyes are blue like sea glass, her hair thin white. She holds out her little hand for Sam to shake. "Who might you be?"

"Sam."

"Just Sam?"

"Just Sam."

"And you're the climber."

"Yes." Sam looks at Justin.

He says, "I told her you were better than me."

Ann says, "You must be very good."

"Not really."

"How is your hand?"

"It's fine now, thank you." Sam thinks, He tells you every-thing.

Justin brings Sam a travel mug of coffee.

"Justin," Ann says, "why don't you make blueberry pan-cakes?"

Sam says, "I wish I could stay, but I don't have time."

"Do you work on Saturdays?"

"I do in the afternoons, but in the mornings, I have to watch my brother."

Ann nods. "How old is he?"

"Thirteen."

"Thirteen!"

"Grandma," chides Justin.

But Ann does not try to hide her surprise. She asks Sam, "Does he have special needs?"

"Yes," says Sam, and her cheeks sting, because she has never said that before. She and her mom never say, Yeah, Noah has problems or issues or needs—not even when he is melting down and people are staring. Sam wouldn't say it now, except that Ann surprised her.

"I won't keep you," Ann says, more gently. "But take a plum. They're very good."

Red plums are lined up on the windowsill like jewels. Justin picks out three. "They're small," he says. And he is trying to toast her an English muffin. She hurries out the door, and he carries the split muffin with butter melting. "Don't be offended," he says. "She's just outspoken."

They are standing in front of the house and Sam is eating the toasted muffin and she is laughing now, because she's got butter all over her hands. She is a mess, loaded down with the plums and travel mug. Justin runs inside and comes out with a wet kitchen towel and cleans her hands. "There."

Ann is standing in the open doorway. "Be careful," she calls out to Sam.

"Thanks," Sam calls back confused, because what does that mean? Drive safely? Watch out for my great-grandson?

By the time Sam gets home, her mom is at the salon and Noah is sitting on the couch with his computer, building the city he is always building, and nothing terrible has happened, except he has not done any chores or homework.

Sam sits on the couch next to him, and he doesn't look up, but he says, "Mom's annoyed."

"I know."

Noah keeps building his walls, and Sam sifts through the mail on the coffee table. Bills, leaflets, ads for chimney sweeping even though they do not have a chimney, a flyer for La Victoria Taqueria. One envelope from NSCC. *Welcome to North Shore Community College.*

Eyes on his screen, Noah tells Sam, "Mom is afraid you'll shack up with some guy who's inappropriate."

"Shack up?" Sam asks, because who says that? "I'm not shacking up with anyone!"

"So, he *is* inappropriate."

Sam laughs and Noah looks up. "What?"

"You're funny."

Noah says, "Why are you surprised?"

"Stop playing that game."

"No."

She checks the chart on the refrigerator. They have a home-work schedule and he is not supposed to miss a day. "Noah?"

He ignores her, but she is used to that. She digs in Noah's backpack for the folder with his math problems and vocabu-lary, and she starts prying him off his computer, threatening and bribing, but the whole time she is thinking about Justin and his great-grandma's house, the shower, and the toasted muffin. How she and Justin stood together for just a second more, until she whispered, Okay, bye. Then just as she turned to go, he kissed her hand.

V

Earth

50

It's time traveling. It's like living in a book in Justin's house. Slipping in between the pages, where everything is old and secret. Sam and Justin step over all the stairs that creak. They drag Justin's mattress onto the floor.

Downstairs there are cut-glass ice cream bowls and they are ruby red. There are drawers all filled with doll clothes. There is a wicker doll carriage with a baby doll inside named Cynthia. Her head is painted wood. Her nose is chipped. For pressing dolls' clothes, there is a miniature iron made of actual iron.

There is a telephone you have to dial, and a gramophone you have to crank. Dishes are mismatched and chipped. Paint blisters the kitchen ceiling, but the house has carved wood banisters, and in the living room there is a window seat with a red velvet cushion. You can sit there and look out at flower beds, and oaks, and maples.

Justin takes care of the whole garden. He mows the grass and pulls the weeds and hacks blackberry canes.

When Sam comes over in the evenings, she and Justin walk out to watch the sunset.

The sky glows, blackening the trees.

You feel like you're floating.

Then when you come in again, the wood floor in the living room tilts gently.

The dining room is pale pink, like the inside of a shell.

On the windowsill above the kitchen sink, Ann keeps a whole family of African violets. She will cut a leaf and cultivate the stem in water. At night she checks on all the flowers, the pink, the white, the purple ones with golden centers.

Justin cooks spaghetti with Sam's help, and then after dinner dessert is gingersnaps and shots of scotch, and ice cream in the ruby bowls. Sam and Justin have chocolate, but Ann has rum raisin. Her favorite candy is maple sugar. Her favorite drink is cognac if it's very fine. Her favorite thing to do is read. Her favorite author is Edna St. Vincent Millay, because she was a good poet and she didn't give a damn.

Ann is all there, and that's amazing. That's the hard part too. Ann is always in the house and she sees everything. Sam is glad she has stopped climbing stairs.

At night they are so quiet. Sam buries her face in Justin's pillow. They fall asleep in each other's arms but shift and wake apart. Sam reminds him, "In four days, I'm starting class."

He says, "I know. You told me."

When they show up together at Red Rocks, they get teased.

Kyle tells Sam, "Have you noticed Bolt doesn't like you so much? When he sees you, he smells Justin."

When Sam comes home, her mom questions her. How old is he? Where does he work? Then she uses the answers against Sam later. Courtney says, "Think."

Sam says, "I do."

"He's twenty-four."

"So what? I'm almost nineteen."

"That's the whole point."

"He's a good person."

"You know that already?"

"It's not already. It's been all summer and last spring."

"Then introduce me."

"Mom! No!"

"Why not? What are you afraid of?"

"Nothing. I just don't want to."

"Well, if you're living with him."

"I'm not."

"Half your clothes are at his place." To Courtney the relationship is like osmosis. "You are never here."

She is right. Sam is not home. She is not anywhere. When she is with Justin they hardly even eat.

They are like air plants. They live on nothing. They sit in bed and talk for hours. Justin tells Sam about his mom, who is now on a church mission. He tells her how they used to be close and then they fought, and that was when he moved in with Ann.

"What did you fight about?" Sam asks.

"Just sin."

"What kind of sin?"

"The regular kind. Drinking and partying and dealing." He says dealing fast and moves on quickly. "Sleeping with my girlfriend."

He tells Sam about this ex-girlfriend who is now living down in Boston. Sam tells him about Corey, but not Declan. Then she does. "He took advantage," Justin says.

Sam thinks about it. "Not exactly."

He says, "I disagree."

They are sitting opposite each other on his mattress. She says, "I was a bad kid."

"No, you weren't!"

"I was."

He says, "You were a kid, not good or bad."

It is strange to hear him say that. It is a relief, but at the same time she doesn't quite believe him. She says, "You weren't there."

"What about your mom?"

"I never told her."

He doesn't say You should have. He says, "I wouldn't have told my mom either."

Sam says, "I wish I'd never told mine about you."

"Why? Is she worried?"

"She's irrational!" Sam says. "She's defensive."

"Because she's never met me."

"And if she does, you think you'll win her over?"

Justin is stroking the arches of her feet. "Yeah, obviously."

Then Sam shakes her head because it isn't obvious at all. The thing upsetting her mom is real. It's not that Sam is sleeping with Justin. It's not that he is a terrible person. It's not even that Sam won't come home in time to help. Courtney knows Sam will be there mostly. What scares Courtney is that Sam will change her mind and decide against college, now that she's with Justin. Courtney is afraid that Sam will give up because she is too happy—and she is right to worry.

51

"Wake me up tomorrow morning," Sam tells Justin the night before class starts.

"Okay."

She is setting the alarm on her phone for eight A.M. "No matter how much I try to stay in bed, don't let me." Under the covers he delves his legs between hers. "And don't distract me."

"I'll sleep on the floor," he says, and that's a joke, because their mattress is already on the floor. "I'll just." He rolls over onto the hard floor, but the way he rolls, he winds the sheets around him, so she is left there in her T-shirt and nothing else.

"Stop!" She's laughing. He rolls back toward her and she says, "Come on."

He spreads the top sheet over her and pecks her on the cheek. "Good night." He lies on his back and closes his eyes.

She lies next to him. Then she rests her head in the hollow of his shoulder. Maybe she should have spent the night at home. It would be easier to wake up there.

"You aren't sleeping," Justin says.

"Yes I am."

"Oh, okay. I thought you were lying awake worrying about tomorrow morning."

"No way," Sam tells him. "I can't wait."

"You're so nervous."

"I'm just afraid I'll oversleep."

"I won't let you."

"You did before."

"I won't let you this time."

"Okay."

"It's better than high school," he tells her.

"Oh, thanks!"

"You don't have to stay all day. You just drive to class and leave."

She lies quiet for a minute and then she says, "I feel like this is a mistake."

"Why?"

"Because I hate school. I always hate it in the end."

"You can change your mind."

"My mom paid my tuition!"

"You can take different classes."

"Stop trying to make me feel better."

"You're gonna kill it."

"And don't be supportive."

"Okay." He's quiet.

"Justin?"

"What, Sam?"

"Just tell me things."

"So you'll fall asleep?"

"Yeah."

He thinks a long time, and when he speaks, his voice is soft, almost a whisper. "The first time I saw you, I knew we would be friends."

"Because I was so weird?"

"You were so smart."

"You mean I was smart climbing."

"You watched me on the wall, and you remembered everything."

"And then I jumped up."

"You one-upped me."

"And you didn't mind?"

"No!"

"Not even a little?"

"Only a little."

"That's what I thought."

"No, that's when I was thinking we're gonna be friends."

"Just friends?"

"Yes."

"So, are you surprised?"

"At what?"

"How we turned out?"

"No, I'm not surprised."

"Why?"

"Because I was right. We are friends."

"Not only," she murmurs.

"Not only, but we are friends anyway. We still would be."

In the morning when Sam sits up in bed, Justin opens his eyes. She carries her clothes down to the shower, and he comes with her. She stands in the water and he soaps her whole body. "Turn around," he says, as he rinses her.

When he turns the water off, he steps out first, but he can't find a towel. They are standing on the tile floor and Justin swipes fog off the mirror and they look at themselves. Her face is flushed. She feels shy to stand there naked, dripping, even though he is naked next to her. Even when she drapes a towel over her shoulders, her happiness is showing.

They get dressed quickly and sneak downstairs thinking maybe they can eat together while Ann sleeps.

No luck. She is sitting at the table, waiting, and it's not like a housemate your own age. With Ann you have to say good morning. You have to use your manners—even though she can say whatever she likes.

"Where are you going?" Ann inquires.

Sam tells her, "I'm starting classes."

Ann says, "Oh, good for you." She is looking at the two of them with their wet hair. "I thought Justin must be going with you."

He says, "No, I'm working in Salem."

Ann says, "You save a lot of water, don't you?"

"Okay, let's make some oatmeal," Justin says.

"I'm not really hungry," Sam admits, but he cooks some up anyway, and he sprinkles brown sugar and wild blueberries on top, and suddenly, she's starving.

52

The building at North Shore is mostly glass, so you can see into some smaller lectures. Sam peeks in and wonders what other people are studying, and if they like it, and if they want to be here.

Outside, you can hear the wind in the trees. Inside, she sits in one of those chairs with a desk that swings over your lap.

First up is stats. It's analyzing data. You put in the numbers, but software will do a lot of the work. There will be a midterm and a final and weekly problem sets. The instructor, Gary Bowen, says, Please do not use computers in my class, so Sam takes out a notebook. As usual, she has the most school supplies of anyone. Her mom got her red, yellow, green, and black notebooks, and mechanical pencils and gel pens and highlighters and notecards. "Okay," Bowen says, "let's dive right in."

The lecture is about data and how to display it in graphs and charts and other ways. Every once in a while, Bowen says something interesting and then he says, "Side note!" And Sam perks up. Side note, there is a really good book you can get called *How to Lie with Statistics*. Pretty much all numbers can be manipulated in the news and politics. That is the takeaway.

Other people are scribbling in blue ballpoint, in pencil, in black pen. The students are all ages. Some of them are bald or gray.

Accounting is taught by this happy older woman named Mary Witchy. She tells the class she is originally from Tennessee. Her hair is white-blond, her shoes are stiletto heels, which seems a little bit insane. Then again, Witchy is a tiny person. Maybe she needs them so you can see her at the board.

She is like a country music singer in love with equations. She sings out, "Assets equal liabilities plus owner's equity. Say it with me!" She draws a great big T on the whiteboard and she says, "Now listen up, because this little critter is the basis of accounting."

Sam does listen. She even chants the equation, and at the same time, she can't wait to leave.

She drives straight from class to the Atomic Bean for her lunch shift, where she makes sandwiches and gets people coffee.

There are two art students from Montserrat College, drawing tiny cartoons of the people who walk in. They are working in ink precisely.

One table over, a dad sits with his little boy, who looks about four. They are eating donuts, and the boy nibbles his all the way around the hole.

The dad asks, "Does it taste better that way?"

"That will be seven twenty," Sam tells her customer at the counter. She tosses salads with blue cheese, spinach, and dried cranberries. She serves BLTs and she remembers how she sat with Mitchell right here at the café and he said he was going to Portsmouth, but he would still see her all the time. She remembers the hot chocolate and how he made Portsmouth sound so pretty.

What were her dad's assets? His magic? His stories? She knows his liabilities.

The dad and little boy clear away their plates. The café empties, until it's only a few people coming in for coffee. Sam has to tell them there are no muffins left. There are never enough to last all day. In the glass case there is just one glazed donut sitting lonely.

Justin texts, *how did it go,* and she says, *okay homework already.* He writes, *can I meet u?* She says she has to help at home.

She makes dinner for Noah because Courtney is working late. Dinner is ravioli, and she talks to Justin on the phone while she is waiting for the water to boil. She tells him about Mary Witchy.

He says, "Is that really her name?"

She tells Justin about statistics. "The book is like twenty pounds." She tells him how you can't use your computer during lecture. And how the art students were drawing their tiny ink cartoons. She does not tell him about the little boy sitting with his dad. She can't bring herself to mention that.

He says, "Do you want to come here after dinner? We're having ice cream."

She says, "No, that's okay."

She eats dinner with Noah, and he won't do his homework. She heaves her stats textbook onto the table and says, "Look what I've got. You have it easy."

He ignores her and she tries to read, as if she is actually more motivated than he is.

Evening light fills the apartment, and she rests her feet on the chair next to her. The pages of her open book look very white there on the table. It is almost eight and Courtney is still at Staples. As her dad used to say, *Your mom is one hardworking lady.*

She remembers a lot of things her dad would say.

She remembers Poems While U Wait. Her dad said words are tools and she thought of screwdrivers and hammers.

She remembers the white rabbit her dad would pull out of his hat. When Sam was small, she believed that trick, and when she was a little older, she half believed, because the rabbit could

disappear and reappear for other people, but she knew his
name was Benjamin and he was always visible to her. And then
eventually, Sam understood her dad was just performing.

She remembers Topsfield. How her dad wrapped her in the
blanket in the car and she was already thinking about next
time. That's how it is when you are little. You think you get to
do good things forever.

Her mom knew better. Her mom always knew.

So, listen to her, Sam thinks now. Just read the chapter. But
when she stares at the white pages, she does not read a single
word.

She wakes with a start when her mom walks in.

"Hey, how was it?" Courtney asks.

"Okay."

Her mom stands there with her hand on Sam's shoulder.
"The first day is the hardest."

"She was sleeping," Noah announces from the couch.

"He never did his homework," Sam reports in turn.

"I'll help him. You rest," her mom tells her. "Just go lie
down." She practically drags Sam to her room.

As soon as Sam sees her bed, she falls into it face-first.

53

She has done hard things before. She has climbed gnarly boulders and banged her knees and cut her hand. She has hung on to a ledge and pulled up, straining every muscle. This is different. She is worn out in her heart and mind.

In accounting, Witchy's favorite equation is Success = Effort + Time.

"Do you think that's true?" Sam asks everybody when they're smoking out at Red Rocks.

"Yeah, definitely," says Justin.

But Amber disagrees. "People always say that, but actually you can work and work forever, and it doesn't help. You don't get anywhere."

"Always look on the bright side," says Sean.

"Well," says Amber. "It's the truth."

Kyle says, "Maybe it depends on the job."

Sam adds, "Or the person."

"There's talent!" Amber says. "It should be Success equals Effort plus Talent plus what's the other one?"

"Time."

"Look at Bolt here," Kyle says. "I tried to teach him tricks. He never learned anything."

"What? Are you saying he's not talented?" says Justin. "Come here, boy."

"You're the one without the talent," Sean teases Kyle.

They are all sitting on the ground and Sam is sitting between Justin's legs. Amber tells them get a room.

Justin risks even more teasing, leaning over Sam. "Maybe I should take you home." She is so sleepy in the smoke.

She says, "No, I'm okay."

Courtney says Sam should cut back her hours at work and concentrate on school. But Sam has already cut back at UPS and she needs cash. How else will she pay for gas and car repairs—not to mention stuff she might actually want, like climbing shoes?

"Can't you just take one class at a time?" Amber says now.

Sam says, "Yeah, but then I'd be in school the rest of my life."

Amber considers this. "Okay, that's fair."

"You got this," Sean cheers Sam.

"Get it over with," says Kyle.

"It's not all bad," Sam says. "I'm taking an elective."

The way it happened was one day she looked through the glass wall and saw a guy showing one of those volcano videos. The room was dark, but the instructor saw Sam watching. He looked straight at her and she shrank back. Then he beckoned, and she slipped inside the door.

"Come join us," the instructor said. There were only a handful of students, so maybe he was trying to recruit one more. "If you are looking for Earth Science, this is the place."

His name is Professor Martin Green, but he goes by Doc Martin. That first day he talked about how the whole world was in flux, which made her think of bubbling cheese pizza and *Dynamic Earth*. He said, You can't even keep up with the maps. Some islands are growing. Some are disappearing. Climate change is heating up the earth and causing sea levels to rise, but at the same time, after a volcano erupts, the ocean cools and sea levels decrease.

Then all at once, Sam asked a question without even realizing it. "So, do they equal out?" Doc Martin looked at her like oh hello! and Sam was embarrassed—but she had to ask. "Do climate change and cooling oceans cancel each other?"

"Good question," said Doc Martin. "They do not. The ocean cools after a volcano erupts, but climate change keeps heating continuously. This is the kind of thing we try to measure."

Then after class, Doc Martin came up to Sam and said, "Good to meet you!" He was tall and heavy with a big beard. He wore a checked shirt, but the checks were tiny compared to him.

"Hi, I'm Sam," she said, and then she confessed, "I am not registered."

Doc Martin said, "Well, we can change that."

"I'm taking Earth Science," Sam tells everybody now.

"Why?" says Amber.

"It's my liberal art."

"No wonder you're so tired."

"Something's gotta give," says Kyle.

"But it's the only one I like."

"What's it about?" asks Amber.

"The first lecture was global warming."

"Good times," Sean says.

They feel bad for her because she is running around trying to take so many classes. She works a lot of weekends, so when she finally shows up with Justin at Red Rocks, everybody says, Oh look who's here! Sometimes Sam thinks Sean, Kyle, and Amber are annoyed with her. Maybe they think she is a coward just doing what her mom wants. Or maybe they are offended that they see less of Justin, now that Sam is with him.

They are all still friends, but it is not the same. It's a lot more Oh hey Sam, you decided to come visit! And they look happier to see Justin. She doesn't think it's her imagination.

It's like that with Noah too, because so many nights she is with Justin. Noah doesn't say I miss you—but he does not want her helping with his homework. When she asks him questions he ignores her. As soon as she sits on the couch next to him, he will take off for his room.

"Noah," she says, "come back."

He doesn't answer.

One night when Courtney is working late and they are eating hamburgers together, Sam asks Noah, "How come you don't even talk to me anymore?"

He says, "What's the point?"

And then she sits there quietly because she knows what he means. What's the point if you are always leaving?

54

Sam is in school for a reason, but geology keeps luring her.

"What is that book?" Ann asks, when she sees Sam reading at the kitchen table.

"Earth Science."

"Oh, how interesting!"

"I should be practicing QuickBooks," Sam admits.

Accounting is important; it's how you get a job. It is money and cash flow and record keeping. Witchy says, "Accounting makes the world go round!" But geology is the world for real— the earth under your feet. It is where you are and what is happening. Accounting is keeping score. You take this, I give you that. You borrow this. I owe you that. You learn how to write up balance sheets—but in geology you learn about the planet before money existed or humans ever lived.

In October, Sam's class drives out to Red Rocks to discuss how glaciers carved out the landscape. They hike in together, and Sam doesn't even realize it, but after just a few minutes, she is up front leading the way.

Doc Martin says, "You know the trail, don't you?"

"Yes." She almost says she is a climber, but then she is too shy to mention it.

Doc Martin uses hiking poles, which is funny because it is not exactly rough terrain. On the other hand, he can point at interesting rocks with them. He looks back to make sure the group is all together. "Where's Colleen?"

Sam says, "I'll check on her."

Colleen is a super-heavy woman who is already out of breath. Sam finds her way behind, leaning against a tree.

"We're almost there," Sam encourages her.

"I'm good," Colleen says. "I'll wait for you guys."

"No, don't stay here by yourself."

"It's my knee," says Colleen.

"You can do it! Lean on me." Sam coaxes Colleen all the way up the trail, where everybody has gathered round to talk about the glacial plane.

They talk about what makes a boulder erratic, and Sam can't stop smiling.

"You're so happy," Colleen tells her. Colleen's face is red, and she is drinking from her water bottle. She has a lot of allergies.

Sam says, "Because look how beautiful it is." A single gold leaf floats to the ground and Sam is curious and glad—like What will happen next? What will we see? It's just so cool to find out the backstory of the ground beneath your feet. It's like you have X-ray vision through the leaves and lichen, underneath the moss and toadstools down to the granite with its tiny crystals. Her dad was right—there are jewels everywhere if you just pay attention.

Meanwhile, when Sam gets back her unit test in accounting, she gets a 79.

"That's not so bad," says Justin.

"It's my fault, because I didn't make myself study."

He looks at her like he doesn't understand that concept. "Why would you have to make yourself learn something?"

"Because I'm not interested in it."

"So maybe bookkeeping is not your thing."

"It *is* my thing," she says, because this is what she came to college for.

When Courtney calls, Sam lets her talk and talk, because she does not want to say anything about school.

Courtney says, "I'm trying to start a rule where Noah can't play his game until he does his work."

"Good luck with that."

"Well, I'm trying anyway. Could you make sure you remind him?"

"He won't even look at me. He hates me now."

"He does not."

"Okay, he's annoyed with me."

Sam can hear her mom thinking. Then Courtney says, "You know what would help?"

"What?"

"If he met Justin."

Sam almost laughs because her mom is relentless. "You're amazing."

Courtney reasons, "If he sees Justin, it won't seem like you're disappearing into some black hole."

"Dinner is not going to help anything."

"Yes, it will," says Courtney.

Sunday evening, Sam leads the way to the apartment. Justin is holding purple dahlias for Sam's mom, as if this will win her heart completely—and it's weird because it almost does. Sam is wearing an old sweater, but Justin is in jeans and a button-down shirt, and also a black vest, and he has brushed his hair. Courtney says, "I love the vest! You look Victorian."

Then at dinner, she serves lasagna and sits next to Justin. Sam sits across from Justin and Noah sits across from Courtney.

"You could grow rosemary," Justin tells Courtney. He is thinking about what she might grow next summer on the balcony, and he is talking to Noah about hockey, which makes Courtney smile. Sam feels like her mom is checking boxes.

❑ Dahlias (!)
❑ Vest
❑ Gardening advice
❑ Ice hockey

He and Noah talk about the Bruins, and Justin knows so much that Courtney says, "Did you play in school?" This is her way of asking, So what about college, what did you study, what are you doing with your life?

Justin answers Courtney, but he keeps his eyes on Sam. "I'm just a fan."

Courtney says, "I hear that you're a gardener."

He says, "Yeah, I work part-time for my uncle on lawn care, but mostly for myself."

"He's gardening in Gloucester," Sam says.

Justin says, "For my great-grandma." Underneath the table, he clamps Sam's feet between his.

"It's an acre," Sam adds, so her mom won't think the job is nothing.

Justin says, "We've got flowers, and fruit trees, and vegetables. We had a big garden over the summer."

"And what about the winter?" Courtney asks. "What do you do then?"

"Snow shoveling and writing."

"What do you write?"

"I keep a journal."

Courtney looks at him blankly, like, A journal? Okaaay. A journal is not one of Courtney's boxes. "A journal for yourself?"

Now Justin looks at her a little bit confused, like who else would he keep a journal for? He says, "Yeah, I'm not going to publish it or anything."

"Noah!" Courtney says. "Come back to the table."

Noah doesn't listen. He is on the couch with his computer as always. But Justin goes over there and sits next to him. He says, "Oh, I love that game."

"Do you play?" Noah asks.

"I used to."

So, Noah starts showing Justin his city, and Courtney tells Sam, "Do you still want that fleece?"

In the bedroom, Courtney pulls out flat storage bins from underneath Sam's bed. "Where is it?"

"Mom," Sam says, because Courtney is so transparent, taking her into the other room and closing the door to talk to her alone. "I don't need a fleece. It's not even cold yet."

"I like him," says Courtney. "Don't look so surprised!"

But Sam is a little bit, because she saw her mom assessing Justin, and adding up his questionable traits.

❏ Journal? What is that about?
❏ Great-grandma? Are you living off her?

Courtney says, "He was looking at you all through dinner."

"Sh! He was sitting across from me," Sam points out, because where else would he look? "It's right there."

Her mom pulls out the fleece and says, "He won't earn any money, though." Now Sam thinks her mom will say, You are too young for this; you are a student and your boyfriend needs a job, not a frickin' journal—but no. Courtney says, "That's why it's great you're learning bookkeeping."

55

"I can't believe she likes you," Sam teases Justin in bed.

"Why? I'm not so bad."

"You're old."

"Oh yeah. I forgot."

"She thinks I'm living with you."

"Well." He is tracing her body with his hands. "She seemed okay with it."

"Yeah." She is warm. "You should . . ." She can't even talk.

"Always bring dahlias."

She is laughing, and at the same time she's sad, because she can't remember anyone bringing flowers to her mom. "I wish."

"What?"

"It was easier for her."

"I think she's glad her kids are older."

"Maybe." Sam slips on top of him. "I'm not sure."

"Why wouldn't she be?"

Sam doesn't answer; it's too sweet. Only later, words return. "Because she is alone."

She wants to tell him about her mom and Jack, and even Adam. She wants to tell about the times that she was little, and all about her dad. For a second, she feels the wanting like that pressure behind your eyes when you're afraid you might burst into tears—but she does not tell him, and she does not cry.

In the morning, Sam finds Ann sitting at the kitchen table with a little flat cardboard box. It belonged to her grandson Eddy and it looks nibbled at the corners. Inside is a mineral collection of twenty specimens glued onto labeled squares. There is a flaky piece of mica and a piece of quartz and there is fluorite and turquoise and a tiny piece of copper and there is pyrite—fool's gold. "Will you look at that," says Ann, because she is a fan of minerals. "I knew I had this somewhere and you know where it was? The broom closet."

Another time, Ann gives Sam a book published by the Government Printing Office in 1894. The title is *Geology of the Green Mountains of Massachusetts*. The cover is rough brown, the pages smooth inside.

"I think this came from the library," says Ann. "Years ago, when they were selling the old books. Look. I got it for a quarter." She is someone who never has to buy a present.

The book includes line drawings of mountains and their composition. Then there are photos taken under a microscope so you can see the crystal structures. Just opening at random, Sam finds a section called *AMPHIBOLITES*. "Last to be described are heavy dark rocks, generally fine-grained, in which the eye recognizes dark crystalloids of hornblende and irregular patches of feldspar and cubes of pyrite." The whole book goes on like this.

"It's very long," says Ann.

Sam says, "And this is just volume twenty-three."

"Yes, I wonder where all the other volumes went. Look at these maps."

"How did they figure all this out?" Sam is thinking about the authors—Pumpelly, Wolff, and Dale.

Ann says, "They must have camped up there."

"I know, but how did they—see everything?" Sam can imagine those three geologists camping and smoking outside their tent and telling stories, but how did they gather evidence? Did they chip off little bits of rock? Were they carrying huge cameras?

Now Sam has her own drawer in Justin's room, and on the floor next to the mattress, she's got the rock collection and *Geology of the Green Mountains*. She has her own mug in the kitchen, and she knows exactly how Ann likes her coffee.

She feels unfaithful to accounting, and to her family. Sometimes she feels like she has traded in her mom and brother. When she turns nineteen, she eats cake with them, but then she drives home to Justin. She goes to bed and she wakes up with him. When she opens her eyes, he kisses her bare shoulder.

Downstairs Ann says, "Good morning." She is never in a rush.

In the evenings they play Scrabble and listen to old records. Ann has all the songs from Freeda's but on vinyl, so they get stuck and you have to lift the needle and set it down again. They cook for Ann, and her favorite dinner is spaghetti. Sam chops the onions. Justin boils the pasta, because Ann can't lift the pot of boiling water.

On Friday night, they eat together, and Ann tells Justin, "Look at your hands!" He says he was clearing out the blackberry canes and she says, "What about the gloves I gave you?"

"I can only find one," he tells her.

"And you didn't wear it, did you?"

He says, "Wearing one is weird."

Ann laughs out loud and says, "Who will see you?" When he doesn't answer, she says, "You're a funny kid." Age means nothing to her. Nineteen. Twenty-four. What's the difference? Even Ann's children are in their seventies. One of them has passed away. Eight years ago, her son, John, died of cancer. He was Justin's grandfather. Ann's daughters live down in Florida, in Boynton Beach, and one is now a widow. So Ann's children

are old, and even her grandchildren are middle-aged. Justin and
Sam are babies. She asks Sam, "What did you learn in school
today?"

Sam says, "Your gross profit is net sales minus the cost of
goods sold."

Ann looks amused. "It's really common sense, isn't it?"

"Yeah, but we get tested."

After dinner, Sam clears, and Justin washes dishes and they
talk about pumpkins, which Justin harvested from the garden.
He says, "But nobody ate them."

"I wish I liked them more," Ann says.

"I thought you wanted them!"

"I like the way they look, but they don't taste like anything."

"You like the seeds," Justin reminds her.

She brightens. "Yes, that's true. My grandfather used to
toast them."

This grandfather of Ann's was born in the nineteenth cen-
tury, which is strange to think about. Ann has a whole stack of
photographs. His name was Edward and his wife was Ann. In
the pictures, Ann's grandmother Ann is wearing a black dress
and a white collar and her hair up. She is frowning and her eyes
are very pale. "She looks like you," Justin tells Ann.

"They look strict," murmurs Sam. Ann's grandparents seem
so stern and straight, but no. They were both radicals. They
lived in a utopian community. It was a beautiful piece of land
near Beverly. Now it's a horse farm, Windy Hill.

"Oh, I've been there," Sam says.

"To go riding?"

"To see my dad."

As soon as Sam speaks, she is embarrassed—and ashamed
for feeling that way. She is afraid Ann will say, And what was he
doing there? Or one of her cheerful questions—Was he recover-
ing from something? But all Ann says is they are good people
there.

"Here are my grandparents with their children." Ann hands Sam a big black-and-white photograph. "Here's Edward and here's Ann." She explains how they were dedicated to living a good life, growing all their own food, building their own dwellings. "Do you see that little girl?" Ann points to a chubby toddler dressed in white. "She was my mother, Edith."

Justin pours the scotch, and Sam serves out ice cream and gingersnaps. She should be studying for her next quiz, but it's hard to worry about any of that stuff now. Ice cream is luscious, and scotch is even smoother. Sam thinks this is a utopia, isn't it? She is in love with Justin, and also his house, and also Ann.

"But it did not work out," says Ann.

"What happened?"

"Naturally, the people didn't get along."

"Why naturally?" says Justin.

"Well, as a whole we are a selfish and self-serving bunch."

"Not always!" Justin defends humanity.

Ann smiles at him, but she says, "I disagree."

Ann says there used to be a lot of utopias around New England. There was Fruitlands, where the people nearly starved, not to mention, they tried to wear linen all winter. Then there were the Shakers, but they died out, because they believed in celibacy. "I think they were pretty frustrated," Ann says. "Look at their baskets."

"What's that?" Justin says. They hear a thumping, scuffling sound.

"Something's on the porch," says Sam.

For a second, they all think it's an animal, because who else would scuffle on the porch? Then they hear a key in the lock, footsteps in the hall, and a big rolling suitcase. A woman steps inside the kitchen and Ann says, "My goodness. Back so soon?"

Justin says, "Hi, Mom."

56

Justin's mom is small. Her hair is gold, threaded with gray. Her boots are muddy, her eyes tired.

"Sit down, Beth," says Ann. "This is Justin's girlfriend, Sam."

Without saying anything, Beth sits down. Sam can tell no one has mentioned her to Justin's mom, but Beth does smile. She is trying to be kind.

Justin gets Beth a drink of water and Ann says, "Do we have any more gingersnaps?"

Sam gets up to check. Does Beth notice that Sam knows where to find them?

"How was it?" asks Justin. He is talking about the mission.

"It was really hard," says Beth, but she says it like hard is good. Her mission was down in Haiti helping at a hospital for women. The idea is to give them medical care when they have babies. "I didn't want to leave."

"You can always go back," says Ann.

For a second nobody speaks. Sam doesn't know where to look, because didn't Beth just arrive exhausted? Ann is wonderful, but she has thorns.

———

The house is different now. Sometimes, Sam comes over and finds a bunch of women with their Bibles open. Then at dinner, Beth will say grace. "Thank you, Lord, for delivering me safely. Thank you for returning me to my family and for all the blessings of this home. Guide us and protect us. Teach us to live in righteousness . . ."

Ann says, "All right, dear."

Sam figures out pretty quickly that Beth is not Ann's favorite grandchild, but Beth lives here anyway. It's ironic because Justin moved here first when Beth kicked him out, but then Beth moved here as well a few years later when she quit her regular job and started working for New Hope, her church. Ann and Beth don't speak much, except sometimes Ann lashes out. As for Beth, she knows better than to proselytize her grandmother. Justin is a different story.

On Saturday, Sam is sitting in the kitchen and she can hear Beth talking to Justin in the dining room. "What's going to happen?" Beth asks Justin.

"What do you mean?"

"Well, what do you intend?"

"We just intend to live our lives."

"What kind of lives?"

Later that day, Beth sees Sam doing homework at the kitchen table, and she is cheerful, as though she never spoke to Justin. "What are you studying?"

Sam shows her and Beth says, "I learned accounting too! I had that same book!" She looks at the open page and then she says, "I have a shortcut for you." She shows Sam a trick for calculating compound interest. It feels awkward getting help from someone who wonders how you intend to live your life— but the shortcut is good.

"Thank you," Sam says.

"I used to do the books for my husband's practice," Beth explains.

"Was he a doctor?"

"Chiropractor." Beth looks sad, but then she smiles. It's strange. Sam can see Beth change her mood. It's like she does it manually. "I'm bookkeeper for my church now, and I love it."

Sam can't tell whether Beth means I love my church, or I love bookkeeping. Maybe both. Beth says, "Do you?"

"Love accounting?" Sam looks down at her open textbook. "I'm trying to."

Beth is kind and she is serious, and she cares about everybody in the world—but she believes a lot of things. She believes in Christ and she believes in family, and most of all—even though she is divorced—she believes in marriage, which is a sacrament and eternal. Ann says Beth must be the exception that proves the rule.

That night in the dining room, where Sam is studying, Justin says, "Look what my mom gave me."

It's a velvet box. When Sam opens it, she sees a little diamond ring. "Whoa!" She snaps the lid shut.

"She wants us to have it."

"*Why?*"

"So our lives will have a purpose."

"No way!"

"That's what I told her."

"She went out and bought us an engagement ring?"

"It's hers."

"Well, give it back!" Sam feels like it's bad luck, somehow. "I'm not wearing your mom's ring!"

Justin says, "I know. Don't worry."

But Beth is like Courtney, making her point silently. She will look at you and sigh. She will leave her ring box on the table. And then she does something Courtney would never do. Beth bows her head to pray—and even if you can't hear the words, you know that she is praying for you.

Justin is used to it. He and his mom were close when he was little and then they fought, but now they're in a kind of truce. When Beth starts lecturing, he says, I know what you think, Mom, and she stops talking. But Beth will look at him; she will look at Sam and Justin together.

Sometimes Sam thinks Beth must like her if she wants her to marry Justin. Sometimes she thinks it's just the principle of it. Beth would behave this way about any girlfriend because she doesn't want her son living in sin. But mostly, Sam thinks Beth is testing Justin. Do you really care about Sam? Are you serious enough to marry her? Okay then, here's a ring. Sam has no idea which is true, but she avoids Beth as much as possible. Sometimes she waits until Beth goes to church before she comes downstairs.

"Good morning," says Ann. "Look what I found on the dining room table!" She is holding the open ring box, and she sounds amused.

"I saw it," Sam says wearily.

"I don't wear rings, myself," says Ann.

Sam looks at Ann's little hands. "Did you use to?"

"Oh sure. I had a wedding ring. I was seventeen."

"Wait, you were seventeen when you got married?"

"Two years younger than you." Ann sets the ring box down. "I did not have an engagement ring."

"You didn't believe in it?"

"We couldn't afford one, dear." Her answer makes Sam feel rude and ignorant, but Ann is not offended. She says cheerfully, "We went ahead without."

Sam asks, "Did your parents want you to get married?"

"Oh yes."

"And did you?"

Ann is almost laughing. "Well," she says. "It seemed like a good idea at the time."

"Did you have other ideas?"

"In hindsight," Ann says, "I would have been an astronomer."

"Really?"

"I would have studied stars."

"What stopped you?"

Sam thinks Ann will say her parents, or lack of money, but no. Ann says, "Well, love, I suppose. My husband. My three children."

It's daunting just listening to this. "We aren't getting married."

"So I hear."

The house is full of whispers, prayers, and arguments. Beth reproaches Sam and Justin silently, and Ann provokes Beth when she can.

At dinner, Beth bows her head and says, "Dear Lord, teach us to live upright lives. Teach us honesty and truth."

Ann interrupts. "Why not be a silent example? Isn't that more Christian?"

Then Beth leaves the table.

"Grandma," Justin says.

"Oh, I'm tired of her," Ann says. "She's no authority."

"Stop," says Justin, but Ann doesn't listen. This is her old house and her big garden. She is queen of her own country, and she will start wars when she likes. They aren't all about religion.

When Beth complains about half-filled coffee mugs on all the tables, Ann warns, "Don't you make Sam feel unwelcome. She is my guest here—just like you." When Beth looks at the cluttered living room and says she can't live in such a mess, Ann says sweetly, "Is that a promise or a threat?"

And suddenly the house that had seemed so airy and mysterious seems small. The rooms are little, and the walls are thin, and everyone is stacked together. Ann lives on the first floor. Beth lives on the second. Justin and Sam sleep up on the third, where Sam feels Beth's disapproval creeping underneath the door.

Early Sunday morning, Sam tiptoes to the dining room to work. She is trying to correct all the problems she got wrong on her accounting quiz. When she got it back, she was so ashamed she crumpled it up into a ball. Now she is sitting at the table smoothing open the crushed pages and she thinks, Look at this. Stop hiding. You don't have to love it; you just have to do it. Start from the beginning.

"Sam?" Ann stands there in her robe and slippers. "Good morning."

"Hi."

"Hard at it?" Ann peers over her shoulder at the test marked up in red and Sam resists the urge to snatch it away. "Correcting your mistakes?"

"Trying."

Sam keeps her eyes on the test, but Ann is in a chatty mood. "Look at what I found for you."

It is another book, this one for children. On the cover is a cartoon mountain with crystals inside, and there are kids with chisels tapping all over, hunting for treasure. It's called *The Rock-Hound's Book*. "I think this went with Eddy's mineral collection."

"Thanks," Sam says, but the book makes her feel much worse, because she can't be reading about rocks right now.

"I thought you could use it when you go climbing. You might find something."

"But I have to study," Sam says. "I don't have time."

"Suit yourself." Ann leaves the book there on the table, and Sam feels guilty, but it's the truth. She is allowed to drop her lowest score, but she has to figure this stuff out and ace the final. The exam is worth 40 percent.

Justin thumps down the stairs and he is sleepy but smiling.

Beth appears all dressed for church and looks at Justin, like Come with me, even though he won't.

"Goodbye, Beth," Ann tells her cheerfully.

Justin leans over Sam's chair because he wants to go to Red Rocks. "It's a perfect day."

She says, "I have to work."

"But look." He pulls open the dusty drapes and sunlight pours through Ann's wavery old windows. It's the very end of November. "You know you want to."

She turns on him. "I can't do what I want to anymore."

And still he doesn't understand. He says, "Why not?" He believes there's time and space for everything, but she is trapped in a dining room, and Beth is returning in just a couple of hours. Focus, Sam tells herself. Wake up, because if you don't, you're gonna lose. You will lose your chance.

She says, "I have to make this work."

But he is not in her position. He has no idea what it's like. She has three weeks left of the semester. He stands behind her chair and she pushes him away.

He says, "You don't have to be mean."

She says, "Don't pressure me."

"You're pressuring yourself," he says. "You're taking this accounting thing too seriously."

That's when she stuffs her books into her backpack.

"Where are you going?"

"Somewhere else."

"Meet me later."

"No, I can't."

"Sam." He follows her out, but she doesn't feel like talking.

She doesn't feel like explaining or apologizing for what she has to do. He says, Wait, but she says no.

She doesn't go upstairs for her clothes. She doesn't take anything. She walks outside with her car keys and her backpack. Justin says, Sam, come on, but she leaves anyway.

57

She drives home and drops her backpack on the floor of her old room, and that night she sleeps in her own bed. Monday, she drives to class and then to work, and then straight to the Beverly library.

Justin texts, *can I talk to you?* He texts again. He calls, but she can't hear because she is in the reading room where you turn off your phone, and she is still correcting her mistakes.

Where she was sloppy, she is cleaning up her math. Where she didn't know what to do, she looks up the practice problems in the book. Wherever she was wrong, she recalculates, and once she starts, she will not stop. She sits at a table with her textbook and her mechanical pencil and her notebook and all she can see is new numbers, the answers she didn't know before.

When she looks up, the evening sky is filling up the windows, and she thinks, When did the sun set?

Walking to her car, she listens to Justin's messages. Then she calls him back.

He says, "You're angry with me."

She says, "I'm just doing my accounting, which I should have done before."

"What's going on?"

"I told you. I have to make this work."

"That's not it."

"That's it!" she tells him. "Why won't you believe me?"

"Because you won't see me. You won't even talk to me."

Even on the library steps she feels the pull of his voice, but she can't miss him now. She stuffs her phone into her jeans pocket, and he is gone.

Soon Ann and Justin and Beth will sit down for dinner. Will Ann ask, Where is Sam? What will Justin tell her? She wonders, and at the same time she doesn't want to know. It is good to be away, to escape those old rooms and those stairs, and even Justin's arms. It hurts to be away from him, and it's also a relief.

After a few days, Courtney asks, "Did you have a fight?"

Sam doesn't answer.

Courtney says, "Well, are you breaking up?"

Again, Sam doesn't answer.

"He was cute," her mom says regretfully.

"Yeah, well," Sam says.

At night when her mom works late, Sam helps Noah with his homework. She retrieves a pile of old magazines from the salon and they piece together an overdue collage on the subject of *The Odyssey*. The key words they have picked are *HOME, TRAVEL,* and *LOVE.*

Sam is cutting out pictures of homes. A log cabin, a houseboat, a bird's nest.

Noah is supposed to be finding pictures for travel, but he does nothing.

"Noah!" Sam says.

"What? I can't find anything."

"Noah! I gave you *Travel + Leisure.*"

He says, "There were no planes in *The Odyssey.*"

"Find a yacht."

"They rowed triremes, remember?"

Sam tells him, "This is for English, not history."

When it comes to love, they can't find anything except people on vacation, clinking glasses, or celebrating diamond rings. In the end, they cut out two horses touching noses and they call it good.

"Okay, start gluing." Sam spreads her own books across the table and opens her computer. Statistics is going fine. Geology is easy. Accounting is where she can't let up.

She sits up late and starts new spreadsheets, preparing income statements and balance sheets for AAA Automotive, the imaginary business in Unit 6.

When Noah finishes the collage, she barely notices. She doesn't say Come on, take care of this mess. She doesn't even hear her mom come home. Sam keeps working at the table with cut-up magazines around her.

"Sam?" Courtney calls softly. But Sam is clawing up a wall of numbers, and she can't answer. She has to keep moving, or she will fall asleep.

Her life is simple now. Work, sleep, study, eat. She is not happy, but that's okay. She is not confident, but she is calm. It's like competing when you have your head together. Every second, you know what you should do.

Every day after her shift at the café, she sits at the library, calculating profit and loss, expenditures and debt. Her spreadsheets start to come alive. She feels she must balance to the penny, or her imaginary business will go under.

On her next quiz she gets a perfect score.

Her mom says, "I knew you would be good at this!" She keeps saying, See? You're gonna write your own ticket! She is already talking about the job Sam will find when she is done— but Sam doesn't think so far into the future. She just wants to crush each problem as it comes.

She misses Justin; she misses laughing with him and kissing—but when she is working, she forgets him.

That's why he startles her. He almost scares her showing up outside the library. She sees this long-haired guy and her heart jumps.

"Hey," he says.

She feels ambushed. "Were you waiting for me?"

"No, I just happened to be standing here."

He unzips his backpack and hands her *Geology of the Green Mountains*. "This is for you." He hands her *The Rock-Hound's Book*. "And this is for you." And he takes out the mineral collection. "These are all from Ann."

"How is she?"

"Annoyed."

"Is that what she said?"

"She asked why you didn't say goodbye."

Sam stands there holding the books and the mineral collection. "Tell her I'm sorry."

"You tell her."

"Okay, I will." She says it definitively, but she can see that he does not believe her. She hardly believes herself, because would she face Ann again? Only in theory.

He tells her, "You didn't say goodbye to me either."

She feels for a second what he feels, to be left like that, but she says, "I couldn't stay."

"You can't even look at me."

Her hand flies up to her face, because it's true. It hurt to leave, but it hurts much more to see him now.

"I know my mom upset you."

"It wasn't her."

"Yes, it was."

"No."

"You ran away."

"I did not!" Sam is looking at him now. "I came home. I ran away when I was with you."

"You wouldn't even talk to me. You just walked out and ignored me."

"I have exams! I can't cut grass and live for free with my great-grandmother."

"That's your excuse."

"It's not."

"It's your excuse because you're scared."

Sam stands before him holding Ann's gifts, and she says, "I am not scared."

"Then say you weren't happy."

She does not say it.

"Say that you don't love me."

She does not say it.

"You're too scared to admit it."

"I'm not," she tells him, because this is not about happy or in love or scared. It's that she has to be responsible—but he doesn't get it. He doesn't even want to understand.

58

After that, she doesn't see him.

Her mom says, "You never go to Red Rocks anymore."

Sam says, "Nope."

"You're all or nothing," Courtney says, and that is true. Sam finishes the semester with an A– in statistics, but As in all her other classes. In accounting, Witchy sends her an email after her exam. *Congratulations, Sam, you earned a 94.7 percent, which was our highest score. It was a pleasure teaching you.*

Doc Martin wishes her good luck even before she takes the final. On the last day of class, he sees her leaving and says, "Hey, Sam."

She stands there nervous in the doorway and he says, "I just wanted to say I hope you take Geology 102 next semester. It's the sequel. It's essentially the history of the earth."

The history of the entire earth. How could anyone say no to that? But Sam says, "I don't think I have space for another elective."

Martin says, "What's your major?"

"Accounting."

For a second, he looks doubtful, or maybe disappointed. Maybe not. He just says, "Got it."

"But I wish I could."

They are standing there together, and everybody else has

gone. It seems like the whole building is quieting down, and as he speaks, she notices the little green checks on his shirt. She sees them individually. Everything at that moment is so clear when Doc Martin says, "Just think about it, if you have time. Far be it from me to steal you for geology—but I gotta say, you have a talent for it."

Those are the words she keeps hearing as she drives off in her car, and at the café, and in the library. She had pushed geology aside—but now she keeps thinking *I gotta say, you have a talent for it*. The words echo in her mind, because who is there to tell? Not her mom. Not right when Sam is getting her degree. Not Halle, home for winter break from Williams College.

Halle is writing an essay about sacred and secular imagery of motherhood—like how the Madonna and child started looking more realistic, so the child is not such a God but more of a baby in his mother's lap.

"Here, look." Halle shows Sam pictures on her phone and there is one of baby Jesus holding a string of coral beads while his mother (the Virgin) reads a book on a windowsill.

It makes Sam think of her mom when Noah was little— except Courtney would never let him play with a necklace; he would break the string. Sam looks at the picture and thinks those beads will go flying and after that Jesus will knock the book over the sill into the garden down below. "The situation doesn't look so realistic to me."

Halle says, "Well, it's still a religious painting."

They are sitting at the café after closing, and when Halle asks how Sam likes her classes, Sam says they're good. She says it was hard at the beginning, but she has a 3.9 GPA now.

"Wow," says Halle as though she is impressed, and then Sam regrets telling her because probably Halle is thinking North Shore is easy and 3.9 is not so hard to get. After that Sam doesn't talk as much. She doesn't mention Doc Martin or Witchy because she feels protective of them. Halle talks about her roommate and her roommate's boyfriend, but Sam doesn't mention Justin.

She has made some friends at the café. Jessie, Haven, Amy. They are work friends and they talk about their aggravations and their cars and little things. Before Christmas, they exchange joke gifts for Secret Santa. Sam gives Haven a giant button that says *NO*.

When she opens her own bag, she finds socks printed with little toasters and bacon and sunny-side-up eggs. As soon as she pulls out those socks, she thinks *You are my piece of toast*. Then all the other metaphors come back to her. *You are my planet. You are my umbrella*—all the lines she and her dad would think up on the sidewalk with his typewriter. Sam used to think Poems While U Wait meant poems you thought up while you were waiting for a customer.

Would her dad even recognize her now? Would he say Sam, I'm proud of you? Or would he say, What's going on? All you think about is tests and grades. Maybe he would say, What are you trying for? Then she might tell him that she has a talent. She has not told anybody else, because it would be weird, and her mom might say, Oh great, geology. But Sam would tell her dad if he were here.

She would say, History of the Earth, the Sequel; should I take it?

And he would say, Why not?

She would tell him, Because I don't have time.

And he would say, But don't you want to know what happens?

She sends an email to Doc Martin and it says, *Dear Professor, I keep thinking about your class and I would like to register but I don't think I will have time to do a good job.*

He writes back, *Dear Sam, That doesn't stop most people. Also, you can drop and get a refund.*

And so she registers, and spring semester she is the busiest

she has ever been. She works part-time at UPS, part-time at the
Atomic Bean, and full-time on four classes. She wakes up be-
fore it's light. She studies notecards at the rink when she takes
Noah to hockey.

By February, her work friends start saying, Sam, we never
see you anymore. By March, her mom says, You'll get sick if
you don't sleep. Sam will drift off on the couch with her books
open on her lap and her dreams are all mixed up. Rocks and
numbers, payroll and orogeny. She is lying there when her
phone starts ringing.

"Sam," her mom says.

"What?"

Her mom is sitting at the table. "Your phone."

By the time she unearths it from the cushions, the ringing
stops. There is no voicemail, just a text from Justin. *Ann fell
call me.*

"Hi!" Sam says.

"Hi." His voice is cold.

"What happened?"

"Ann fell on the ice and broke her hip."

"What was she outside for?" Sam thinks of Ann lying help-
less in the snow. "Where is she? How is she doing?"

"She's okay. Not great. She wants to see you."

VI

Dreamer

59

"Who is that?" Ann is tiny in her hospital bed.

"It's me, Sam."

"Just Sam?"

"Just Sam."

"Sit down." It's a double room with a curtain down the middle. Sam can hear voices on the other side, but at the moment Ann has no other visitors. Sam pulls up a pale blue chair.

"Where have you been?"

Sam is startled by the question. "In school, taking classes."

"Is that all?"

"And working. Helping my mom."

Ann gazes at her. "You've been in quite a rush."

"It's true." Sam looks down but she cannot hide. "Thank you for sending Justin with the books and mineral collection."

"Are you using them?"

"Not yet. I have to keep up with accounting."

"And what have you learned now?"

"Well—notes payable, notes receivable."

"What else?"

"Wait, tell me how you are."

Ann frowns. "Oh, I'm expecting to hear my fate."

"Your fate?"

"Where they send me. Whether I will walk again."

"If anyone can do it, you can."

Ann says, "Flattery will get you nowhere."

"I wasn't—"

Ann smiles. "I was pulling your leg."

"I can't always tell."

"I like that about you." Ann's tone is light; her eyes are fierce.

"I'm sorry," Sam murmurs.

"For rushing out?"

"Yeah."

"A little gun-shy, are you?"

The nurse comes in to take Ann's vitals. She says the doctor will be rounding too, and Ann should eat, so Sam gets up to go.

"Come again," Ann says.

"Okay."

"Come back and talk to me."

"I will."

She walks out to the slushy parking lot and starts looking for her car, up and down the rows.

"Sam." It's Justin in his station wagon pulling up beside her. When he rolls down the window, he looks good, as though he's over her. "Hey, Sam. Thanks for coming."

"Of course!" This is how she talks to people ordering their coffee. "She's amazing."

He nods but he says, "I don't know what's going to happen."

"She's sharp."

"Was she scolding you?"

"Not really. A little bit." Sam is shivering, standing there.

"Are you okay?"

"Yeah. I said I would come back."

"Great!" He is cheerful too.

———

The next time she visits, Sam brings Ann rum raisin ice cream, and right before she leaves, Justin appears. They sit for a few minutes with Ann and don't say anything.

Finally, Ann says, "I hope we're all still friends."

Sam nods, embarrassed.

Justin says, "Sure."

But Ann looks at Sam and says, "I hear that you're not climbing anymore."

"I'm doing other things," says Sam.

"Do you want some more?" Justin holds up the ice cream for Ann.

"No, you can put it in the freezer," she tells him. "There's a kitchen down the hall."

"I'll go," Sam volunteers. "I have to go anyway. I have a midterm."

Ann asks, "For which class?"

"Geology."

Sam finds the top for the ice cream carton and starts heading out.

"Good luck, dear," says Ann.

Sam doesn't have a chance to visit the next week. It's work and school and Noah and other things preventing her, like staying up late with practice tests. Trying to memorize vocabulary. She has no time for anything, but when Justin texts her *ann wants to know where youwere,* she apologizes. *Sorry I had tests. I can come Th.*

He answers, *They might transfer her.*

Then Sam rushes to the hospital on Thursday, as early as she can.

The room is full of people. Beth, and Justin, and nurses coming in and out. Ann tells Sam, "They're moving me to Pilgrim."

"That's a good thing, right?" says Sam.

Beth is packing up Ann's clothes. "Grandma, do you want these books?"

Ann looks bothered. "Justin, will you take away this . . ."

"Lunch?"

"You can call it that."

"Grandma, I'm going downstairs," Beth says. "I'll be right back."

"I'll be here," Ann says. The nurses are stepping out to grab some paperwork. Beth is gone. The only one left is Justin as Ann turns to Sam. "Tell me about your midterm."

"It was fine."

"Show it to me."

Sam opens her backpack and Ann says, "What's that?"

"Nothing," Sam says.

But Ann is too quick for her. She sees a big yellow SAT prep book and she says, "Why are you studying for SATs now? Didn't you already take them?"

Sam doesn't want to say she is taking them again, so she pulls out her midterm and shows Ann her score, a 98. "This is the one I got wrong. This question here. Stromatolites."

"Let me see that." Ann holds the test up. "Where are my reading glasses?" Justin hands them to her and she says, "Oh yes. Presence of blue-green algae. What was the date that you forgot?"

"Three point five billion years ago."

Ann says, "What a lot of time has passed."

"I know," says Sam.

"Will you take another?"

"Geology course? My professor says I should."

"And will you?"

Sam hesitates. Then she says, "I would have to transfer."

"Where would you go?"

"Well, I wouldn't, because I'm in the middle of accounting."

"But if you did."

"U Mass Amherst."

Ann takes that in, and her eyes are full of light. "Oh, be a scientist."

"That's what you tell everyone," Justin says.

"You mean that's what I told you!"

Beth is back with blankets and a new nurse with a wheelchair. "We're going to take you downstairs now," the nurse says.

Ann says, "Not so fast."

The nurse looks a little nervous. "We've got the ambulance waiting."

"That won't be necessary. My granddaughter is driving me."

The nurse says, "I'm sorry, ma'am." Because those are the hospital rules. You get transferred in an ambulance.

"But I told the doctor no," says Ann.

"It's for liability."

"It's ridiculous. This is not an emergency."

"I realize that, ma'am, but it's hospital policy."

"It's a waste of money."

Beth is trying to help Ann into the wheelchair, but she shouts, "I don't want to!" Beth tries to calm her, but Ann swats her away. She wants to stand up. Sam knows Ann wants to run away, but she doesn't have the strength.

"It's just a short trip." The nurse is wheeling Ann down the hall.

Beth leads while Justin and Sam trail after. "Bury me and get it over with," says Ann.

Outside the hospital, the ambulance is waiting and two guys load Ann in her wheelchair, ramp lifting slowly. Rising up, she is quiet and cold. She looks at Beth like You've betrayed me. She glares at Justin. And finally, she looks at Sam.

"You got this." Sam tries to be encouraging.

"Oh, have I?" Ann shoots back. "I wish we could trade places."

Beth leaves with Ann. The ambulance pulls away without a siren, and Sam sinks down on a metal bench. She feels cursed, even though she knows Ann was just upset.

"She didn't mean that." Justin sits next to her.

"Yes, she did." Sam stares out in front of her. It's just that Ann's moods change so fast. "She's sweet one minute. Then she's scary."

"Scared."

"I guess." It's hard to imagine Ann scared of anything.

Justin says, "It was good of you to come."

"It wasn't good."

"Oh, okay. What was it then?"

"Just what I should have done."

"You like feeling guilty."

"No, I don't."

He says, "I was just trying to thank you."

"Oh."

"And you act like you were making reparations."

It's freezing on that bench. Sam's jacket is thin. Her head is bare. "I didn't make you very happy."

He looks down at his salt-stained boots. "Yes, you did."

"I mean the way I left."

"That doesn't matter now."

"But you were angry."

He does not deny it. He just says, "You're cold, and I should go."

"Yeah." She thinks he will get up to leave, but he does not. They are sitting there with their legs almost but not quite touching. "You were right. I didn't say goodbye—or tell you anything, even though I wanted to."

"You didn't want to."

"Yes, I did, but it was hard to say."

"What was it?" She shakes her head, but he presses. "What did you want to tell me about?"

"My life."

"Your life."

She is embarrassed. She can hear her mom. *Sam, you're nineteen*, because how much life does she have to talk about? Not much, if you count years. Nothing compared to Ann, or the whole earth.

A bus pulls up wheezing. Doors open, flooding them with light, and they shake their heads and the bus drives off again. She says, "It's okay, we'll talk later."

"No, tell me now."

60

They sit together on the bench, and then they sit in his car with the heat on, and Sam tells him about her life, but not in order, not the way it happened. She does not tell Justin about Topsfield or about Kevin with *L.O.V.E.* tattooed on his hand. She doesn't tell him how her dad would mist her in the greenhouse or how they walked along the beach or how he never wanted ribbons. None of that. She says how angry she was and unforgiving when her dad returned.

Her voice is steady; she is not crying at all, until she says, "Now I've lost my chance." Then she starts crying hard. She is almost out of breath. "And I can't tell him anything."

The sun has set. Justin is brushing tears from her face. "What would you say?"

"That I'm more like you than I thought. That when I was younger, you were trying and trying all the time—but I didn't see it. Sorry." She takes a breath. "And I do want to get away. I always want to and I don't want to be like he was, but I always am now. I'm always thinking of something else. I don't know what to do. I'm trying to be an accountant, but."

"But what?"

"I just think." He looks into her eyes, but she is shy to say it. He takes her hand and she holds on. "Maybe I do want to transfer and major in geology."

He sits back half laughing.

"Why is that funny?" she demands.

"Because I thought you were talking about us. I thought you were going to say you want to be an accountant, but you miss me."

"I do."

"Now that I mention it!"

"No, I miss you."

"How much?"

So much, she thinks, that I tried not to remember you. So much, I didn't want to see you. "The problem is I can't do everything at once."

"But I would help."

"How?"

Slowly, he kisses her. His nose brushes hers. His lips touch hers. Then he draws back. "I would ignore you."

"Oh great."

"You would go away to Amherst and I'd stay here with Ann and we'd never see each other."

"If I get in."

He pounces. "You applied already." She doesn't want to answer, but he says, "Admit it."

"Yeah, I did."

61

It is cold and snowing but it's spring. Sam is working and taking all her classes and helping her mom with Noah, but she is also with Justin. She cooks with him, and after dinner, they sit together with a bowl of ice cream and two spoons. She falls asleep with him, and when she wakes up, she slips into his arms.

They climb on Sunday mornings and their hands are raw. They drink coffee from a thermos, and their shoes are soaked with mud. No one else wants to come out in this weather, so they go alone, and they keep trying the tipped boulder, and every time they fall.

The weather starts to warm and rain dissolves the last bits of snow when Sam and Justin try for what seems like the millionth time, and as usual, they fail.

They end up walking back to Justin's car with their mats rolled up on their backs and they are bruised and filthy, hair and arms and faces streaked with mud.

Sam says, "You know what I hate about that rock?"

"You can't figure it out."

"I *can* figure it out—but it's taking forever."

"Yeah," Justin teases. "By the time you're smart enough, you'll be too old."

They drive to Ann's house and she is sitting on her front

porch with a blanket draped over her. "Success?" she asks, as always.

"It's too big," says Sam. "It's way too technical."

Beth is pulling up. She is home from church and she is smiling, because she loves it so much, even though nobody in the family goes with her. The garden is fresh and beautiful; the crab apple is budding. Justin takes advantage of the moment and turns to Sam. "Are you going to tell them?"

That startles her, because what is he doing, putting her on the spot like that?

Ann is already asking, "What is it?"

Beth covers her mouth with her hand, and Sam thinks, Oh no! She thinks we're getting married, after all. Sam shakes her head. "It's nothing."

Justin looks at her like, Are you being shy? How can you not tell everybody? "She got into U Mass Amherst."

Beth says, "Oh, my goodness."

Ann is talking too. "Are you going for geology?" But Sam can't hear the rest, because she is rushing inside.

"Sam?" Justin calls after her.

She is running up to the third floor, but she isn't fast enough. He catches her on the landing and she accuses him. "I didn't say that you could tell them."

"I didn't know it was a secret." He follows her up to their room.

"It's not."

"Except nobody can talk about it?"

"I might not even go!"

"Why?"

"Do you *want* me to leave?"

At first, he doesn't answer. Then he says, "No."

"So why are you telling everyone?"

"Two people. Beth and Ann."

"Why are you telling them?"

"Because it's good news."

"You think it's good."

"Didn't you apply for this?"

"I wasn't supposed to get in."

"Well, you did!"

She is hunting for clean clothes to take down to the shower. "Why do you think I'll go there?"

"Because you're ambitious."

"That doesn't mean I'll go."

She grabs her clothes and escapes to the shower on the second floor but when she comes out, he is waiting outside the door, because, after all, he has to shower too. He says, "I'm sorry I told them."

She says, "It's okay."

He says, "I won't do it again." Then he says, "I'm ambitious too."

She stares at him because really? He is smart and he is strong. He climbs like a dancer. His body remembers every move, but he is the least ambitious person she has ever known. Even her dad was always practicing and hustling. "What are you ambitious for?"

He has to think for a second, but then he says, "Probably for taking care of people."

"Ohh," she groans, because her own ambitions are secret and selfish. When she applied to transfer, she never told anybody but her references, Witchy and Doc Martin. Now that she got in it's like getting caught. "I'm afraid to tell my mom."

"Why?"

"After she paid my tuition and got her hopes up and she thinks I'm finally finishing?"

"She'll be proud."

"For giving up and leaving?"

"You did this amazing thing."

He has no idea how Courtney counts up Sam's credits. Sam's

mom knows the accounting requirements by heart and Sam only has one more semester if she takes summer school. Courtney always talks about it. "There's no point telling her if I'm not going."

"But you will go, so you have to."

It bothers her that he thinks it's obvious, that he is so happy for her, that he doesn't mind that she might leave, and that he can't imagine she might be afraid. "Why do you keep saying I'll go when I can't even afford it? Do you even know how much money it would be?"

He is a person who dropped out because college was a waste of money, but when it comes to Sam, he says, "It's just two hours away."

"You make it sound like you won't even miss me."

"I'll miss you," he says. "What's wrong with that?" He acts like missing is what everybody does.

"Come with me." She says it so quietly he might not hear.

"I can't."

Sam sits down on the landing. She can't argue, because Justin drives for Ann, and cooks, and gardens.

"I owe her." Justin sits next to her. "You don't even know what she did for me."

"What did she do?" Sam thinks he's going to say Ann posted bail, or something.

"She trusted me."

"I mean, she's your great-grandmother."

"She didn't have to. And I promised I would stay. When she was at Pilgrim she said, Promise me, because she doesn't want Mom praying over her."

For a while they don't talk. They just sit there, Sam in clean clothes, and Justin still muddy.

"It's not realistic," she says at last.

"College?"

"Yeah."

"Why does it have to be realistic?"

"I've put her through enough." Sam is talking about Court-ney.

"Which scares you most?" says Justin. "Going, or telling her?"

62

It's hard, because Courtney keeps talking about how they will celebrate when Sam gets her certificate. She is thinking pizza and a beach party or maybe dinner at Passports. That's Courtney's favorite, because they always serve fresh popovers. She doesn't know Sam is considering even more school, and after that she won't be certified for anything.

Sam keeps imagining the conversation. She will say, Mom, I applied to transfer, and Courtney will start yelling. Sam, what are you thinking? You're almost done! You can't start taking student loans now. And Sam will say, Don't worry. I'm staying here; I'm not going into debt. I know how much loans cost over time. Believe me, I can calculate the interest.

Then, every once in a while, Sam thinks her mom will react differently. Sam will say, Mom, I have a chance to go to U Mass Amherst, and Courtney will say, WHAT? Are you kidding me? You got in *there*? You can go and be a scientist? You can't turn that down. Even if your loans take a hundred years to pay, you have to go!

Of course, her mom won't say that. Almost definitely not. But if she did, that would be even worse, because then the decision would be on Sam. She would go and mortgage her whole life and she might not even pass her classes, because how is she even qualified? People come to U Mass from all over. It's a cut above. That's what her own professors say. "Don't be intimidated," Witchy tells Sam. "You're a smart gal, okay?"

As soon as Sam hears the word intimidated, she feels it. The fear that makes you clumsy. The ice that makes it hard to swallow. Probably the admissions committee made a mistake—but they don't contact her. Nobody rescinds Sam's acceptance. All her official messages are about money. Her bill is ready for viewing.

She has six days left to register, and she has to tell her mom. The longer she waits, the worse it gets, and the more offended her mom is going to be that Sam kept this secret from her.

She comes home Thursday night, just as her mom is making dinner.

"Where's Justin?" Courtney asks.

But Sam didn't bring him, because she has to do this thing alone.

She sits down with her mom and Noah and they eat spaghetti and meat sauce and sprinkle Parmesan and Sam says, "You guys, I have to tell you something."

Courtney looks petrified, and Sam knows why. With Beth, it's Wait, are you engaged? But Sam's mom goes right to pregnant. "Stop it, Mom! I'm fine. I applied to U Mass Amherst."

For a second nobody says anything. Noah looks at Sam, and Sam looks at her mom.

Courtney is puzzled, and then hurt. "You never told me that."

"I didn't think I would get in."

"You got in?" Courtney is holding her fork in midair.

"I'm not really going."

"They accepted you?"

"It was just my professor's idea."

"Which professor?"

"Doc Martin."

"Which one is he?"

Sam looks down at her bowl. "Earth Science."

"Oh, Sam."

"Sam, Sam, Sam," murmurs Noah, which is his way of saying, Now you're busted for real.

"Don't worry," Sam tells both of them.

Slowly, Courtney says, "You'd have to take out so many loans."

"I'm not going to," Sam promises. "I'm not enrolling."

"Why did you apply, then?" Noah asks logically.

"I just—wanted to see."

Courtney says, "You wanted to see now—after all this?"

"Yeah."

Courtney says, "You've worked so hard for your certificate. You're so close!"

"I can still do it!"

"But you don't want to."

"I mean I do, but—"

Courtney puts down her fork. "I knew this was gonna happen."

"What?"

"I knew it."

"How could you know?"

"I was the one who told you about geology."

"What are you talking about, Mom?"

"When you were little and you couldn't sleep, I would tell you about geology and all the rocks."

Sam has no memory of this. "You did not."

"Oh yeah, I did."

"That never happened!" Sam says, because where is all this coming from? This whole conversation is so random. Ninety percent of the time, Sam imagined her mom furious. Ten percent overjoyed. What is this?

"I used to talk to you about geology when you were lying awake."

Sam shakes her head because there's no point arguing. "Whatever you say, Mom."

Courtney smiles wistfully. "You are really something."

"But you still think I should stay here and get a job, right?"

"After working like you did? Hell yeah," says Courtney.

"Okay, thanks," says Sam.

Maybe it's her quiet voice. Maybe it's the way she sits there looking at her bowl. Maybe it's just that her mom knows her too well. "That's what I would do," says Courtney, "but you're not me."

There is every reason to stay. There is Justin. There is Courtney and Noah, who both need her. There is money, which Courtney points out more than once. It's so much money. There is only one reason to go, which is that Sam wants to learn.

She thinks about that all the time. In class, and at the Atomic Bean, and with Ann at the kitchen table reading the course titles in geology. "Okay, there's The Earth," she tells Ann. "And The Earth Honors."

Ann says, "Of course, you should take Honors Earth."

"Watershed. Biogeochemistry," Sam reads slowly. "Petrology. Genesis of igneous and metamorphic rock. Recognition of crystallization history with polarizing microscope."

"I'd like to try that," Ann tells her. They sit there trying to imagine a polarizing microscope and the crystals you would recognize in there.

"I can go later," Sam says. "I can work a year first."

Ann says, "Yes, that's true. You could."

"Or in a few more years," Sam says. "After I've saved money."

"But there's no time like the present," Ann points out, which

is one of those phrases that gets weirder and weirder the more
you think about it. No past, no future. No time but now.

"You would go, wouldn't you?" Sam says.

"Absolutely."

"Even if you couldn't afford it?"

"How else will you get to use that microscope?"

Ann watches from across the table as Sam opens her admissions portal and sends in her deposit.

63

All summer, Sam works to earn money for the move. Her mom is upset because she should take her last accounting classes to have a backup plan, but Sam wants cash. She is looking for a place in Amherst, and roommates, and a job there too.

Sometimes, she can't sleep because the whole thing costs so much. Even with her student loans, she is not sure how she will pay for everything—like food. And once she gets a job, how will she find time for coursework? She could take fewer classes each semester, but that would mean more years in school. She sits up at night thinking Honors Earth. Petrology. What will that be like? What is Quaternary?

Justin says, "You'll sleep better if you climb."

She says, "I can't," because she is leaving in four weeks and she can't miss work.

"Come on," he says. "Come anyway."

They go out to Red Rocks Sunday, carrying their mats. The air is thick with insects. You can hear the whole forest humming. The atmosphere is heavy when they find their boulder, the tilted one. It feels like it's going to rain, but they climb anyway. Sam's arms are slick with sweat, and her shoulders, and her back.

They take turns on the tipped boulder. They keep jumping up and falling, falling, falling, until the thunder starts. The storm is booming in the distance, and then right overhead. A minute later the sky cracks open. It's raining so hard and fast that Justin takes off his hat and holds it upside down and it starts filling up with water.

Sam's face is streaming. Her T-shirt is like wet tissue paper on her skin. When they walk back to Justin's car their feet squish in their shoes. Their mats are waterlogged and hard to carry, but the rain feels so good.

The next time they come to Red Rocks it is dry. Sam climbs until her shoulders ache. Her feet scrabble against the rock, and her arms stretch until she thinks they'll break, and still she fails, and so does Justin.

Two weeks before she leaves, Sam gives notice at the café and everybody signs a card that says *Oh, the Places You'll Go*.

One week before, Ann gives Sam her pink African violet to take with her. And Halle's dad insists on giving Sam a super-light barely used computer.

Halle's parents say, You are on your way and we could not be more excited for you. Sam, you will do amazing things.

"No pressure." Halle hugs Sam around the shoulders like, I'll protect you from them.

Jen cuts Sam's hair shoulder length at the salon. Courtney says, Finally! Jen says, You've gotta look professional, but in the mirror, Sam looks scared.

"Are you worried?" Courtney asks as they walk from the salon to the car.

"What do you think?" Sam says.

"I think you'll figure it out."

"I'd better," Sam mutters. She is visualizing her loans.

"You can do it!"

"Maybe."

"Are you worried you're not smart enough? Because you are."

"Thanks, Mom."

"I'm serious."

"I know."

They sit together in the car and her mom says, "Are you worried about Justin and the long-distance thing?"

"No."

"What then?" Courtney asks.

"You."

"Me! What are you worried about me for?"

"I just—"

"What?"

Sam forces the words out. "I just—I'm leaving you alone."

"I'm not alone."

"With Noah."

"He'll be okay," her mom says, even though Noah is not doing great in school, and he can't really handle other people.

"How are you going to watch him and work and do everything?"

"I just will," Courtney says in that voice Sam recognizes: half nervous, half offended.

"But now it will be harder."

"Listen, you have one job," Courtney says. "You have to go in there and crush it, okay?" Sam doesn't answer, so Courtney keeps talking. "You are a student, and you have to think like a student. You know the motto of Dean College?"

"What?"

"To the strong and the faithful, nothing is difficult."

"*Nothing?*" Sam says. She is also thinking, You didn't finish there.

"Are you listening? You are gonna get it done. And I'm going to be fine, because you know why? You know my secret weapon?"

"Determination?"

Courtney waves that away. "I have my whole life ahead of me."

Sam doesn't feel like Courtney has her whole life ahead of her. She feels like her mom can never stop, and that she'll be working two jobs and watching Noah forever, but she says, "Okay."

"I'm young," Courtney tells Sam.

"Okay, Mom."

"I'm thirty-eight!" Courtney is laughing now.

"What?"

"You're hysterical," says Courtney.

The truth is, Sam's mom is flying. She can't stop talking about how Sam is starting at U Mass. She tells all her clients. She even gets advice from one lady who used to work there teaching American history.

"But I'm not taking history," Sam tells her mom.

"You know what? I'm gathering information," says Courtney.

"Stop!" Sam pleads, because what if she comes back? What will her mom say then? And how will Sam face everybody?

The only place Sam can escape is on the boulder. Climbing, she holds on so hard her mind can't wander. Falling, she can laugh at her mistakes.

At night she dreams she's holding on with her right hand. She is dangling and her dad is whistling. She can hear him whistling closer and then he starts cheering. Come on, monkey! Now she flies up. She is floating, and her victory is shining like the sun. She is so warm. No cold, no doubt, no pain inside her.

"I have to go back," Sam tells Justin in the morning.

They climb that day and the next, and then the third day, they climb with Sean, and Kyle, and Amber.

It's supposed to be her goodbye party, so Sean brings Freeda's pizza. Amber brings her special brownies. Kyle has enough beer for everybody, but Sam hardly drinks any. All afternoon she climbs and falls.

Sean lends Sam his extra-thick purple mat, but she gets bruised anyway.

"Hey, have some pizza," Kyle says.

Sam doesn't answer, because she's got one good hold, and she can't stop trying.

"Try the brownies," Amber coaxes her.

The afternoon is cooling down and getting beautiful, and the others kick back where Bolt is playing in the ferns, but Sam keeps climbing and falling.

Sam drops onto the mat, but she is not resting, she is studying the way the boulder tips over the ground. The outside of the rock is smooth; the underside is tricky. You have to navigate that dark place and pull up from below.

Justin says, "At least drink water."

But Sam is thinking, Is there a way to climb the underside in fewer moves? If she goes lateral and shifts her weight earlier, she will have more energy for the edge.

"Sam?" Justin asks.

She jumps up again, but she starts slipping. She chalks her hands and tries once more. Her shorts are muddy. Her thighs are bruised, her knees scraped up, her climbing shoes are dented from weird holds. It's like the rock is molding them, and her sore feet too.

By evening the others barely watch her anymore. She is climbing underneath the edge and she is shifting her weight, swinging her body, feeling her way.

"Hey! Sam!" Justin calls out in surprise. She is half over, half under, on the lip of the boulder.

When she falls, Sean says, "That was cool."

She's up again, and she feels the wisp of a breeze on her bare arms. She climbs up and holds on to the edge, and feels with her feet where she can't see, and then she reaches, and she tries to spring, but falls again.

She lies on the mat and looks up at the trees. Everything hurts, and at the same time, she knows. She's solved the problem in her mind. The question is whether she has enough strength left to follow through. Her hands are burning. She stands and shakes out her arms. This doesn't feel like life or death. She isn't angry. She isn't tense. She is just quiet.

Once again, she climbs, clinging to the edge and feeling with her feet. The distance seems so far. It's so long and slow, and her own weight is so heavy. She feels like she is traveling the whole world, and she is far away. She hears voices, but she is barely conscious of Justin and Amber and Sean and Kyle. She is reaching and reaching, and then she is in that silent place, pulling up slowly. Scrabbling her feet, catching hold.

She is standing high atop the boulder, and everyone is shouting; Bolt is barking—but Sam is winded. It's not like the dream where she was floating. In real life, joy comes in a rush, so fast, so sweet, she can't hold on to it. She bends over, breathing hard, and what stays with her is the trying. Not the moment she pulled up, but all the hours falling.

She climbs down a little way and jumps the rest. She drinks some water and Bolt licks her knees, and Justin kneels and tapes her ragged hands. Everyone is talking except Sam.

"What were you thinking up there?" Justin asks.

"My dad," she says, because she wishes he had seen her. She names the problem Dreamer. That's for him.

The end-of-August air is warm, caressing, as they take the trail out. The world is blue, no longer green. The next day Sam and Justin will load her car and then they will drive out together so he can help her move. Justin will leave Sam there. He'll come home early the next morning.

Amber says, "You're gonna hurt tomorrow."

Sam shrugs. "I'm hurting now."

"Ice," says Kyle.

Amber and Kyle are carrying the cooler filled with empty bottles. Justin has the empty pizza boxes, *Hot and Delicious.* Remember this, Sam's dad told her once at Freeda's, and she memorized the napkin holders and the stacked boxes and the shakers full of chili pepper flakes. Did Mitchell know she could not forget him? He didn't say Remember me.

Kyle is talking about Sam's climb and Amber says, "I wish I had it on my phone."

"That's okay," Sam says. "You are my witnesses."

Amber says, "I don't even have a picture."

"But now I wish I could start from the beginning," says Sam.

Amber looks at her like I love you, but you're weird. "What are you talking about?"

"So I could figure it out all over again."

"Well," Kyle says. "You are a climber."

Amber is still talking about her missed photo. "You were too fast for me."

But they are walking slowly now. Slower and slower, until they can hear the highway through the trees. "I don't want to leave," Sam says, except she knows she will. You'll do great, everybody says. You'll be back, they say, as she tries to memorize these leaves, these words, this light, this air.

About the Author

ALLEGRA GOODMAN's novels include *The Chalk Artist* (winner of the Massachusetts Center for the Book Fiction Award), *Intuition, The Cookbook Collector, Paradise Park,* and *Kaaterskill Falls* (a National Book Award finalist). Her fiction has appeared in *The New Yorker, Commentary,* and *Ploughshares* and has been anthologized in *The O. Henry Awards* and *The Best American Short Stories.* She has written two collections of short stories, *The Family Markowitz* and *Total Immersion,* and a novel for younger readers, *The Other Side of the Island.* Her essays and reviews have appeared in *The New York Times Book Review, The Wall Street Journal, The New Republic, The Boston Globe,* and *The American Scholar.* Raised in Honolulu, Goodman studied English and philosophy at Harvard and received a PhD in English literature from Stanford. She is the recipient of a Whiting Award, a Salon Book Award, and a fellowship from the Radcliffe Institute for Advanced Study. She lives with her family in Cambridge, Massachusetts.

allegragoodman.com
Facebook.com/AllegraGoodman

About the Type

This book was set in Sabon, a typeface designed by the well-known German typographer Jan Tschichold (1902–74). Sabon's design is based upon the original letterforms of sixteenth-century French type designer Claude Garamond and was created specifically to be used for three sources: foundry type for hand composition, Linotype, and Monotype. Tschichold named his typeface for the famous Frankfurt typefounder Jacques Sabon (c. 1520–80).